The Outcasts
of Eden

The Outcasts of Eden

A novel

D J Presson

This story is a work of fiction. Names, characters, businesses, events and incidents are the products of the author's imagination or used fictitiously. Any resemblance to actual persons, living or dead, business establishments, events or locales except as noted by the author, is coincidental.

ISBN: 0692715592
ISBN 13: 9780692715598
Library of Congress Control Number: 2016908163
Kwill and Keebord Publishing, LLC, Hendersonville, NC

To Clara, may your generation be better stewards of the planet, and each other, than your forebears.

And God proceeded to take the man and settle him in the Garden of Eden to cultivate it and to take care of it. And God also laid this command upon the man: "From every tree of the garden you may eat to satisfaction. But as for the tree of knowledge of good and bad, you must not eat from it, for in the day you eat from it you will positively die.

Genesis 2: 15 – 17

Now the serpent proved to be the most cunning of all the wild beasts of the field that God had made. So it began to say to the woman: "Is it really so that God said you must not eat from every tree of the garden?" At this the woman said to the serpent: "Of the fruit of the trees of the garden we may eat. But as for eating of the fruit of the tree that is in the middle of the garden, God has said, "You must not eat from it, no, you must not touch it that you do not die." At this the serpent said to the woman: "You positively will not die. For God knows that in the very day of your eating from it your eyes are bound to be opened and you are bound to be like God, knowing good and evil."

Genesis 3: 1 – 3

And God went on to say; "Here the man has become like one of us in knowing good and evil," and with that God put him out of the Garden of Eden to cultivate the ground from which he had been taken. And so he drove the man out and posted at the east of the Garden of Eden the cherubs and the flaming blade of a sword that was turning itself continually to guard the way to the tree of life.

Genesis 3: 23-24

Overture

TENZIN WANGCHUK DRANK his frothy buttered tea and waited for the sign that it was time to leave. Steam rose from the cup that he cradled in his hands, warming them, the steam mingling with the cold dry air. He stared out the window of the tiny hut at the inky black outline of the massive mountains in the distance. The spotless snow was no longer lit in the cold blue light of the moon, which had slid behind the mountains hours before. He watched, as a tiny flash of light appeared on the very highest peak. The first rays of the rising sun gleamed on the dark surface of the mountain with a bolt of golden light. He finished the last of his tea and said the prayer of his ancestors.

"I will walk as if my feet are kissing the Earth. I bring peace and calm to the surface of the Earth and share the lesson of love. I walk in that spirit."

Tenzin stood up with the graceful ease of his youth. He slipped his cup into the leather satchel that hung on a strap across his body. The satchel already contained a slender copper teapot battered and tarnished from years of use. The only part of the teapot that showed its bright copper origins was the lid, worn smooth and shiny from his and his ancestors' fingers. He had already placed a small bamboo whisk, his knife, a tin of black tea and another of yak butter into the satchel. The weight of the satchel and the items it contained rested against his hip and pulled against his brightly colored robes.

He walked out of the hut and greeted his yaks with loving-kindness. He offered his young hands and soft voice in greetings of love, scratching their noses and rubbing them along their backs and sides, mingling his scent with theirs. The yaks had been waiting for him just outside the door, like dogs waiting for their master. They stretched their noses to sniff his hands and his body and greeted him in return. Three of the females were pregnant, their bellies swollen with the life they carried within them. He scratched each of them and rubbed their flanks. The bulls waited some distance away. Their long shaggy winter coats were beginning to drop, the hair falling in clumps and blowing in the wind around the hut, hanging like spider webs in trees and on fence posts.

As the sun rose in the sky, it bathed the snow-covered heaven-high summit of the Himalayan peaks in a blaze of glory, setting them alight with bright yellow hues of molten gold. He set out with happiness in his heart, bathed in the golden early morning light, his walking stick in hand. A woolen cap covered his head and his ears. His robes of saffron and magenta wrapped him in warmth. He set out on the ancient ritual of spring that had been carried out by his ancestors for centuries, the annual trek with the yaks to the high mountain meadows. They followed him willingly, their hand-wrought bells tinkling a greeting to the sun, to the mountains, and to the world.

⤳

CHAPTER 1

—— ⚬ ——

The Reading of the Will

"Where's Morris, damn it?" asked David Reed, looking impatiently at his Rolex. He was standing at the window huddled conspiratorially with his father at the plush law offices of Morris & Deacon. They were waiting for the reading of the Last Will and Testament of his uncle, Robert Prescott Reed. He stared out the window at the historic landmarks of the Capitol Dome and the Washington Monument in the distance. "Let's get this circus over with so I can get on with my life," he said irritably.

"David," chastised his father, Patrick Reed. "Have some respect for the dead and for Roberta and Jackie." Patrick looked over at his niece Roberta, and his sister-in-law Jackie Reed, sitting quietly at the other end of the room in front of the lawyer's desk. Jackie had hardly changed since Patrick's brother Robert had married his lovely French bride thirty-five years before. Fashionable and chic, she made a very stylish widow. Roberta, on the other hand, had never been Patrick's cup of tea nor her father's either. She had been an embarrassing thorn in Robert Reed's side for most of her life. An environmentalist and life long hippie, she had come into the meeting displaying her clear contempt for them and these proceedings wearing Doc Marten boots, jeans and a Rolling Stones T-shirt under a beat up leather jacket. Her unkempt dirty-blonde hair hung in long, untidy braids. Although Roberta was in her early thirties she still looked like a teenager, and had obviously inherited her mother's excellent genes. Despite her unkempt appearance, she was strikingly pretty with fine regular features. She wore no makeup and had a flawless complexion and big blue eyes.

"We all know this is just a formality," said David conspiratorially. He watched Roberta with obvious disgust as she stared at the folder containing her father's Will on the lawyer's desk. "I'm going to be named CEO, Dad. There's no one else who can keep this company running without any bumps."

Arthur Clark, Robert Reed's long-time business partner, overheard the self-important boast and turned around to stare at David.

"What??" David asked sarcastically. He returned Arthur's incredulous stare with a high-pitched disrespectful tone. "C'mon! I've worked for that tyrant my whole life. I know how he thinks and what the clients want and expect."

"David," Patrick Reed chastised quietly. "It's unseemly to be so transparently grasping. Show some dignity, son."

The door to the office opened and everyone turned to see who was entering, expecting Robert Reed's attorney Stan Morris to walk in. An assistant came in with a tray of ice and beverages and set them on the credenza.

"Shit!" hissed David under his breath, looking at his watch again.

David pulled his son away from the window. "Let's pay our respects," he said, following Arthur over to Jackie and Roberta.

Arthur bent down to kiss Jackie who was dabbing at her eyes and nose with a delicate embroidered hankie. "How are you both doing?" he asked with genuine concern.

Roberta looked up at him and gave him a thin smile. She said nothing, and then turned her attention back to the folder.

"I can't believe he's gone," said Jackie, as fresh tears rolled down her cheeks.

"So what far-flung part of the globe are you off to next in your misguided and infantile attempt to save the planet?" David asked Roberta mockingly.

Roberta stared back at David with clear contempt. "I don't know David, but as far away from you as I can hope to get!"

David turned away, his look of taunting superiority replaced by withering rejection. Roberta had been able to unnerve him ever since they were kids and he struggled to regain his composure. "Where is that damned Morris?" His voice had a slight hint of hysteria to it. He breathed deeply to settle himself down.

The side door to the office opened, disguised from view as part of the wall's wainscoting and chair rail, and Stan Morris, old and frail, came into the room. David and Patrick attempted to stop him as he made his way to his desk, but he curtly waved them off, moving around them to stop in front of Roberta and Jackie. He bent down with some effort to whisper condolences, and Roberta gave him a thin smile. He took her hand in his for a moment and looked at her with deep concern clearly showing on his face. He dropped her hand and walked to the desk to sit down. All the men moved in towards the desk. They took their seats behind the women.

"We are here for the reading of the Last Will and Testament of the late Robert Prescott Reed, recently deceased. The Will is dated less than two months ago, written on New Year's Eve, December 31, 1993." Morris spoke with well-practiced gravitas. "I will start with the personal assets."

" 'To my loving wife Jacqueline Reed, I leave the bulk of my personal assets and estate including the house in Chevy Chase, Maryland, the apartment in New York City, and the condo in Aspen, as well as our personal banking and investment accounts.' "

Jackie dabbed at her eyes with her handkerchief, and Roberta reached over to hold her mother's hand.

" 'Next, I bequeath $1,000,000 in cash to the American Freedoms Fund as a charitable contribution to be used to further the cause of freedom from government intervention in the business and personal lives of Americans, freedoms which I have long cherished, espoused and supported in both my business and personal life,' " continued Morris.

Everyone shifted uncomfortably waiting for the lawyer to go on.

" 'Next, I bequeath my yacht, The Green Machine, to my brother Patrick.' " Morris stopped again, and looked up at the assembled group.

"Well, just get on with it, Morris. You know what we're waiting to hear!" said David, much too heatedly.

" 'And finally, to my nephew David Reed, who has been like a son to me and whose long years of service to Reed Public Relations has been invaluable, I bequeath ten percent of my shares in that company.' "

"What do you mean, ten percent?" asked David. "That's got to be a mistake."

Morris did not answer and moved on.

" 'And to my daughter Roberta, my namesake, my adversary, the one person in my life who has been on the opposing side of every environmental issue I have worked on in my career, the person who calls me a deceiver, a manipulator, a monster and has sought to humiliate and embarrass me in public. To the one person for whom I have worked tirelessly to build this company, and to whom I now pass this mantle, I bequeath the rest of my shares and interests, and confer on her the title of CEO and President of Reed Public Relations.' "

Jackie gasped as she heard this unexpected bequeath.

"Wait a God damn minute!" said David. "What did you say?"

"Holy shit!" said Patrick.

Arthur Clark stifled a laugh, and then unable to contain his reaction, began laughing out loud in hard side splitting guffaws as the irony of the news descended on the group.

Roberta's eyes widened in disbelief as the reality of what she had just heard set in. "Oh God, no," she pleaded, slowly shaking her head. "No, no, no!"

CHAPTER 2

How The Truth Becomes a Lie and a Lie Becomes the Truth

THE BUFF-COLORED FAÇADE of the Ozark Bugle in Little Rock, Arkansas was one of many architectural jewels in the sleepy southern capital. Robert Reed felt keenly aware of the history that had taken place in the newspaper's current building since its' dedication sixty years before in 1903. He was proud to be working at the historic venue. Landing a job as a cub reporter at the paper at the age of twenty-one had been like winning the lottery, but after five years of being a stringer with no byline, he was eager for a shot at the big time. He and his wife Jackie had had their first child, a daughter they named Roberta, one year ago, and he needed to kick his career into gear or find something else to do. Living on salads and beans was not going to cut it with a wife and daughter to support.

1963 was turning out to be a watershed year of historic events in America, and Robert Reed was itching to create a journalistic stir at the paper. The news coming out of the big city papers were making the careers and fortunes of reporters all over the country. To begin the year on a controversial note, Attorney General Robert F. Kennedy made the news in January, when, in a report to his brother, the President John F. Kennedy, he concluded that race problems remained entrenched in the American culture despite the administrations insistence on civil rights for all Americans. In his inaugural speech in defiance of the President, Governor George Wallace of Alabama defiantly proclaimed "segregation now, segregation tomorrow, and segregation forever".

In February, Betty Friedan caused a media frenzy when she published her book, *The Feminine Mystique,* awakening the sleeping female warrior of liberation for countless women who felt trapped by their homemaker roles. In March, Edward Lorenz published his scientific paper, *Deterministic Nonperiodic Flow,* in the Journal of Atmospheric Sciences, establishing the foundation for chaos theory with the idea that the energy created by the flap of a butterfly's wings in Brazil could set off a tornado in Texas. Alfred Hitchcock released his film, *The Birds,* successfully proving that, in theory at least, chaos can turn even placid winged beauties into the most terrifying villains in the history of filmmaking.

In April, Dr. Martin Luther King, Jr. was arrested in George Wallace's hometown of Birmingham, Alabama for "parading without a permit". In May, Eugene "Bull" Connor, Birmingham's Public Safety Commissioner, ordered fire hoses and police dogs unleashed on demonstrators protesting segregation. In June, Governor Wallace created a media show by blocking the doorway of the University of Alabama before finally stepping aside to allow black students James Hood and Vivian Malone to enroll. Emboldening his fellow white racists to stand firm in their unconscionable hatred, including white supremacist Byron De La Beckwith, who the very next day, assassinated NAACP leader Medgar Evers in Jackson, Mississippi. Two weeks later, John F. Kennedy gave a historic speech about freedom in West Berlin, declaring "Ich bin ein Berliner".

In August, Dr. King gave a speech before a crowd of a quarter of a million people at the steps of the Lincoln Memorial in the so-called March on Washington, where he boldly and eloquently described his dream of a future when men would be judged not by the color of their skin but by the content of their character. Now in late September, Robert Reed wondered what new pivotal events would occur before 1963 would pass into oblivion and 1964 would begin, and he was itching to be part of it.

Arthur Clark was working the high school sports beat at the Bugle, but had expressed an interest in hard news reporting. He and Robert had quickly become best friends at the paper. Robert liked Arthur because he was upbeat, entertaining and easy-going. They were walking up the back stairs of the building to their fourth floor office, Robert stealthily steering them away from the bank of crowded public elevators to take the stairs, lamely telling Arthur they needed some exercise after their big lunch.

"Arthur, listen, I have something I need to talk to you about," he said. He stopped mid-way up the stairs and lowering his voice. "I had a very interesting call last night from Trevor Skeets, my old roommate from college. He's a biochemist at Stanton Chemical now. He made me a proposition on behalf of the company that could be our ticket out of here." He pulled Arthur aside, as someone passed them going down the stairs, and waited for the person to exit on a floor below.

"Why all the secrecy?" asked Arthur.

"I don't want anyone else to scoop this," answered Robert. "Listen, you know that book by Rachel Carson about DDT and how it's killing the birds and ruining the environment?"

"Yeah, sure," said Arthur, "she's all over the news right now. I read it. It's good stuff. Makes you think."

"Stanton Chemical wants us to write a series of articles in support of the chemical industry, refuting the science in the book, and calling her credentials and the validity of her findings into question," said Robert conspiratorially. "They want us to publish the articles in the Bugle, presented as if they are a thoughtful and reasoned look at the book and the debate it's stirred up. With any luck it'll be picked up by the big city boys."

"Why would we do that?" asked Arthur. "Her reasoning seems sound and what she says makes sense. I mean, if you use chemicals to kill off the insects, some of those chemicals are going to end up in the ground water, rivers and streams and in the creatures that eat the insects, and then they get eaten and the fish get eaten and on it goes. I don't understand why we would want to refute it?"

"Because no one has told the other side of the story, and it's our chance to ride a big news story instead of reporting on chicken shit news about late library books and grandma's missing cat!" said Robert sarcastically. "Shit, the most controversial thing we've ever reported on is the affair the high school principal had with the history teacher. Besides, what makes Rachel Carson right and the chemical companies wrong? I mean, why don't we at least look into it and see where it leads? She's a marine biologist, what makes her qualified to write about chemicals and birds and all that?" he said, repeating exactly what Trevor Skeets had told him the night before. "Maybe it's not the pesticides? Maybe it's something else? I mean, if we were to follow her advice, we'd all end up back in the Dark Ages again and the insects and diseases would run rampant," he concluded with what he hoped would sound like a reasonable argument.

"I guess it's a good idea," said Arthur hesitantly. "At least we can run it by Bingham and see what he thinks."

"Good man," said Robert, smiling broadly and slapping Arthur on the back. "Believe me, this is our big moment. You won't regret it! If I can get Bingham to agree to let us do the stories, we should see where it leads us. If they like what we do, who knows! And having a powerful company like Stanton Chemical owing us a favor can't be a bad thing, right?" asked Robert rhetorically with a glint of avarice in his eyes.

CHAPTER 3

—— ✿ ——

The War is Truly On

ROBERT AND ARTHUR sat at a table at the back of the bar at the Hay-Adams Hotel in early January, the famous hotel and its bar nearly as legendary as its fabled White House neighbor across the street. The historic residence had many times in the past been the site of the nation's drama and bloodshed, a symbolic reflection of the national mood, both merry and heartbroken. It was hung once again with black wreaths, swathed in the dark and somber hues of mourning as the nation continued to grieve over the assassinated young President. Mrs. Kennedy had moved out of the residence in December, a shell of her former vibrant self. President Johnson, aware of the questions of conspiracy swirling around him and his home state of Texas, could not bring himself to order the wreaths removed. The nation had buried its handsome young prophet, his death extinguishing forever the hope and dynamism of its youth who were now girding themselves with the armor of suspicion, finding no one to whom they could give their trust, no one to show them the way out of the valley of their fears.

Robert and Arthur were meeting Trevor Skeets for drinks, and had come in early to take in the ambience of the famous hotel. As they watched the people and sipped their drinks, they wondered about the schemes being hatched by the individuals whispering in hushed conversations in the quiet atmosphere of the lounge. The deadly rip current of events in the last months of 1963 had people jockeying for power now in January, as the turmoil of transition became an opportunity to move up in the chain of command.

Robert saw Trevor Skeets and another man walk in and he and Arthur stood up to greet them.

"Skeetsy, so good to see you! It's been a long time."

"Robert, how are you? How's that beautiful wife of yours? You know I still haven't forgiven you for winning that bet!"

"Just as beautiful and sexy as ever. Let me introduce you to the other half of the writing team. Arthur Clark, Trevor Skeets."

"Great to meet you, Arthur," said Skeets, shaking his hand. "We loved the articles, they were just what we wanted. Robert, Arthur, let me introduce you to Stanton Chemical's President and CEO, Henry Mueller."

The men exchanged handshakes all around. They sat down as the young waitress in a frilly white blouse and black mini skirt came to the table.

"What's your poison, gentlemen?" asked Arthur. "Henry, Trevor? What'll you have?"

"Vodka martini, very dry, and just slightly dirty," answered Skeets, leering suggestively at the waitress.

"Same for me," said Mueller.

"Two more rounds for us as well," said Arthur.

"Damn!" said Skeets as the waitress walked away. "What a rack on that piece of ass! Who wants to bet I can get lucky with her later?"

They all laughed. "You're so charming," said Robert sarcastically. "I'm sure you'll just sweep her off her feet. Maybe I'll take that bet."

"No, way! I lost to you last time with Jackie," said Skeets.

The waitress brought their drinks to the table on a tray, leaning over next to each man as she made her way around the table, revealing an ample bosom that spilled readily over the top of her blouse. She stopped next to Skeets to place his drink on the table, and he surreptitiously ran his hand up the side of her leg, inside her mini-skirt, and brushed his thumb against her panties. She flinched slightly, spilling some of his martini on the table.

"Whoa there, honey," said Skeets, winking at her, and removing his hand before anyone saw it. "Let's keep it in the glass. It's easier to drink that way."

The waitress looked hard at Skeets and he smiled conspiratorially. "Don't worry, honey. I'm a big tipper, and I got a big wad burning a hole in my pocket." He winked and gestured crudely from his groin. The waitress rolled her eyes and groane, but said nothing. He sneered back and reached into his pocket to pull out a bundle of bills. When she saw the roll of money she relaxed and smiled at him. "What did you think I was talking about?" he laughed. "Bring us back a towel to wipe the table, and keep these drinks coming!" He peeled off a twenty-dollar bill.

The waitress smiled flirtatiously, deciding the money was worth the abuse. "You heard him, gentlemen," she quipped. "I'm going to hold him to it." Everyone laughed as she walked away swaying her hips and tucking the twenty into her bosom.

"So Robert, thanks for coming out to D.C. to meet with us," said Skeets. "We were really impressed with your articles. Henry and I got to talking about this and we have a proposition for you."

"Okay," said Robert. "We're all ears."

"What those articles did for us," began Mueller, "in deflecting criticism and casting doubt onto Rachel Carson and this new environmental movement, creating confusion in the mind of the public, well, we'd like to expand on that idea. Our industry, hell, our very way of life in America, is being threatened every day. If we don't crush all these movements, all this hippie bullshit! If we don't counter the attack against American capitalism and unfettered free enterprise our way of life will be over. We, all of us," he said, drawing a circle with his hand to include everyone in the bar, "and all of America as we know it, is under siege. These hippies and radicals are taking this country down. We need a voice; a megaphone of our own."

"Henry, we can write more articles, but I don't think the paper will go for it. We've exhausted that topic, and the paper's getting some heat for printing them," said Robert.

"That's not really what we had in mind," said Skeets. "We were thinking of something much bigger."

"Yes, I've talked it over with four CEO's from other chemical companies, and some CEO's at the big oil companies and they're all on board with it. We think it's time," said Mueller.

"Time for what, Henry?" asked Arthur.

"We want to set you up in your own business. A public relations business," said Skeets.

"Public relations?" asked Robert.

"Yes, we want to set up a firm that can help us tell our side of every story, a firm that works for us. We need to even the playing field and we think you are the men to do it," said Mueller.

"In Little Rock?" asked Robert.

"No, no, not in Little Rock," said Skeets, snickering conspiratorially and vigorously shaking his head. "Right here, my man, in the most powerful city in the most powerful country in the world. Right here, in Wash-fucking-ton, D.C., and you, my friend, and you Arthur, will be right smack dab in the thick of it!"

Robert looked at Arthur, a smug smile of self-satisfaction spreading across his face. He had been right, having a powerful company like Stanton Chemical owing them a favor had been a very good thing indeed.

CHAPTER 4

⸻ ⸻

The Carefree Days of Youth

ROBERTA SAT UNDER the shade of a large oak tree with her two best friends, a blanket spread under her, absorbed in the book she was reading, Rachel Carson's *Silent Spring*. She wore a loose cotton skirt, and short-sleeved cotton blouse. The arms of an Eastford College sweatshirt were tied around her neck to ward off the cool spring breeze that periodically blew. She had her shoes off, her toes sliding sensuously up and down the soft wool blanket, enjoying the feel of freedom in the warm spring sun. Behind her, a banner was hung across the entrance to the main hall of the quaint New England college campus where she had spent the last four years of her life. It read *Best of Luck Eastford College - Class of 1984.*

Evan Manning was tickling her with a daffodil, trying to get her attention. She swatted it away and kept reading.

"Roberta, I'm talking to you," pleaded Evan.

"I hear you," she answered, not looking up from her book.

"Answer me! Why won't you go out with me?" Evan had been hounding Roberta for four years to go beyond the friendship stage and move on to seriously dating, but no matter how much he tried to convince her that it was a good idea, she always said no. This time she just looked at him and rolled her eyes in exasperation.

Roberta had met Evan during her first year at Eastford College. She had been working the booth for the National Conservation Society during the college's annual Arts Walk, distributing pamphlets, asking for donations and signing up new members. Evan was wandering by when the sign above the booth caught his attention. In bold green four-foot letters it said, SAVE THE PLANET. Intrigued, he had walked over to Roberta and asked, "What's wrong with the planet?"

"What do you mean?"

"Your sign says SAVE THE PLANET. What's wrong with it?"

She handed him a pamphlet. "If we're not careful, we'll lose it."

"How do you lose a planet?" he asked sarcastically. "It's a pretty darn big thing to lose, isn't it? I mean, does it roll behind God's washing machine, or get thrown in the jar with the change from His pocket?"

She had looked at him for a moment with her mouth open but no words coming out. "Well, no. I mean we'll lose the species that inhabit it."

"Oh, well. That's quite different," he had said, picking up a pamphlet.

"Are you interested in the ecology movement?" she had asked him.

He smiled at her condescendingly. "The ecology *movement*. I hate that word. The civil rights *movement;* the women's *movement:* the Surrealist *movement;* everything's a movement but we don't seem to be getting any-where. We're still just as stupid as we were when we came down from the trees." His look challenged her to dare say something intelligent in response.

She hesitated as she thought about it. "I never really thought about the actual meaning of the word. A group of people coming together to achieve a common goal, a movement toward a shared belief."

He watched her as she stared at nothing, forming her thoughts in her mind. She turned her turquoise blue eyes back to his and smiled broadly, and he felt his loins melt and his heart skip a beat. "When you really think about it," she said with conviction, "if we'd never come down outta those damn trees we wouldn't have to have this movement to save them, would we?"

It was that moment that he had fallen hopelessly in love with her, and had unfailingly pursued her every day of their four years together at Eastford College.

"Leave her alone, Evan," said Summer. "She has a lot on her plate right now." Summer Sparrow was Roberta's best friend in the world, and they did everything together. Summer knew more about Roberta than anyone else and they told each other everything. "So, have you and your Dad made up yet?" Summer asked as she searched for a New York City rock station on her tiny radio. *Love is a Battlefield* by Pat Benatar came through its tinny speaker. "I need to get a boom box," she said to no one in particular.

"No, and I don't think we ever will after our last big fight," sighed Roberta, answering Summer's question. "We just can't see eye to eye on anything to do with the environment. You know, I used to think he was such a hero, a real champion of the Earth. But this issue of clear cutting forests really has us at each other's throats. We had a big fight again last night on the phone. I'm starting to think he's just a big liar. He refuses to understand anything I say about the devastation of the environment and the abuse of the Earth by big businesses like American Pride. And when I brought up Rachel Carson and how moved I am by her book he went ballistic! My Mom had to take the phone away from him before he had a stroke or something! I want to get my master's degree in environmental science. He wants me to get a business degree and come to work for him at his environmental public relations firm. I used to think that was what I wanted, but now," she paused shaking her head "I don't know."

Summer looked at Roberta sympathetically. "He's from a different generation. He thinks the Earth is only here for man to exploit and plunder, and he has the power to influence what people think. He will never change, Roberta," she said sadly.

Roberta looked at Summer with resignation. "I must have done something really bad in a previous life to be punished with a father like this!"

Summer understood her friend perfectly and tried to cheer her up. "But in some ways, you're lucky. At least you can get away from it all like you do every summer. Where are your parents whisking you off to this time? Paris, London, Rome?"

"Oh my God! They tell me that it's part of my education," laughed Roberta. "They've been sending me to a major European city every summer since I was twelve, plus my mother's family in France insists I come to visit them every year." She placed the back of her hand on her forehead and adopted a swooning posture. "Like a heroine from an Edith Wharton novel, *I must take a tour of the Continent.*"

"Don't knock it! You're the most well-travelled twenty-two year old I know," said Summer enviously. "You've been everywhere!"

"I think I might skip this summer and stay home, though," Roberta said thoughtfully. "I'd love to take a trip across the good ol' U.S. of A, and see the Grand Canyon, Yellowstone, maybe go all the way to Oregon. Just bum around and be free, instead of going to stuffy museums and meeting people my parents deem to be the *right* people."

"Hey, that sounds like fun!" exclaimed Evan, his eyes wide with enthusiasm and a big mischievous grin on his face. "My uncle has a VW camper van we could use. It would be great. We could sleep out under the stars in the desert, make a campfire, tell ghost stories, and cuddle in the sleeping bag," he said, winking comically at Roberta.

"That would be so cool!" exclaimed Summer, suddenly very excited too. "We could roast marshmallows and cook over an open fire every night, out on the open road during the day, no one to tell us what to do or where to go. Footloose and free!"

"Wow," Roberta said wistfully, warming to the idea. "Could we really do it?"

"Why not? What's to stop us?" asked Evan.

"I don't know. Nothing, I guess," said Roberta. She sat thinking for a moment as Summer and Evan waited for her answer. "Let's do it!" she exclaimed finally.

"Woohoo!" shouted Evan, jumping to his feet, and grabbing his books. "I'll call my uncle."

"My parents are going to kill me!" exclaimed Roberta, jumping up too.

"At least you'll die happy," said Summer, grabbing Roberta's hands and dancing a happy little jig around the big oak tree.

CHAPTER 5

—— ✎ ——

The Call of the Open Road

"TOTALLY AWESOME, MAN! I love this song!" said Steven from the back seat of the van. "Turn it up, turn it up!"

The VW camper van that Evan's uncle had let the kids borrow for their summer trip had a state of the art sound system, and Evan cranked up the volume as Van Halen's *Jump* came on the radio. Roberta sat in the passenger seat in the front of the van with a map in her lap, periodically giving Evan directions and pointing out places of interest on their route. Summer and Evan's younger brother Steven shared the back seat of the van.

Evan had the classic, All-American good looks for which the girls at Eastford College had gone wild. Steven, five years younger than Evan, had just graduated from high school. He was a rebel version of Evan's clean-cut All-American style. Steven's long shaggy hair and playful, dimpled grin made him popular at school. He was the bad boy all the good girls wanted to go out with, and his velvety brown eyes and devilish smile could lure them into doing things their parents had forbidden. Academics were definitely not his strong suit. Music was his passion and he carried his guitar with him almost everywhere he went, using his lucky pick, which was always in his pocket, to create the songs to the lyrics and melodies that were continually rolling around in his head.

Summer and Steven sang along to David Lee Roth's high-energy vocals, Summer's lovely soprano voice harmonizing beautifully with Steven's sexy tenor. Steven was playing along on his guitar, hitting Eddie Van Halen's chords perfectly.

Roberta was singing along in the front seat, bobbing her head in time to the music. She looked over at Evan and pointed to a spot on the map. "It looks like the campgrounds are about twenty-five miles up this road," she said to Evan, speaking loudly to be heard over the radio. The song ended and Roberta reached down to turn the volume back down, just as the DJ was announcing his next set coming up after the commercial break.

Summer leaned in from the back seat. "I think we need to stop at the next town to find a grocery store. I'm thinking of making a Paella for dinner."

"Mm, that sounds great! I love Paella!" said Roberta.

"Pie what?" asked Steven.

"Pie-a-ya!" Roberta and Summer said in unison.

"It's a Spanish dish with rice and shrimp and chicken and sausage, flavored with saffron," explained Summer to Steven. "I can put it right on the campfire in one big pot. I hope I can find all the ingredients. Saffron may be a little unusual out here in the boonies. Look, there's an exit up ahead. Maybe there's a grocery store."

Roberta turned around in her seat. "You'll love it," she said to Steven. "It's really good. I had it in Barcelona last year."

"You should open a restaurant, Summer," said Evan, turning his head to look at her, as he put the blinker on to change lanes on the highway.

Summer pursed her lips and made a face filled with doubt.

"He's not kidding," added Roberta encouragingly. "The food has been outstanding on this trip." She turned to Evan. "Maybe we can find a good bottle of wine to go with it. My treat."

"No, you bought the beers last night," said Evan. "It's my turn to treat. "

"Hey guys, look, this exit coming up, a Safeway," said Summer.

"Perfect, and there's a gas station across the street," said Evan.

Evan maneuvered the van onto the exit ramp and into the parking lot of the grocery store, stopping in front of the entrance. "I'll go gas up and meet you back here. You, my sexy friend," he said lovingly, running his finger down Roberta's nose and then tapping the end with his finger, "pick out a couple bottles of wine."

Roberta smiled and blushed at being called sexy, and shyly lowered her eyes from his gaze.

Evan threw the gearshift into Park, while Steven and Summer piled out the back of the van and headed into the store. Roberta kept Evan waiting while she collected empty food and beverage containers from the front seat. She looked around for a recycling bin for the glass bottles but there was none, so she reluctantly had to throw everything in the trashcan at the front of the store. She couldn't wait until the day when recycling would be available everywhere.

Roberta went to look for the wine, and Steven and Summer walked around the store together. Steven was pushing a shopping cart, and Summer was pulling items off the shelves and putting things into the cart.

"So how'd you learn to cook so good? Are you a chef or something?" asked Steven.

"My Mother got me started, I guess," explained Summer. "When I was eight or nine I wanted to help her make dinner, and she showed me how to make salad dressing, a vinaigrette. She showed me once, and it was my job every day from then on; minced shallots, French mustard, salt, pepper, vinegar and oil, mix it up. *Voila!* Salad dressing! I grew up on a commune with three other families. We had a big old rickety farmhouse and we grew our own food, and kept chickens, goats, and rabbits, and a dairy cow. Each day I picked lettuce, tomatoes, peppers, onions, whatever was fresh and ready to eat that day. I started asking my parents to give me cookbooks for my birthdays and for Christmas. I love to cook. I read cookbooks like most people read romance novels."

"Roberta's right," Steven said. "You should open a restaurant."

"Yeah, it's my dream to have my own restaurant, but my parents are making me finish college first," said Summer reluctantly. "They're both professors at Eastford. They're like, really big on academics and all that. It sucks. I hate school. I hate being stuck inside all day listening to boring lectures. I want to be outside. I want to be creating something. I want to be working in a garden and cooking up fabulous recipes. What about you? Will you follow in Evan's footsteps?" she asked. "He's got to be the smartest guy I've ever met."

Steven rolled his eyes and sighed. "Tell me about it! Try bein' in that dudes shadow all your life! My Mom worships the ground he walks on. My Dad died about five years ago. My Mom just fell apart and Evan kinda took over at home. But that shit's not for me, man, I ain't goin' to college. I only finished high school cuz they were both on my ass constantly. I'm in a band back home. I play lead guitar, do a little songwriting. We've had a few gigs around town, but it's time for us to hit the big time, get serious, man. The drummer's got a friend that has a recording studio. As soon as I get back home we're cuttin' a demo tape, try to get a recording contract. I've been workin' at the record store after school and weekends for a year, man, savin' up my money. It's gonna cost a thousand bucks to cut the tape. We're each puttin' in two hundred. My Mom thinks I'm savin' for college. She's gonna fuckin' explode when I tell her, but I don't care. It's my dream, man, and I gotta go after it. You know what I mean? It's like, a higher calling."

"Yeah, go for it, for sure," agreed Summer. "You only live once. You gotta do what's right for you!"

Roberta came around the corner and spotted them halfway down the aisle. "Hey, there you guys are," she said. She was carrying two bottles of wine and lifted them for Summer to see. "Not much of a selection. Is this okay?"

"Perfect!" said Summer. "I actually found everything I need. They even had the saffron. We're just about finished, we'll meet you at the checkout."

Evan came in from the parking lot, and found Roberta standing in the checkout line holding two bottles of wine and four plastic wine glasses. "I'll take those," said Evan.

Roberta handed the items to Evan, and then picked up a Life magazine from the checkout stand with a photo of a ruggedly handsome man about her age on the cover. The caption under the photo read, *'French Environmental Photojournalist Michel Manon. His life's purpose is a higher calling'.* "This looks interesting," she said, handing it to the fat checkout lady who had long, glittery pink fingernails nails and a cigarette dangling from her mouth.

Steven and Summer stood in a different check out line with their shopping cart. Steven picked up the same Life Magazine, perusing the cover photo and the caption, and threw it in the basket on top of the groceries. He got out in front of Summer before she began unloading the cart.

"Hey beautiful," he said to the young checkout girl. He looked behind them to make sure there was no one else in line. "What's your name?"

"Amy," said the girl shyly.

"You're really pretty, Amy," said Steven leaning in. "You've got great eyes. I'm sure guys tell you that all the time though, huh?"

Amy giggled shyly, her face turning bright crimson. "No, not really" she said, melting under his intense and alluring stare.

"I'm Steve, this is Summer. We're in a band. That dude over there," he said, pointing to good-looking Evan, "is our lead singer. The chick he's with does harmony vocals and plays piano. I'm on guitar. Summer's on drums. We've been invited out to Portland, Oregon to be the opening act for Fleetwood Mac." Summer stared at Steven with a look that said *what the hell are you talking about?*

"That is so *totally* awesome!" said Amy.

"Yeah, it's really cool, man," continued Steven. "It's our big break. We're drivin' out to Oregon. Came all the way from Vermont. Campin' under the stars at night, checkin' out this amazing scenery during the day. Just, you know, bein' free."

"That is *so-o-o cool!*" gushed Amy.

"Yeah, man, it really is. So, you know, we're a little strapped for cash. Like, think you could help us out?" Steven looked at her fingers keying prices into the register, then back to her face, showing an impish grin. "You know what I mean?" he asked.

Amy got the message and started passing every other item through without keying it in. The store manager walked by and eyed them suspiciously. She stopped keying, pretending to look for a price on an item, and he walked on. Steven smiled and winked at her. Summer handed her some money after she had totaled everything.

"Thanks man!" exclaimed Steven. "You're an awesome chick. Keep an eye out for us in Oregon, man. We'll be in the news," he said picking up the paper grocery bags.

"Hey? What's the name of your band?" shouted Amy, as he headed towards the door.

Steven turned around, a flash of genius in his eyes and a dimpled grin on his face. Walking backwards out the door, he shouted back, "A Higher Calling!"

CHAPTER 6

Every Life Needs a Purpose

"To the chef!" said Evan, raising his wine glass in a toast to Summer. A roaring campfire blazed brightly in the middle of their campsite, and the four young travelers sat in a circle on aluminum lawn chairs, finishing up the delectable paella that Summer had made.

"To the chef!" said Roberta and Steven in unison.

"Thank you, thank you!" said Summer, standing up and taking an exaggerated bow. She sat back down and took a swallow from her wine glass.

"I'll never be able to do anything like that!" said Roberta. "You're so amazing. What an awesome meal!"

"What do you mean?" asked Summer. "It's very easy. You're amazing too!"

"Yes, you are amazing," said Evan, reaching over and taking hold of her hand.

Roberta smiled at Evan and squeezed his hand. "No, I'm not. Not really," she said. "I mean, look at this guy," she said, reaching out for the Life Magazine. "Twenty-five years old and already an award winning environmental photojournalist. Look at these photos!"

Roberta thumbed through the magazine to show Evan the photographs from the article; a polar bear riding an ice floe, an adorable snow-white baby seal with big black eyes staring sweetly up at the camera followed by the blood-stained ice under the baby after being clubbed to death in a brutal baby seal hunt. A mother elephant protectively cradling her baby in her trunk, a mother lioness lovingly nuzzling her sweet cub, and nomadic people in brightly colored garments leaving their tracks in the shifting sands of a far off desert.

"He risks his life to get these photographs. He knows his purpose in life and takes huge risks to achieve it. He's dedicated and he's uncompromising. It's what I want to be, but I am deluding myself into thinking I can be somebody like this. I'm just a spoiled suburban kid with a comfy life. I've never done anything worthwhile."

"You're too hard on yourself!" countered Evan. "I think you're fantastic, and you're going to do great things in life. And just look at you, you're beautiful too. You're like every man's dream."

"You're judging me by the way I look, not by what I've done," said Roberta, pulling her hand away.

Evan took her hand back and placed it again inside of his. "You're smart, you're passionate, you're incredibly beautiful, you're funny," he said.

Roberta laughed suspiciously and looked around to see if someone was behind her. "Are you talking about me?"

"Yes, I'm talking about you! Who else would I be talking about? Don't you know how incredible you are?" he asked.

"No, I guess I don't," said Roberta hesitantly. "I just wish…I just want to do something important! I want to make a statement with my life. I feel like I've always been the good girl, the quiet one who doesn't rock the boat. I want to accomplish something big. I want to make my mark in the world."

"Give yourself time, you're not even out of college yet," replied Evan. "You're going to do great things with your life, I just know it. People like this guy," he said, dismissively thumping the magazine, "that kind of life only comes along once in a while. Not everyone can do that. Stop worrying! Have some fun. The big important stuff can come later. We're on our way to Portland, we just ate a fabulous meal cooked by our best friend, and you're with people that love you." Evan looked at her very seriously, the love he felt for her evident in his eyes. "You're a fantastic person and you can accomplish anything you want."

"I'm not as confident about that as you are. It seems so easy for you," said Roberta more heatedly than she intended. "Your life is all laid in front of you. You know what you want to do and how to get there; an MBA from an Ivy league school, a job on Wall Street, a nice little wife with nice little kids with a nice little life of country clubs and private school and church on Sundays. I just don't feel so sure of everything like you do."

"That's unfair," he said, pulling his hand away, his feelings obviously hurt. "You make it sound so shallow. What's wrong with a nice life, as long as you love the people in it, and take care of them? I don't think your life and my life are mutually exclusive."

"Maybe not," she answered hesitantly. "I don't mean to hurt your feelings," she said apologetically. "I think I'm just...I don't know." Roberta sighed and looked over at him. "I'm fighting with my father and it colors my whole outlook. Mark my words, though, I'm going to make a statement somehow."

"You can make a statement when we get to Oregon," Evan said encouragingly, easily forgiving her for her earlier comment about his shallow outlook. Reaching for the bottle of wine, he said, "Right now, you should relax and have more wine. Steven, where's your guitar? Play us a tune!"

Steven took up his guitar. He went through his tuning routine and then deftly belted out a couple of original tunes. He paused for a second and took a swallow of his wine, and then launched into the next song, one he was still working on called *Summer*. The words of the song started out sweet and caring, and Evan and Roberta cooed in agreement, and then he ad-libbed some funny lines about paella and everyone laughed.

Evan put his arm around Roberta and she leaned over to rest her head against his shoulder. Summer lit up a joint and passed it around. Roberta took a hit and instantly felt her mood lighten and her cares lift away. She looked up at Evan, seeing him smiling and laughing and singing along, struck by how handsome he was. It seemed as if she had never really seen him before, and she was suddenly very aware of what a good friend he was and how much she loved him. She leaned in to kiss him lightly on the lips. Evan locked his eyes onto hers, love plainly visible on his face in the warm glow of the firelight.

As Summer and Steven blended their voices in perfect harmony, Evan stood up and took Roberta by the hand and led her away to the van.

CHAPTER 7

Why He Fights

MICHEL MANON PREPARED for his next photo assignment with the same swift action and meticulous attention to detail that he had always done. When disasters occurred he had to act fast and be ready to fly to the far reaches of the globe at a moment's notice.

Michel had come by his passion for photography very early in life. As a boy, he had received a camera from his grandfather for Christmas. His grandfather was an accomplished amateur photographer himself and he taught Michel how to develop and print the photos he took in the tiny darkroom in the potting shed behind their modest stone *maison*. Michel was spellbound the first time he saw the images appear as if by magic on the blank white paper, and he was soon scouring his hometown for interesting photographic subjects.

He had a natural eye for composition and seemed to understand the effect of light instinctively. As he trekked further and further along the ancient roads that led out of the village, the people would seek him out, invite him into their humble homes and tell him the stories of their lives. Many of them had been involved in *la résistance* during the Nazi occupation of France in World War II, and he would snap their photos as they sat for hours weaving their spell of diabolical and cunning escapades to valiantly outwit the German soldiers. He would run home to develop the negatives and print the film, presenting them to the teary-eyed storytellers as a gift for their children's children.

Soon after receiving the camera, the purpose of Michel's life came to him suddenly and forcefully in one great bolt of understanding. He knew from the moment it happened what he would do with his camera and his talent. He was walking through the woods near his parent's home one beautiful fall day and came upon a dove that had been shot by a hunter. He stared at the creature with tears in his eyes as it cooed up at him, flapping its wings helplessly with its injured body.

The anger he felt toward the hunter welled up in his heart, and he began shooting pictures of the dying creature as it passed through its final agonizing ordeal. He ran home to develop and print the film in his darkroom, and tears rolled down his cheeks as he watched the images appear. The eyes of the creature stared back at him from the watery solution and seemed at first to implore him for help. Slowly, with each additional photo he developed, the light of life in the eyes of the dove grew dimmer, and then went out completely. The images were seared into his mind's eye of nature's beauty suffering at the hands of man, leaving him shaken for days afterward, and his lifelong activist fervor was born.

His talent and his activism would eventually take him around the globe, producing stunning photographic images and heart-wrenching words of outrage and compassion as he spoke to countless organizations, governmental agencies and United Nations committees. Among organizations like The Sierra Club, The World Wildlife Fund, The Nature Conservancy, The Cousteau Society and others, he was a hero of mythic proportions and he was known to school children around the world as simply Michel.

No one would deny that his talent was enormous, and he was blessed with the rare ability to shoot a great photo and write the words to go with it that could start the observer's blood boiling or melt their heart. The force of the impact that his talent wielded in pictures and print was irresistible, and many common, everyday people around the globe had been moved to action by one of his books or articles.

By the age of twenty-five, he had already won numerous prizes for the beauty and insight of his photographs including two Pulitzers; one for his photos of the baby harp seal hunt by Canadian fur traders, their sweet-natured faces and soft white fur set inconceivably against the blood red carnage in the aftermath of their clubbed demise, and the other for his stunning photos showing the eternal majesty of the ancient herding communities of the Maasai people in Kenya.

Michel was thankfully aware that he had the somewhat rare privilege of living an integrated life. His work and his passion were one and the same creating a synergy that coalesced to produce stunning and moving images for the world to see. He had risked his life many times to snap a prized photo. His risk-taking was not due to egotistical motivations, but from a deep-seated desire to bring pictures of suffering and beauty to the world that no one else could get.

His next assignment would be heart wrenching and difficult, but the images of horror and misery must get out to the world. He quickly packed two hard-sided camera bags with the precious cargo of his trade: three camera bodies, various telephoto, portrait and wide angle lenses, sun shields, several lens caps, cleaning solution, packets of lens paper, hundreds of canisters of 35mm film, and extra canisters of canned air to clean the dust off the cameras and the lenses. Where he was going there would be minimal creature comforts, and nowhere to buy anything he might have forgotten.

He then packed two large steamer trunks with hundreds of bars of soap, toothbrushes, toothpaste, bottled water, shampoo, dishwashing liquid, chocolate candy bars, American cigarettes, canned and dried food, and toilet paper. Into a backpack he put several changes of underwear, a few T-shirts, an extra pair of jeans, a towel, a box of matches, a medical facemask, several Moleskine journals, a travel guide, a map, and a French-English dictionary.

He looked around the apartment, eager to be on his way, yet worried he was forgetting something important. He took several seconds to close his eyes and imagine himself at his destination and the desperately poor and tragically injured people there, thinking hard if there was anything else they might need. He didn't know what he would encounter, but knew from the news reports and his contacts at several aid agencies that this was a disaster of immense proportions in human suffering. He could think of nothing else, and he closed the trunks, the camera cases, and his backpack, and loaded his car for the drive to the airport and the Air France flight that would take him to his destination of Bhopal, India, and the disastrous release at a Union Carbide chemical plant of methyl isocyanate gas that had killed, maimed, suffocated and blinded hundreds of thousands of desperately poor people.

CHAPTER 8

Roberta Finds Her Voice

THE LITTLE VW camper van full of friends had finally arrived in Portland. They arranged to stay with Summer's twenty-four year old cousin, Dylan, a college dropout and radical environmental activist whose door was always open to anyone who needed a place to crash. A parade of college friends, teenage runaways and potheads made their way to the apartment throughout the night, each one bringing something with them by way of payment; a pizza, a bottle of booze, a six pack, or a joint. Dylan was passionate and articulate, and the amorphous group talked all night about what was wrong with America. The land, water and air were being destroyed by big business and government inaction. Dylan was extremely intelligent, and he had a command of facts at his disposal that supported his arguments. He was prepared to break the law to make his point, and he boasted about his radical activities that included many protests that ended in police altercations and being dragged away in handcuffs.

They talked about the legislation that would be needed to protect the environment, and something new that he called *sustainable development* that placed responsibility on the corporations and enforcement on governments to guard against stripping the planet of its natural resources. They argued about the slow progress of working within the system to encourage people to vote for pro-environmental congressmen and senators on a local and national level versus the immediate effects of working outside the system, using guerilla tactics to bring the plight of the planet to the world's attention. Dylan became heated when he talked about the whitewashing, or green washing as he called it, that was being perpetrated on the American people by companies like the logging and paper giant American Pride, who were clear-cutting forests in the Pacific Northwest. They had recently begun using their connections and influence to gain access to old growth forests. Their big money contributions to the President's political campaign guaranteed them favorable treatment at the White House and in Congress, and they were a perfect example, he told them, of American greed and corruption at the highest levels.

Eventually someone made the connection between Roberta Reed and Robert Reed, and there was a tense moment when Dylan thought they had been infiltrated by a spy in their midst. He haughtily challenged Roberta to prove her commitment to the environmental movement by going along with a group of protestors that were driving up to a logging camp near Antelope to protest American Pride's recent logging of an old growth forest. Evan was dead set against it. He tried to persuade her to steer clear of the confrontation these people had in mind, but Roberta was determined to go. She felt that she had finally found the opportunity to put her words and feelings into action. Summer and Steven agreed to go along, too. Evan did not like the sound of it and pulled her aside to try to convince her not to go.

"But this is exactly what I was trying to tell you last night in Wyoming," argued Roberta. "I want to do something to make a difference. I want to make an impact, and this is the only way to do it."

"Roberta, this is one of your Dad's clients. You can't!" exclaimed Evan.

"On the contrary, it's the very reason I should go!" Roberta shot back. "Who better than me to counter the massive cover up my father has foisted on the American people?"

Evan looked at Roberta, and pleaded," Please don't do this, Roberta."

"Look, you can stay here if you want to," she exclaimed. "You aren't obligated to come along, but I've made up my mind. I'm going!"

CHAPTER 9

Father And Daughter Part Ways

ROBERT AND ARTHUR were celebrating the successful launch of the public relations campaign to counter the negative publicity American Pride had been receiving over the issue of clear-cutting and their logging activities in old growth forests. The campaign was working, and according to polls conducted by RPR, the results showed that the negative feelings against American Pride had begun to shift.

They were hosting an elegant cocktail party at Robert and Jackie's beautiful Chevy Chase, Maryland mansion. Robert and Jackie were the consummate host and hostess, with Robert handling drinks and jokes, and Jackie handling the caterers and wait staff and looking breezily beautiful. The guest list consisted of a stunning array of the glitterati of American business and Washington power brokers. Besides the guest of honor, Earl Montrose, the CEO of American Pride, CEO's from some of America's top companies were in attendance including Henry Mueller and Trevor Skeets, who had recently been promoted to Executive Vice President at Stanton Chemical. Charles Conway, the CEO of Purity Oil, Alexander Trinket, the CEO of Healthful Tobacco, and James Bishop, the CEO of Standard Motors, along with a smattering of congressmen and important people from the Hill including Robert's old friend, Senator Harry Markham were there.

The public relations campaign that Robert and Arthur had contrived for American Pride was two-pronged. The issue of clear-cutting of forests, specifically old growth forests, was in the news and American Pride was feeling the tide of public opinion turning against them. The CEO, Earl Montrose, tried to mitigate the negative press by casting aspersions on the protestors, but that seemed to enrage the public even more. He turned to Reed Public Relations for help.

The first prong of the campaign was intended to influence policy-makers in Washington, D.C. through well-placed articles, white papers and opinion pieces purportedly written by knowledgeable stakeholders with interviews on the Sunday news programs by hired guns from Congress whose re-elections depended on money from the wood and paper industry. This part of the campaign focused on the role the U.S. played as a leader in the world economy, and warned of apocalyptic devastation to the mighty U.S. if American Pride was forced to change the long-standing practice in the logging industry of clear-cutting. Alleging that the industry would be forced to lay off tens of thousands of people, and opening up the threat of a worldwide lumber shortage, allowing American economic and political enemies in Japan and Russia to step in and drive the U.S. industry out of business.

The second prong of the campaign was intended to pull at the heart-strings of the public and win their sympathy. Using a heavy rotation of radio, television and print ads, this aspect of the campaign focused the nation's attention on the people and families employed by the lumber industry whose lives would be negatively affected, comparing them to the brave and fiercely independent people who had journeyed west to settle the Pacific Northwest. The most effective of these was a television ad showing a sepia-toned photograph of an 1880's-era logging camp of lumberjacks holding axes and hand saws that faded out to become a lumber camp of today, while a voice overlay by a famous actor told about the patriotic legacy and rugged individualism of American Pride and its' workers. It warned of dire economic consequences were Congress to limit the industry. The term "old growth forests" was never mentioned in any of the ads, but instead foretold a warning that Big Brother was putting the brakes on American industriousness, threatening the jobs of honest, hard-working people "just like you and me."

The pleasant summer evening had allowed Jackie to open up the huge sliding doors that led out onto the flagstone pool deck. Their guests sipped drinks and nibbled hors d'oeuvres offered to them from wait staff with silver trays while being quietly entertained by a jazz combo playing seductively from a corner of the patio. Jackie had commandeered Robert's secretary to help her with the party preparations, and together they had floated hundreds of lit candles in the pool, and strung yards of twinkling party lights in the trees surrounding the flagstone pool deck.

Trevor Skeets had trapped one of the waitresses, plying her with what passed for him as charm. His blatant sexism had not changed in twenty years, and in fact, had grown worse with age and success. He was delivering the punch line on a dirty joke about sexually liberated women he had heard from Johnny Carson on a recent trip to Hollywood. The joke fell flat, and the waitress stealthily slipped away from him. Dejected, he turned around to see who was within reach, and walked over to Robert Reed and a small group of men on the other side of the pool.

"I have to say, Robert," Earl Montrose of American Pride was saying as Skeets joined them, "I think you outdid yourself on this new public relations campaign. What a stroke of genius to compare the people in our logging camps to the migration west in the 1800's."

"Thanks Earl," said Robert. "I can't take all the credit though. David over there," he said, pointing to his nephew David, "came up with the idea for the TV ads. I love those sepia photographs that morph into your logging camp."

"Well, whoever I should thank, it's brilliant. The white papers and magazine articles describing the economic impact to the U.S. and the Sunday news shows with our trade association fanning the flames of fear of the Japanese...I mean, it's brilliant!" exclaimed Earl.

"Glad we could be of service," said Robert, feigning humility.

"We wouldn't use anyone else," added Skeets to the compliments going Robert's way. "This man is brilliant when it comes to diverting attention and subverting the truth."

"Well, let's just say I am good at presenting a different side of the argument," said Robert, seething at Skeets' blatant characterization of his business.

Skeets felt Robert's annoyance, and launched into the joke he had told the waitress, hoping to have better luck with a male audience. Just before he got to the punch line, Arthur came running up to the group from inside the house, and pulled Robert aside.

"You've got to come and see this!" whispered Arthur in Robert's ear. "Now!"

Seeing the look of urgency and shock on his face, Robert quickly followed him into the house. A knot of people was gathered around the television, including Harry Markham. Robert momentarily wondered if the President had been assassinated or one of his clients had been involved in some kind of disaster. He made his way to the front of the group and his jaw dropped as he recognized Roberta's face on the screen, drenched in rain and mud, chained to a huge tree.

The view through the rain spattered camera lens showed logging equipment and bulldozers sitting idle around the camp. Loggers were standing around with their hands jammed into their pockets, kicking at the ground in boredom and frustration. A reporter was standing next to Roberta with a microphone in his hand. Robert reached out to turn up the volume He slowly sat down in the silk upholstered chair in front of the television.

"Why would you go to such extraordinary lengths to get your point across?" the reporter asked Roberta. "Isn't it enough to simply protest with placards and signs?"

"No kidding," said Senator Markham under his breath.

"Unfortunately, it's not enough," said Roberta to the reporter. "I would prefer not to have to go to these lengths, but American Pride's campaign to destroy America's treasured old growth forests must be stopped. This tree is estimated to be over four hundred years old, older than the American republic itself. It has a right to its continued existence. The lumber industry must take steps now to sustain their own industry, and begin planting their own reusable forests for the future, or we will soon have no old growth forests left on this planet."

"I understand from some of your...um, colleagues here," said the reporter with some hesitation, as the camera panned the scene to reveal ten others who were also tied or chained to trees," that your father's public relations firm, Reed Public Relations, was hired by American Pride to counter the rising tide of public opinion against these logging practices. Doesn't that present somewhat of a conflict of interest for you?"

Roberta's heart thudded wildly, and she wondered who had told the reporter that her father's firm represented American Pride. She looked over and saw Dylan watching her with a self-satisfied grin on his face, and she was momentarily chastened that she had agreed to take part in this. She struggled to regain her composure and think about how to answer the reporter's question.

"Yes," she said slowly, tears stinging her eyes," that's true, but cutting down these trees is wrong, and I'll fight against anyone, including my own father, to prevent them from being removed!" A slight edge of hysteria had crept into her voice at the end, and she was visibly shaking.

"Is there anything you'd like to say to American Pride, and your father, specifically?" asked the reporter.

"Oh, shit," said Senator Markham.

"To my father, no," she said, looking at the camera and somehow hoping he would see how sorry she was but also how determined, "but to American Pride and companies like them, just two words: sustainable development. We can't continue to use up natural resources at this pace and expect to maintain our existence on this planet. American Pride must realize that a shortsighted gain to make a profit at the expense of long-term planning is not the answer." Roberta paused for a moment to catch her breath, and then added. "If they cut this tree, they'll have to take me with it."

Robert sat motionless in his chair, trying to make sense of what had just happened. Arthur pulled Earl Montrose aside, whispering assurances that they would get started immediately on damage control.

Senator Markham yanked Robert up from his chair and spoke quietly into his ear, pulling him along by his elbow as he made his way to the kitchen and out the back door. "I do believe, Robert Reed, you've got a humdinger of a situation on your hands! Yesiree, a humdinger! Sorry, I can't stick around to see how it all turns out. Can't afford to appear to be on the wrong side of this issue. Call me in the morning and we'll schedule a private meeting with the trade association to see how we want to handle this."

As Markham snuck quietly out the door, the stunned group of party guests began talking heatedly, and the phone began ringing, and continued to ring for the rest of the night. In the days and weeks that followed, he and Arthur scrambled to come up with a counter attack to save the American Pride account. In the campaign of damage control he cooked up with David's help, they used Roberta's protest tactics against her, appropriating the term "tree-hugger" to deride the environmental movement and its members as a throw-back to the 1960's, and that era's drug-addled flower children who wanted to bring down the American way of life. They engineered a smear campaign that used the now derisive slur repeatedly in print and on television. Her father refused to speak to her after the incident, and in less than a month her mother had whisked her away to stay with her relatives in France to give her father time to cool off.

Interlude

TENZIN CLIMBED THE mountain passes with the sun, his yaks fanning out behind and beside him. As the sun rose higher in the sky the golden hues descended down the mountain range, and onto the valley below, bathing every flower, every leaf, every drop of dew and every blade of grass in warmth and light.

Twenty springs had passed since his first trek. Tenzin wandered with his small herd of yaks through the mountain meadows, following an ancient route, grazing them on tender grasses, clover flowers, and lichen. The air is thin at this altitude and life is precious, yet a number of species thrive in the short burst of spring and summer at the top of the world and Tenzin felt one with the Earth. The jagged peaks rose above the valley floor more than 22,000 feet into the heavens and seemed high enough to impede the march of the stars across the sky. The broad fertile valleys meandered through the sturdy mountain ranges, showing off their spring green alpine meadows like delicate flowered skirts, abuzz with activity, teeming with life in the sun of late May. Dogwood and lychee blossoms painted the landscape, their petals blowing in the wind and showering the meadows like pink and white rain; Himalayan blue poppies showed off in hues of lavender and were visited by gigantic, wooly mountain bees. Dark winged alpine butterflies darted delicately around pink buddleia. In the canyons below, the power of rushing waters from the three rivers that sliced through the rock walls of the canyons, swollen with snow melt, could be heard, the sound carried upward on the wind.

"The color of the mountains is the Buddha's body; the sound of running water is his great speech," whispered Tenzin.

He and his yaks ascended the mountains on a dangerous trek, especially for the little calves in his keep, across rocky terrain and through rushing river tributaries. He stands guard and is watchful and patient. The yaks give the monks the milk from which the butter is churned that flavors the frothy tea that sustains them in the cold, dry, thin air. The mountains give the yaks nourishment in the spring and summer. His annual trek along ancient mountain paths to the high meadows at 13,000 feet of altitude is part of the rhythm of his life, the giving and the taking, the interconnectedness between him and his yaks and the Earth, that has continued for more generations than he can count.

In the far distance, he can see his village below and the monastery where his brother monks reside, and where he and his yaks reside during the winter months. Colorful prayer flags crisscross the landscape of the village and the surrounding hillsides, fluttering in the wind. The prayers of the monks, spoken in chants and written on the flags, are carried on the wind to the ears and the hearts of men and women everywhere. Smoke from the alters of burnt offerings curl in ascent to the sky, a symbol of the monks' belief in the interconnectedness of life that flows between all creatures like smoke. Tenzin sees the smoke and sends a prayer on the wind to the world.

"As Wind carries our prayers for Earth and all life, may respect and love light our way; may our hearts be filled with compassion for others and for ourselves; may peace increase on Earth, and may it begin with me."

CHAPTER 10

Sacrifice Should Not Always Be Rewarded

"THERE'S GOT TO be something we can do! This isn't fair!" shouted David Reed, pounding on the table in the luxurious boardroom at Reed Public Relations.

"I think we should give her a chance," one of the people at the table said to him.

"It's what her father wanted, we can't go against his wishes," said another.

"No! This can't be allowed to stand! She can't possibly run this business," said another.

Arthur Clark used his pen to tap the table in an attempt to regain order in the room. Eventually, everyone settled down and he spoke.

"Let's have an orderly discussion, shall we?" he demanded. "I think you all know my position about this. I've known Roberta all her life. I have been more like an uncle to her than just her father's business partner. She's energetic, intelligent and very passionate about the environment, and she comes with tremendous credentials. She took her master's degree in environmental science, and has worked for some of the most respected environmental foundations in the world. She has co-chaired a UN sub-committee on the new science of climate change and has connections to some of the best minds on the planet regarding conservation and green initiatives. She may not have a degree in business, but with our help I think she can learn. I also think she can bring this firm a new and fresh way of thinking about its' role and how we serve our clients. And lastly, it's decreed in the Will, and is what Robert Reed wanted. There's nothing we can do."

"Arthur, are you out of your mind?" asked David. "You know damn well that if we let her loose in here, she's going to find out things that could destroy this firm and all of us with it. Robert Reed was no namby-pamby bleeding heart! He made our clients look green even when they weren't. Christ, he invented the whole idea of green washing!"

"But that should never have been a strategy," said Margaret Newberry, an advisor to the firm, and a non-voting member of the board of directors. "Right now, a lot of businesses are looking for ways to actually be green, and not just pretend to look it. I agree with Art, we need to give Roberta a chance. She can take this company into the 21st century with a new perspective. She has the credentials and the gravitas to make us look good to the whole world!"

"Need I remind you all that my son David received ten percent of Robert Reed's shares in that Will, and I still own sixteen percent, and with Arthur's twenty-five percent, that gives us enough as a voting block to vote her out and override the Will."

"I hope you aren't serious?" said Margaret. "I, for one, will not go along with a boardroom coup." Several of the other advisors and board members at the table murmured in agreement.

David looked threateningly at Margaret, hatred in his eyes. "You have no voting shares and are here only as a courtesy, Margaret, so shut the fuck up! This is a family matter!" he declared.

The room erupted in shouts and recriminations. Arthur again tapped his pen on the table to regain quiet. "Quiet down, all of you. I will settle this matter immediately. I will not vote against Roberta. Truthfully David, I agree with Margaret. We need to take this firm in a different direction, and you are not the man to do it."

David jumped up out of his chair and locked eyes with Arthur. "Listen you old goat, I worked my ass off for that tyrant for more than ten years, doing his dirty work and kissing his ass. I am the *only* one who can take the reins of this firm. I deserve it," he said angrily as he walked to the door. "You haven't heard the last of this, Arthur!" he shouted as he stormed out of the room.

CHAPTER 11

Mom Is Usually Right

ROBERT AND JACKIE Reed had reached the stratospheric heights of the social and political culture of Washington, D.C. Their magnificent mansion in the exclusive enclave of Chevy Chase, Maryland was the showy result of Reed Public Relations' success in the heady atmosphere of power brokers that bartered favors and made fortunes in the nation's capital.

Roberta had grown up in the home. Although she knew she had lived in Arkansas briefly after her birth, this was the only home she had ever known. Roberta's baby sister had died of influenza when Roberta was six, and so she had been raised as an only child, doted on by her protective mother.

Although Roberta and Jackie had a close relationship, as a teenager Roberta had chafed at the constraints of her mother's constant vigilance, made all the worse by the tragic death as an infant of her second daughter. She had relied on her mother to provide a buffer between she and her father when she was in college. Her rocky relationship with him sometimes strained her relationship with her mother, but they always managed to come back to equilibrium, finding common ground in their deep and abiding love for each other.

They were sitting at the table in the breakfast room of Jackie's elegantly appointed home looking at the cards and letters of condolence that had poured in after Robert Reed's death. Hattie, the sweet Jamaican maid that had helped raise Roberta, had placed a tray of tea and cookies on the table. Roberta sipped her tea as Jackie started on a fresh stack of envelopes, reading each one and then clipping it together with the envelope, to use as a reference in her future correspondence with the sender.

"We've received condolences from so many of your father's friends and all the employees at the company," said Jackie, waving her hand over the stacks of mail. "Secretaries, writers, editors, graphic artists, mail clerks and managers from San Francisco to London. They all wish you well, too, in your new role."

"I've gotten dozens of phone calls too," said Roberta. "I have to say, I am really perplexed as to why Dad did this?"

Jackie picked up a card from the pile and handed it to Roberta. "We received a lovely card from Harry Markham. He and your father have been friends for as long as I can remember. He has always been very kind to me."

"Really Mom?" asked Roberta, rolling her eyes. "Senator Markham's had a mad crush on you for years. I'm surprised that Dad actually put up with it. I'm sure, now that Dad's gone, he'll be sniffing around here a lot more."

"Roberta, really! Don't be crude," scolded Jackie.

"Well, it's true isn't it?"

"Oh Roberta! Your father always knew it was just a harmless flirtation," said Jackie defensively. "He knew I never seriously looked at any other man. He was my Prince Charming, your father, so handsome in his tuxedo. What grand parties we've had in this house," she said wistfully. "I know so many important people because of your father. Movie stars, Presidents, Prime Ministers, and I even met that lovely Princess Diana. It was exciting to be married to your father and I loved every minute of our life together." Jackie wiped a tear from her eye. "No one could ever take his place, not even Harry Markham, but he and your father had many mutual interests, and they go way back. He's like family."

"Oh yes, how convenient for Dad to have such a powerful friend in Congress who could trade favors and influence legislation to help his clients get away with their rape of the planet!"

"Roberta!" said Jackie in exasperation. "I know you and your father had differences but must you speak that way about him now, at this time? He was a good man, and he did good work."

"Have you been living under a rock all these years, Mother? How many times did you have to break up our fights? Honestly, after the fallout over the Oregon incident, if it hadn't been for you, he and I would have never spoken to each other again. We had more than differences; we were at each other's throats! Dad hated me, and everything I stand for. He was a corporate apologist, a spin doctor, and his whole corrupt life was one big lie!"

"Roberta, *arrête!* I don't believe any of that! I kept out of your father's business, yes, but you broke his heart with what you did in Oregon, but he didn't hate you, Roberta. He just didn't understand you. You humiliated him on national television. And then, after that, to find out..." Jackie reached out to take hold of Roberta's hand, and Roberta looked her mother in the eyes, a deeply hidden secret of emotional pain from Roberta's past registering on both of their faces.

Jackie patted Roberta's hand with motherly affection. She smiled resignedly, then moved on. "All I know is he was a good husband, and he provided me with a good life, and I will always love him." Jackie squeezed Roberta's hand for emphasis. "And he must have trusted you after all. Otherwise, why would he make you CEO of the company?"

"I wish I knew. I am as stunned as everyone else. And it's not going to be a smooth transition either. David called the board together two days ago and tried to convince them to vote me out. I have my first employee meeting on Monday morning, and I meet with the board in the afternoon. I haven't even set foot in that office for ten years. I'm so nervous." Her face showed her anxiety, and Roberta unconsciously bit her lip.

"What are you going to wear?" asked Jackie.

"What?"

"What are you going to wear?" repeated Jackie. "You have to make a good impression on your first day. You must look confident and ready to take on the world. It's very important. What you wear on your first day will be the first of many important decisions that you make."

"I don't know," answered Roberta, looking down at her jeans and sweat-shirt. "I haven't even thought about it. I don't have anything appropriate to be CEO of this God-awful firm!"

"Well, that is something I can help you with!" exclaimed Jackie, standing up and pulling Roberta off her chair. "Come, my darling! We have some serious shopping to do!"

CHAPTER 12

A Makeover Can Do
Wonders For Your Attitude

MIN-MIN, THE ORANGE tabby, stretched lazily in the warm sun streaming in through the curved bay window of the townhouse on Dupont Circle, her morning routine of eating and sleeping unchanged. Everything about the cat's environment was the same, but the woman who exited the home at 8:15 on Monday morning was decidedly not. She had dressed with great care, choosing the right suit, heels, and jewelry to make the right impression.

The office of Reed Public Relations was abuzz with activity. The busy receptionist was answering phones and directing calls to the myriad people who helped make the firm successful; artists, writers, editors, managers, assistants and department heads. Packages to be couriered to clients were stacked on the corner of her desk. The faxes coming in from offices around the world, and the sound of the copy machine printing off hundreds of pages added to the cacophony that made the office hum.

David and Patrick Reed were locked away behind closed doors waiting anxiously for Roberta to arrive, and plotting ways to get rid of her. Robert Reed's executive assistant, Holly Branson, paced nervously in front of the reception desk, waiting for her too, wondering if firing her father's assistant would be Roberta's first official act as the new CEO. Arthur had walked by the front door several times, hoping to catch her as she walked in, and ease her into the lion's den. He was worried that she would come into the office wearing braids and Birkenstocks, and fall flat on her face on her first day.

David and Patrick wandered out to the front reception desk, and stood next to Holly and Arthur. A manager walked over, and then a writer and a graphic artist. A couple of assistants came out of the kitchen holding coffee cups. They all waited, chatting nervously and trying to appear nonchalant.

Roberta Prescott Reed, chic and sophisticated in a new tailored suit, her curly blonde hair cut to perfection, shiny new briefcase in hand filled with the many plans and ideas she had for the company she had inherited, stepped off the elevator and through the office door of Reed Public Relations, ready to kick some ass.

CHAPTER 13

She's Better Than She Realizes

ROBERTA WALKED INTO the office and right past the throng that rushed to greet her at the door. She walked down the hall and into her father's office. Everyone who had been waiting for her at the reception desk followed close behind her, shouting and jockeying for attention. She placed her briefcase onto the desk and turned around to face the large group that had followed her into her new office.

She held up her hand to indicate silence. "I know you all want time with me and I will make sure that each of you is put on my calendar. Right now, I want to spend time with Holly and Arthur. The rest of you will be notified when I am ready to meet with you."

"Wait a minute!" said David.

"Yes," Roberta said, giving him a hard look.

David was momentarily stunned by the new Roberta standing before him, a formidable person standing at her father's desk, her face a reflection of unbowed determination. The hair, the suit, the makeup, the shoes, the briefcase, and most importantly, the look on her face; it all came together in a way that oozed power. "Don't you think I should be here too?" he asked meekly.

"Not at the moment," said Roberta with finality, opening her briefcase. "Now all of you, please, give me thirty minutes with Holly and Arthur."

The group filed out of the office and Holly closed the door behind them. Arthur walked around the desk and took Roberta by the shoulders.

"Look at you!" he said approvingly.

"You look wonderful Roberta, like a completely different person," said Holly smiling at her.

"You handled David perfectly. I've never seen him quite so dumbstruck before," said Arthur.

She smiled up at him and kissed his cheek. "I'm sure he'll get his swagger back in no time," she said. "I wanted to make sure I set the tone from the beginning to let him know I'm no shrinking violet." She began pulling papers and files from her briefcase. "Let's get started. I need you both to be prepared for a very long day."

Arthur and Holly sat down opposite the big desk where Robert Reed had previously held court, lording over the minions at RPR for more than thirty years. Roberta took the chair without hesitation, and looked up at Arthur and Holly, their faces each showing the inner dialogue going on in their heads.

"I've made some notes with ideas and goals I have for the company," she said, placing her hand atop the pile of notes and files she had pulled from her briefcase, "but I want to begin first by saying to you both that today marks a new era at RPR. This is not going to be the same company. I am not the same leader, and we will not do business in the same way as my father did. My effort, with your help, is to clear away the smoke from my father's leadership here, and open up the windows letting in sunshine and fresh air. We are an environmental PR firm, and our goal is no longer to foist disinformation and propagate confusion, but to actually do the work of true environmentalism in business. I anticipate and am fully aware, that this will not go over well with some of our team members," she noted, using a term her father had never used.

"I will act swiftly to let go of those that cannot see the new vision, and I will bring in new people that can." She paused for a moment, and then continued. "I asked to meet with both of you first to let you know that I will be relying on you to be the cheerleaders of our new mantra and to spread the word to your colleagues with pride and eagerness. Keep me informed of malcontents and divisive individuals. Protect my flank as I try to move in this new direction." She looked at Holly and Arthur with determination. "Honestly, I cannot do this without you both, and I hope you will stick with me. I may appear as solid as a rock, but I am truthfully, quite scared." She smiled thinly, her eyes imploring them with her honesty.

"You don't have to worry about me, Roberta," said Holly eagerly, "I'm all in! I can't wait to get started!"

"Me too!" exclaimed Arthur. "We're here for you, my dear, and only you."

Roberta let out a sigh of relief and smiled. "Thank you. That's what I was hoping to hear," she said gratefully. "Now let's start with item one on my list."

CHAPTER 14

Life Can Be Cruel

Evan stepped from the train and onto the platform at Grand Central Station. His morning commute from Nyack on the 7:20 took about 50 minutes. He used the time to read, work or relax, sometimes being lulled to sleep at the end of the day by the gentle sway of the locomotive as it snaked it's way along the tracks. His office was only five blocks from the Grand Central Terminal. He walked briskly regardless of the weather, mentally and physically preparing himself for battle, entering the office totally awake and renewed with energy and enthusiasm.

Roberta's prediction of Evan's life that night ten years ago on their camping trip had been prescient. He had received his Master's Degree in Business Administration from Princeton University, and had landed a position at Vista Communications. In eight years there he had risen through the ranks to become an Executive Vice President and their lead contract negotiator on a variety of mergers and acquisition projects.

Despite the unrequited love that Evan had felt for Roberta, he had moved on with his life after the one and only romantic encounter in the VW van in Wyoming. He had eventually married a girl who had caught his attention at his hometown church. Jane was an old-fashioned girl, quiet and sweet, and she brought out Evan's deep-seated desire to protect and nurture someone. Three years before Roberta had inherited RPR, Evan had married Jane. They had lived a peaceful life in Nyack, New York, and he looked forward to coming home each evening on the train from his job in Manhattan.

Sending Roberta an invitation to the wedding had been fraught with anxiety. Although he had maintained his friendship with her, he still felt a twinge of remorse whenever he saw her. He wanted to make sure that nothing spoiled Jane's special day. He loved Jane very much, although in a different way than he had loved Roberta. After much soul searching, he finally relented, figuring that even though he had wanted their relationship to blossom into love and eventually marriage, she would always have a special place in his heart. Being friends with Roberta meant sharing the special occasions of his life, and so he placed the invitation in the mailbox. She had eagerly accepted and had come to the wedding with nothing but gladness in her heart for her friend's own happiness.

Within a year Jane had become pregnant with their daughter, Cassandra. During Jane's pregnancy she and Evan had shared the excitement and discovery of having their first child. They eagerly prepared for Cassie's arrival, discussing each and every detail together. The nursery was painted, tiny clothes were purchased, and a comfortable rocker was placed in a sunny corner of the room. Evan's love for Jane grew deeper as her body grew with their unborn child, and he felt truly blessed, thinking that his life could not be happier.

Unbeknownst to him, it was the fairy tale before the nightmare.

Having not had any warning signs of a change in Jane's feelings for him, Evan was taken completely by surprise four days after Jane and the baby came home from the hospital. Sitting in the rocker in the baby's room quietly nursing the newborn, she calmly announced to Evan that she no longer loved him and had not for some time. She explained that she had hoped that Cassie's birth would change her feelings for him, but instead of rekindling her love for her husband, the baby's birth had convinced her that she could no longer abide life with Evan. For Jane, the manifestation of this acknowledgement of her feelings was so extreme, that it could only be described as revulsion. She literally could not bear to be near him.

Jane's personality changed so drastically after Cassie's birth that Evan was sure that it was an extreme case of post partum depression. As her behavior and demeanor became more and more erratic, he went to the NYU medical library to research the subject. He indeed found that the hormonal changes a woman's body goes through after childbirth can bring on severe bouts of depression, and that in some cases, the levels of estrogen are dangerously high and can result in disturbing behavioral changes. If the hormone levels remain high for too long, there is an increase in the chance of developing cancerous tumors. He made copies of the articles and brought them home but Jane refused to read them. He pleaded with her to at least see the doctor but she refused that suggestion as well, allowing that the only thing that would make her happy was for him to leave her alone.

Her mood towards him became increasingly surly, and they went days with only cursory and obligatory conversation passing between them. Evan was heartsick and overwhelmed with worry and he tried to deflect her deepening depression by accommodating her every need, but the more he tried to comfort her or concern himself with her welfare, the more she pulled away, literally shrinking away in disgust if he touched her.

Six months to the day after Cassie was born, Jane found a lump in her right breast. The biopsy showed cancerous cells and she underwent a double radical mastectomy and had begun enduring rigorous chemotherapy. Evan took leave from work to be by her side. She suffered from violent spasms of vomiting and the indignity of having her hair fall out. Evan tried his best to make her comfortable, cleaning her face after she vomited and gently guiding her back to her bed, sometimes carrying her frail body when she was too weak to walk, but in the end, all she wanted was for him to leave her alone.

Eventually he came to realize that his very presence was jeopardizing her ability to recover. Her feelings for Evan had grown more intensely negative as if *he* were the cancer she was fighting. She told him that life was too short and too tenuous to live with someone you do not love, and she strengthened her resolve to have her divorce from him if she lived through her ordeal. Her sister and mother had taken over the daily care of Cassie, and Evan moved into the guest bedroom of their beautiful home, taking the train into Manhattan each day, the work he did for Vista Communications the only respite for him from a bleak and sad existence.

CHAPTER 15

Know Your Enemy

ROBERTA'S FIRST DAY was slipping rapidly into early evening, and her final meeting of the day with David and Patrick Reed was next. She had purposely kept them waiting, asking Holly to put them last on her calendar. She wanted to keep them off balance and at bay. After David's blatant attempt to initiate a boardroom coup, she knew he could not be trusted.

Holly had proven invaluable all day, quickly providing detailed information as Roberta and Arthur met with each employee to discuss their clients and the administrative or creative work they did for the firm. Holly and Arthur sat on either side of Roberta like protective sentinels, purposely making the employee sit opposite them at the solid oak desk, carefully watching them as they responded to questions. Holly made notes during the meetings, capturing not just their words but also their moods and mannerisms, something that would help Roberta make decisions about each one. Roberta asked the majority of the questions while Arthur sat silently as each employee discussed the main focus of their work, to whom they reported at the firm, and their long-term goals. She made a note of those that had reported directly to either her father or were reporting to David. She asked each of them to give their opinions on client management, client history and their assessment of the clients' dedication to their environmental responsibility. A few were quite open and honest with her, and she made notes when someone said something interesting or controversial. Some were cagey and fearful, and although she made an effort to connect with each one, there were several for whom her notation about them said simply: FIRE.

David and Patrick walked into Holly's outer office, and made a bee-line for the closed door to Roberta's inner office. Holly quickly blocked their way.

"Have a seat," she said, motioning to the chairs situated against the wall. "I'll see if she's ready."

David looked at Holly with a menacing look, and was about to give her an angry retort, when Patrick stepped in. "Thank you, Holly," he said, moving David toward the chairs, and taking a seat himself.

Holly picked up the phone on her desk and buzzed Roberta's desk. "David and Patrick are here."

"Send them in," said Roberta, sitting up straight and taking a deep breath. "And bring in the Purity Oil and Stanton Chemical files, please."

"Will do." She replaced the handset onto the cradle, and walked over to open the door to Roberta's office. "You can go in now," she said to them, letting them know in no uncertain terms that they must go through her from now on to gain access to Roberta's inner office. As they entered the room, she left the door open. She walked to the filing cabinets and retrieved the files. She placed the files on the desk in front of Roberta and took her seat on the other side of her.

Roberta stood up as they entered. "Patrick. David. Thank you so much for waiting until the end of the day for us to meet. I'm sorry that my interviews with employees took so long. I appreciate your patience," she said, smiling. "Please, have a seat. Can we get you anything? Coffee or a soft drink?"

"Or a stiff drink?" asked Arthur playfully.

They all laughed except David, who was seething with anger at being made to wait all day.

"Roberta, I'm not fooled by your little act," he said. "What the hell do you think you're doing making me wait all day to get in here? I'm the most senior person in this firm."

Roberta ignored his petulant tantrum and made a note on her pad, saying nothing.

"I'm not sure how you figured that," said Arthur hotly. "Roberta is the most senior person at the firm, and I believe *I* am just below her."

David ignored Arthur, and continued looking at Roberta. "You are not capable of running this firm, Roberta. You are in way over your head. Move over, little girl, and let the adults take over."

"David," she said, looking at him with a hard stare, her head held high and her jaw firmly set, "I am well aware that you are still angry that my father made me CEO of the company, but it's done and we must move on for the good of the company. I hope you can let go of your anger and we can work together." She decided that, for the moment, it was best not to confront his insubordination directly, but to play to his ego. "I value your input and will rely on your expertise in a number of areas, and I hope we can get along for the good of the firm. There are two accounts that I am particularly interested in getting your advice on."

The tight and menacing glare on David's face slowly softened as her words of encouragement took hold. He sat down in the chair in front of her desk. "Which accounts?"

Roberta was relieved that she had used the right tactic in diffusing the situation, and she sat down quickly to take advantage of his momentary interest in compromise. "Purity Oil and Stanton Chemical."

For the next hour she peppered him with questions about these two clients as she thumbed through the files on her desk. David was circumspect in answering her, and she felt certain that there was something he was holding back on. There were things that had gone on at the firm that he did not want her to know, and they involved these two clients. She knew that they had been her father's first clients, and they would need to be reassured that even though leadership at the company had changed, they would continue to receive excellent service, although not the *same* service. Despite an impassioned explanation of her vision for the company's future, and the real environmental impact she hoped to achieve with all of her clients, the legacy of mistrust that her father had relied upon had been ingrained in David. He did not trust her or her lofty motives. He insisted that both clients were threatening to move their business to a new firm, and it was only because of him that they had not jumped ship.

"I would like you to schedule a meeting with each of them," she said finally. "Will you arrange it?"

"Yes, but I will need to be there," answered David warily.

Sensing his hesitation, she added, "Absolutely. I want you to continue to take the lead on a day-to-day basis. I would certainly rely on your expertise to manage both of these client but I need to introduce myself, and we will both want to reassure them that their client team and account management will not be disrupted."

"I think they'll agree to that as long as I deliver the message," he said.

"Good." She stood up, signaling the end of the meeting. "I don't know about you, but I think we've had a very good first day." She extended her hand to David across the desk. "I'm looking forward to a fruitful partnership with you David." She came out from around the desk and stood next to him, placing her hand on his shoulder and walking him out the office door. "Get with Holly to coordinate with my schedule, and if I have to move some things around to accommodate them, I will."

"Will do," said David walking down the hallway to his office. He felt somewhat befuddled by how Roberta had managed to make him feel so agreeable, not even aware how smoothly she had handled him during the meeting and how deftly she had steered him out the door.

"Congratulations on a very good first day!" said Arthur, watching David walk away. "I think your father made a very wise choice making you CEO."

Roberta smiled up at Arthur. "I wish I knew why?" she asked, looking at Arthur with a question on her face.

Arthur said nothing for several seconds, and then answered, "Maybe we'll both understand it one day. But it was a wise choice nonetheless." He took off his glasses and rubbed his eyes. "I'm beat! I don't know how you're still going?"

"Why don't we start back up first thing in the morning," she offered, guiding him gently out the door. "Go home and get some rest. It's been a long day."

"I think I will at that," said Arthur, kissing her cheek.

Holly sat down at her desk in the outer office and began typing up the notes for the day. Roberta stopped at the door to her office and said, "The same goes for you too! As soon as you're done with those notes, go home. You were absolutely indispensible today. I couldn't have gotten through it without you," she smiled. "I'll see you first thing tomorrow morning."

Roberta walked back into her office, closing the door behind her. She walked to the bar at the other end of the room and poured herself a scotch. She picked up the notepad from her desk and sat down with a heavy sigh on the couch in the corner, reviewing the notes she had made from her meeting with David. She frowned as she read back through them. Despite her adroit manipulation today that allowed them to come to a temporary truce, he would have to be watched. He was not to be trusted, and she knew that he would be waiting for an opportunity to stab her in the back.

She took a couple of swallows of her scotch, reading through all the notes from her interviews, counting up how many people at the firm were against her, and would not be able to make the transition to her new vision for the company. Something about her conversation with David had put her on edge, and she suddenly felt very alone, realizing the enormity of the task ahead of her.

What had ever possessed her father to turn the business over to her? What had motivated him to do such thing? She was an activist, not a corporate apologist or cynical spin-doctor. She, like most activists, had been convinced that the term "corporate environmental public relations" was an oxymoron and she had fought against her father and his tactics for most of her adult life. Didn't he realize the terrible moral position he was putting her in? She shook her head very slowly in response to her own question. Could it be possible he had done it in revenge? She knew in her heart he had been capable of great treachery and guile, but she still could not believe that he hated her so much, his own daughter, that he could use revenge to make a decision of such importance for his beloved company.

She put the glass down and reached for the phone on the table and dialed a number. She closed her eyes and waited, counting the rings.

"Hello?" said the voice on the other end of the phone.

Her eyes welled up with tears of relief upon hearing the voice on the other end.

"Hello Evan? It's Roberta," she said slowly, her eyes still closed. "I need your help."

CHAPTER 16

Know Your Limitations

ROBERTA MADE EVAN a generous offer to come into the firm as her CFO. What she realized with stunning clarity at that moment was that there was no one whom she could completely and totally trust, no one who had her back and could play an equal role in the balance of power against David and Uncle Patrick that she needed. The idea had hit her like a bolt of lightning, and she had dialed Evan's number and poured out her heart to him, explaining her vision and what she was up against. He had said yes without hesitation.

They had talked well into the night, their longtime friendship quickly evaporating any hesitation at total honesty either of them had. He confided the situation with his marriage and Jane's illness to Roberta and she was supportive and empathetic to the emotional turmoil he was suffering through. Jane's feelings had not changed, and so, when Evan told her about Roberta's offer to come to Washington to help her run the business, he saw Jane's eyes light up for the first time in several years.

Roberta's offer was an opportunity to change his life's tragic direction, and gain some needed perspective away from Jane. Within a month he was working full time at RPR. His personal situation at home had made him apprehensive to make any long-term decisions, and with Roberta's insistence, he had been living in the carriage house behind Jackie's expansive mansion in Chevy Chase For a year he had been making the morning commute to the RPR office in downtown Washington in Robert's classic Jaguar roadster, which Jackie had been reluctant to part with, and for which she had eagerly pressed the keys into his hand.

During the first three months that Evan worked at RPR, he flew back and forth to New York on the weekends on the shuttle to La Guardia. In contrast to Evan's weekly life with Roberta and RPR in the heady atmosphere of Washington, his weekends at home in Nyack were mixed with the joy of seeing Cassie, and the unendurable agony of seeing Jane. Her contempt for him had only grown more intense since he had moved to Washington, and it wasn't long before she asked him not to come back to the house in Nyack, but instead to go to his mother's in upstate New York, where he could arrange to see Cassie. Soon after, she presented him with a proposal for a divorce settlement and the name of her attorney.

Evan's life in Washington took his mind off of the open-wound of anxiety and confusion he felt about his wife's illness and their doomed marriage. He was dedicated and energetic and he plunged into every aspect of the company's affairs with a headlong fervor. Evan's first task for Roberta, after providing her with a detailed analysis of the company's financial situation, was to help her put together a proposal to acquire a Paris agency. They had continued to acquire small agencies run by a new generation of young, environmentally dedicated visionaries in strategic locations around the world.

Evan turned out to be the perfect combination of warmth and toughness that she needed, and he truly embraced her vision for the company. He had a kind and easygoing way about him that disarmed people, yet he was equally comfortable with the hard financial aspects of putting a deal together.

RPR was heavily involved in Washington political life, and Roberta, like her father, was considered an A-list guest for social events with powerful and influential people. There were no sought after invitations in town that she was not on the event planners "Preferred Guests" list, and she and Evan unwittingly made a beautiful and complimentary couple. Although Evan had already achieved great success in the heady reaches of Manhattan, there was nothing like being at the top in Washington, D.C.

Roberta's office was inundated with invitations by telephone and mail for congressional fundraisers and black-tie events that seemed to be happening all over town all year round. Politicians found it necessary to get right back into the fray of campaign fundraising just as they were getting settled in and comfy with their friends, foes and colleagues on the Hill. Roberta ignored most of these events for very good reason. It would be impossible to attend them all, and her extensive travel schedule would permit her to attend only those that were important to her business and her clients. The only invitations that she planned for in advance were those issued by Senator Harry Markham's office.

As Roberta had predicted on that morning that she and her mother had sat at the kitchen table drinking tea and reading cards of condolence, Harry Markham had indeed come calling. After a suitable period of time to allow for mourning, he had proposed marriage and Jackie had accepted. Roberta was unsure of this strange yet predictable turn of events, but she knew that Jackie was a women who craved the limelight, and could not go long without a powerful man at her side.

Jackie had known Evan since Roberta's college days, and she and Harry loved having him living at the carriage house. Harry teased Roberta in private that she was "lettin' a right tasty catch slip off her hook" but Roberta's protests fell on deaf ears, and she would inevitably walk away from Harry shaking her head in frustration at his clumsy matchmaking attempts.

Evan's feelings for Jane grew colder over time as her complete rejection of him finally found its emotional bottom. The deep feelings he still had for Roberta grew stronger the more they worked together, but he had kept them locked away inside, allowing them unfettered working room to do what was best for her business.

CHAPTER 17

The Extent of the Deception is Staggering

ROBERTA'S NEW VISION and direction for the firm of teaching corporations the interconnectedness of the global environment and their responsibility to it, had fired her imagination beyond her wildest expectations, and she was soon engulfed with the dynamic energy of her mission.

A year since taking over the reins at RPR, her life's work had continued to take her to far-flung parts of the globe. She had walked into the office that first day ready to do battle, with a detailed and comprehensive plan locked away in that fancy briefcase her mother had given her, to radically change the way the company did business. Patrick and Arthur had soon retired from active day-to-day management, although they maintained their shares in the company, keeping the balance of power in check between the two sides. After seeing Roberta and Evan in action, Arthur left feeling confident that she could manage the business with no difficulty on her own.

As it turned out, David had been invaluable in keeping Purity Oil and Stanton Chemical. Roberta knew they were suspicious of her motives and Evan had counseled Roberta that to maintain both her vision and her integrity, she may one day have to come to the decision that some clients were not cut out to stay on with the firm. She did not want to lose anyone. She wanted to give all of her clients a fighting chance to come around to her way of thinking.

Robert and Arthur had pioneered a field that reflected the values of the post-World War II era in which they were raised, where the end always justified the means and the definition of success was the achievement of power and money. The Cold War taught them to believe that America was under constant threat from its enemies, and the legacy of McCarthyism taught them that extremism in the defense of freedom was no sin.

Robert and Arthur did not have to believe in everything they preached, they only had to believe in the mission. The pulpit from which they preached sat in a church of their own making, and required only that they worship the shiny, squeaky-clean image that their clients wished to project. This was a harsh and startling realization for an idealistic young girl to come to grips. Roberta shuddered as she thought of the types of services her clients had come to expect of RPR under her father's direction, and the challenges she continued to face to change her clients perceptions of their responsibilities to the planet.

RPR's clients had always been treated to an array of services unique to a Washington, D.C.-based firm. Under the direction of the Executive Education Program at RPR, executives who were required to testify before Congress were coached and drilled during mock hearings. In RPR's plush conference rooms, congressional protocol, etiquette, demeanor and body language, and the difficulty of staying cool under pressure in the intimidating and hostile atmosphere of Congress were discussed and practiced around the massive solid mahogany table. This service was invaluable and was very often quite legitimate, but could also be used to twist or manipulate the truth. In going through RPR's files late one night, Roberta had been appalled to learn that the firm had represented the tobacco companies whose CEO's had sworn before Congress that they *believed* that smoking cigarettes did not cause cancer. Although this seemed ludicrous on the surface, they swore this as their *personal belief* not evidentiary fact, and RPR had used this as a way to foster confusion in the public about the damaging health effects of smoking.

During the past year, the revelations that she and Evan had found of the extent of RPR's propaganda machine had made her sick with anger and disbelief. In another of her father's brilliantly cynical ideas, RPR established The Green Earth Award. Administered under the name of a bogus environmental association located at RPR offices, the award was an effective means of focusing public recognition for their clients' good environmental practices. The annual contest was open to any aspiring company that wished to submit its' product or idea, and was advertised in magazines and environmental publications. Each year thousands of entries were received from companies large and small in hopes of winning the coveted prize, but the top prize always went to an RPR client. The deceptively brilliant result was the useful archive of great ideas RPR had at its disposal for the benefit of its paying clients.

In its' most contemptuous abuse of the public's trust, RPR contributed its' creative energies to the US automakers, petroleum, coal and plastics industries when it became involved in producing counterclaims in the debate surrounding the greenhouse effect and global warming. Planetary scientists and climatologists were warning that high levels of carbon dioxide gas emitted into the atmosphere. Mostly as a result of the burning of fossil fuels, chiefly from automobiles, but also from other industries that used petroleum to manufacture their products. Dirty fuels such as coal used in the power industry, combined with widespread deforestation, resulted in an increase in the Earth's naturally occurring greenhouse effect, causing the build up of dangerous levels of heat in the Earth's atmosphere. As a way to counter this new claim they shrewdly created an association called Scientific Probes into Atmospheric Challenges to Earth, or SPACE.

The credentials of highly compensated scientists working for this bogus scientific association were used to supply the veneer of validity. Just as they had done thirty years earlier with Rachel Carson, their sole purpose was to sow doubt by challenging the science. This machine of deception worked tirelessly to churn out thousands of press releases and articles derisively refuting the evidence, and arranged television interviews and lobbied Congress. The disinformation and propaganda campaigns that her father employed depended heavily on his cynical view that the average American knew precious little about science, and was incapable of evaluating competing arguments among scientists.

Despite Roberta's dynamic efforts, she was up against the world of wariness and distrust that her father had created. The first casualty of war is truth. The manipulation of information by the wedded bedfellows of politics and commerce had resulted in a crisis-fatigued, overly suspicious public who found it extremely difficult to make decisions on highly critical issues because they did not trust the information they were getting. The political personalities and opinion celebrities of modern society manipulated the truth to their own benefit, and the few lonely voices speaking the truth were lost among the din of false voices shouting for attention.

Since the very first day Roberta took the reins of RPR, she had slowly changed their tactics from management of disinformation and propaganda to a more direct approach of educating her clients about the very real public relations benefits of adopting a far-reaching and documentable environmental policy. Her efforts had been met with strong resistance from both inside and outside the firm, and the diabolical thinkers her father had surrounded himself with were replaced with some of those very same collaborators who had stood with her against the lumber industry in that forest in Oregon.

In direct contrast with her father's mushroom theory of spreading disinformation, Roberta and her colleagues at RPR actively encouraged and communicated their client's efforts to become responsible corporate planetary citizens. She had not yet been forced to step upon the pulpit her father had built to preach a false sermon, and from a different generation indeed, she had earnestly continued the painstaking and delicate process of dismantling it.

CHAPTER 18

Evil

DAVID REED PARKED his Porsche 911 in the church parking lot and sat for several minutes watching the parishioners enter through the door of the church. Today's church was first Sunday of the Month, the Presbyterians. He didn't particularly like this one, and only half-listened to the fire and brimstone sermons. Second Sunday of the Month were the Methodists, and he liked them. They were the least judgmental, and the sermons were tolerable. Third Sunday of the Month went to the Episcopalians. He had no particular religious sensibility, and the only reason he attended these churches was to keep in the good graces of some of his clients. On the last Sunday of the Month, he played golf.

The one thing he liked about these three churches is they demanded nothing of him. As long as he bowed his head, and put money in the plate as it passed by, and donated generously to the summer Bible Camp, they left him alone. The preachers sometimes used a passage from the Bible to drill some kind of message about politics or bad behavior into the heads of the congregation, but for the most part, they droned on about nothing, repeating the same old lines, and the same old passages, as if they never once thought about how ludicrous what they were saying really was. These were not highbrow Christian philosophers, they never suffered from a moment of doubt, and the congregations liked it that way.

David had learned this little trick from Robert Reed. "David," he had said, "find the churches in the best neighborhoods in Washington and Chevy Chase, and go in and make friends. That's the best way to get clients. You wouldn't believe the rich and powerful bastards that rip off their fellow man during the week, and go to church on Sunday."

David spotted his mark and stepped out of the car, flicking the lock on the key fob, and smiled at the little beep-beep the Porsche made. He sauntered up to the steps nonchalantly, getting behind the man he wanted to meet. David purposely bumped into him, and oozed charm as he patted him on the back, shaking his hand and introducing himself by way of his profuse apology. The man introduced his wife and kids, and David joined them in their pew. The man had recently been in the news, and his company was under investigation. At the end of the service, David would walk out with them, they'd invite him to join them for breakfast, and he'd talk sports and ask him if he played golf. He'd talk business and drop a few names. He'd schmooze about the PR game and the man would open up to him, ask for his help, and by the end of the week, David would be his savior.

Robert Reed had been a con artist, and David had learned the art of the con at Robert's side. He believed he understood his brilliant uncle better than anyone. He had built a magnificent business on deception and lies and David knew exactly how to play that game. He was still seething with anger over Robert Reed's betrayal in giving Roberta the majority shares in his company. He had spent his life doing the man's bidding, licking his boots and kowtowing to his whims, only to be kicked in the teeth when it came time to pay back his years of service.

He had to admit Roberta had shown real spunk. Despite her adolescent, loony tunes attempt to save the planet, she actually had hit on something. The business was garnering more accolades from clients than ever before. The tide in the country was turning and she was at the forefront of it, but there were still clients that needed David's brand of PR. Purity Oil and Stanton Chemical would never buy Roberta's vision. Though they paid lip service to it. They confided to David that they wanted nothing to do with her mission of corporate environmental responsibility. They had set Robert

Reed up in this business for a reason, and they felt betrayed by him for putting his radical daughter at the head of the firm. They expected the same mushroom theory treatment of keeping the public in the dark and feeding them shit that Robert Reed had pioneered. They wanted to look green, but fought tooth and nail against any and all regulation that would force them to actually *be* green.

David had been stoking the flames of their disenchantment with Roberta ever since day one. He had insisted on several occasions that setting him up in his own business might be the only answer to keeping her do-gooder nose out of their messy business. Trevor Skeets had finally confided to him in a moment of alcohol-induced honesty at the very same Hay-Adams Hotel bar that they had first made Robert Reed the offer, that neither Stanton Chemical nor Purity Oil would ever give David the deal they had given Robert Reed. In a martini-fueled speech of slurred words Skeets had told him, "David, you shuust don't measure up to the man. Besides, we kinna like things the way they are. Her environmennal cridenshuuls give us the perfect cover. Hey, don't feel bad. You shuust keep raking in all those eshorbitant fees we're paying you and enjoy yoorshelf. Ish all good, buddy."

To make things worse, not only had he been insulted by that perpetually tanked-up Skeets, Evan Manning ran around like he owned the place. He and Roberta were joined at the hip, and were becoming their own version of the D.C. power couple. They had their photos taken at functions on Capitol Hill and the White House with senior cabinet members, senators, celebrities and rock stars. Roberta seemed to be connected to anyone and anything that was new and cool, and Jackie and Harry Markham kept her looped into the old guard that *wanted* to be cool. She and Evan saw eye-to-eye on everything, finishing each other's sentences and feeding off of each other's creative energy like a tag team. Their high-energy buzz floated through the office like a virus. David's input at meetings was either ignored or ridiculed, and he was treated like a superfluous appendage most of the time. He smiled and he pretended to be a team player, all the while biding his time until the first big disaster when Roberta's holier-than-thou attitude would come crumbling down around her ears, and she would be forced to choose between her principles and that pulpit of lies that Robert Reed had built.

CHAPTER 19

An Attempt at Planetary Cooperation

Roberta exited the cavernous conference center in Berlin, Germany where the 1995 United Nations Conference on Climate Change was taking place. It was the first meeting of the Conference of the Parties following the Framework Convention in 1992 in Rio de Janeiro, Brazil three years earlier. Despite the fall of the Berlin Wall and the rapid thaw in political relations between East and West, Berlin's weather was not reciprocating the warming trend in relations. The city that had been the symbol of the Cold War's divisions was living up to its past, at least as far as the weather was concerned, showing no warmth to the 117 delegates and 53 observers from countries around the world, whose vastly differing priorities and concerns presented a growing number of obstacles in their attempts to negotiate an agreement on reducing carbon emissions.

Roberta buttoned her coat, tightened her scarf, pulled up her gloves, and released her umbrella against the freezing rain. Still the cold April wind blew right through her, chilling her to the bone. She longingly thought about the conference in Rio, and the soothing warmth of that Atlantic coast city. Perhaps the warm sunny weather of Rio had lulled the participants into a false sense of calm. Berlin would certainly do nothing of that sort, she thought, as she began walking toward her hotel.

She had attended the Rio conference as a representative from *Environmental Action,* the environmental foundation she had worked with prior to the upheaval of inheriting her father's company. She had unexpectedly bumped into her father in Rio. He had been attending on behalf of clients who were opposed to the climate change commitments being asked of the participating countries. They had nervously hugged each other hello and made obligatory small talk, and then went their separate ways.

The disinformation put out by her father's firm on behalf of the petroleum industry had helped subvert the goal of the attendees in Rio, resulting in an onslaught of counter claims and opinions in the media back home objecting to the science of climate change. Despite the appearance of progress, and 155 signatories to the 1992 agreement on a framework, it was generally agreed by environmental groups pressing for stronger commitments in Berlin, that the results from the meeting in Rio could not be considered much of a success.

After three days, the current framework sessions were proving to be just as stubbornly difficult to move forward as had been the ones in Rio. Trinidad and Tobago had submitted a draft protocol on behalf of the Alliance of Small Island States, requiring a 20% reduction in greenhouse gas emission by 2005. Samoa called for the adoption of the Small Island States protocol, and was supported by Fiji, Mauritius, Micronesia, Papua New Guinea, Norway and South Korea. They argued that island nations would be harmed most by the weather-related disturbances and flooding expected to be caused by climate change even though they were the least responsible for the greenhouse gas emissions creating the current crisis. China and India, along with 77 other developing nations, had selected The Philippines to present their list of objections. At the top of their list was an objection to being included in the existing CO_2 reduction commitments due to economic hardship, framing the issue as a way for rich nations to take advantage of and continue to suppress progress in the poorer ones.

Some progress had been made. New scientific methodologies had been agreed upon for measuring CO_2 emissions, but debate continued on choosing the best methodology for estimating the Earth's ability to remove CO_2 from the atmosphere by the Earth's oceans and forests. The calculations were difficult, and computerized projections based on best-case and worst-case scenarios depended on how quickly the planet's forests were depleted and kept the participants engaged in debate for most of the day. The other major task before the negotiators was the issue of financial support for developing countries and the additional industrial, scientific and financial resources that they would need in order to implement energy-efficient technologies. The group of 77 developing nations eagerly participated in those discussions.

The opening plenary was still several weeks away, and the rumors were flying, including one that claimed the head of the German delegation, Dr. Angela Merkel, Federal Minister for the Environment, Nature Conservation and Nuclear Safety from their host country, would be elected as President of this Convention.

Roberta reached her hotel, an early 19th century structure on a side street near the Brandenburg Gate, the site of so many historic speeches by US Presidents. She folded her umbrella before entering the hotel vestibule. The driving rain pelted her face and eyes, momentarily blinding her. She rushed through the door and bumped into someone entering at the same time. He turned around and she saw the face of Michel Manon, the man that she had idolized for so long, the man who had spurred her determination to make a statement with her life from the first day she saw his ruggedly handsome face on the Life magazine cover.

"Excuse me!" they both said at the same time.

"No, it was my fault," said Roberta. "I was desperately trying to get in the door and wasn't looking ahead of me."

"It is understandable. The weather is *pas bon*, even for zee ducks," said Michel, smiling broadly and holding the inner door open for her. *"Après vous, mademoiselle."*

"Merci. Vous êtes très gentille," responded Roberta in excellent French.

They walked together into the hotel lobby, which was sumptuous and warm in ancient dark wood paneling and rich upholstered furniture. A lively fire burned in the original marble fireplace, and she instantly felt better as the warm air of the room hit her face and seeped into her bones.

"You are Américaine, *n'es-ce-pas?* You speak French?" he asked.

"Well, I speak very little French, I'm afraid," she answered, stopping just in front of the stairs. "I'm out of practice," she said with a sweet smile. She gazed into Michel's soft brown eyes, regretting that she had let her French slip over the years.

"Haven't I seen you somewhere?" he asked. *"Ah oui, je me souviens.* I have seen you at the conference," he exclaimed, answering his own question.

"Yes, I am attending the conference," she answered. "Roberta Reed, Reed Public Relations," she said, removing her glove from her hand and extending it in greeting.

He took her hand and felt a thrill pass through him like an electric shock.

"Public relations?" he said inquisitively. She thought she detected a hint of derision in the way he said 'public relations'. He held onto her hand for an extra second longer than necessary. "I am Michel Manon. Photographer."

"Oh, you need no introduction, Monsieur Manon," she said smiling, still holding his hand, which despite the cold outside was quite warm. "I must confess that it was an article about you that first inspired me to take a public stand for my environmental convictions."

"Ah, oui? Formidable!" he exclaimed enthusiastically.

"I'll tell you the story sometime. You'll get a kick out of it, I think," she offered jovially.

"How about now?" he asked impulsively. *"C'est très mauvais le temps.* Perhaps you will do me the honor of having dinner with me here in the hotel. The food is not too bad. Fortunately, the chef is French," he said with an impish grin. "I would love to hear your story."

"That would be lovely," she agreed, thrilled by the idea of having dinner with her longtime idol. "I would like to freshen up a bit. Shall we meet back down here in an hour?" She began climbing up the stairs to her room.

"Parfait!" He followed her, stopping at the landing. "In one hour."

Roberta got her key in the door with difficulty, her hand shaking from excitement. She flung her handbag and briefcase onto the bed and quickly tore off her clothes. She put on the fluffy hotel robe hanging on the back of the bathroom door, and wiggled her toes into the soft cotton slippers. She started running the bath water in the claw-footed tub in the luxurious bathroom. She found the bubble bath on the ledge of the tub on a small silver tray, and after smelling it to make sure it would not clash with her perfume, poured a small amount into the running water, and threw in a washcloth.

She still had about a half bottle of wine leftover from the previous night. She poured herself a glass of the German Gewürztraminer, and padded back into the bathroom. She placed the glass on the ledge of the tub, and eased her body into the luscious, fragrant water. She placed the washcloth, hot and wet from the steaming bathwater, on the back of the tub, and leaned against it, sipping her wine and letting the cares of the day melt away. She soaked and sipped for twenty minutes, letting her mind go blank, breathing slowly in and out as all of her muscles relaxed.

She toweled off and put the robe back on, leaving it dangle open as she caressed her body with a luxurious perfume-scented body lotion, a gift from one of her clients whose products she used exclusively. The giant American cosmetics company La Jeunesse had enthusiastically embraced her vision and revamped their entire line of products to be manufactured with environmentally focused processing and ethical testing without animals.

She refreshed her makeup and then slid into her cashmere Yves St. Laurent sheath. She slid into suede pumps, added handmade silver and onyx earrings and necklace from a gallery in Paris and draped a black and silver silk wrap from Morocco around her shoulders. She took one last look in the mirror, and walked out the door and down to the lobby to meet up with the man of her dreams.

CHAPTER 20

—— ↶ ——

Is It Love?

ROBERTA SPOTTED MICHEL standing in the lobby as she descended the wide, red-carpeted stairs. He was standing at the fireplace speaking to a slightly disheveled man in a rumpled raincoat. Michel was stunningly handsome in contrast, and had prepared for their dinner with a freshly shaved face, black turtleneck, and black and gray tweed jacket over gray flannel slacks. He had come down to the lobby with anticipation, and had already been waiting for fifteen minutes for her to return to him, feeling compelled by that little thrill he had sensed before when he had taken her hand.

He looked up from his conversation and was suddenly aroused at the sight of her. He quickly excused himself and walked over to the bottom of the stairs, reaching out his hand to her as she descended the final steps. That same thrill he had felt the first time came back with renewed force, and ran from his hand to his heart, all of his senses came alive, and he felt as if he had suddenly been reawakened from a dream.

"*Vous êtes absolument belle, Roberta! Très charmant,*" he said appreciatively, kissing her hand.

"Thank you," she murmured quietly.

Michel led her by the elbow into the quaint dining room of the hotel. He had called ahead to ask for a quiet table in the back of the room, and the maître d' graciously obliged, showing them to a private little corner. The décor in the hotel's small dining room mirrored that of the rest of the antique hotel, but with a decidedly cozy French bistro ambience to reflect the national origin of the executive chef.

"This is so nice, Michel. I really didn't have any desire to go back out in that cold wet weather," she said, taking the seat he pulled out for her.

"You must look out the window," he said, pulling aside the curtain. "The rain has turned to snow. The flakes are fat and fall slowly to the ground, and it is quite pretty," he said, sliding her chair under her. "It may make the walk back to the conference center a bit treacherous in the morning."

"I love the way freshly fallen snow deadens sound, and makes everything look clean and pure," she commented. "At least momentarily."

"Yes, until the street grime blackens it with soot. That is why I hate New York in the winter. It is an ugly city in snow," he said honestly. "Paris, on the other hand, is beautiful in any season."

"I was recently in Paris. I have an agency there," she said, as the tuxedo-attired waiter stood by silently waiting for a pause in the conversation. "It is one of the most beautiful cities in the world. My favorite."

Michel continued looking at Roberta, in no hurry to acknowledge the waiter. "I cannot wait to hear more about you, your life, and your business. Would you care for an apéritif? Un Dubonnet ou Lillet Blanc, *peut être?*"

"You know, I would love a Lillet," she said, remembering the light blend of Bordeaux wine and fruit liqueurs of that apéritif. "I haven't had it for a long time. It sounds just right at the moment," she smiled.

Michel looked up at the waiter who quickly stepped over to the table. "*Un Lillet apéritif pour la dame, et un whiskey,* Johnny Walker, *pour moi. S'il vous plaît.*"

"*Dankeschön,*" said the waiter, bowing slightly.

Roberta opened her menu, which the maître d' had placed atop the place setting in front of her. She sat back and perused the menu, resting the large portfolio on her lap.

"Everything sounds very tempting," she noted aloud. "It is a sort of French-German hybrid in the way the chef prepares the dishes. A Wiener schnitzel with Lyonnais potatoes and a light red wine sauce, and French sausages cooked in German beer and apples. I like it. It's unusual."

The provenance of every item was listed on the menu, identifying the farm from which it came. There was a little asterisk at the bottom of the menu explaining that the restaurant sourced its produce, meat, poultry and fish from gardens, farms, ranches and fisheries guided by humane treatment and principles of sustainability.

"This menu reminds me of my friend Summer Sparrow. She owns two restaurants in California, and like this one, she adamantly sources all the ingredients locally and humanely," she commented. She made a mental note to write Summer an email later, telling her about this restaurant.

"That's an unusual name. *Très jolie,*" said Michel.

"Remind me to tell you a story about her," Roberta said. "What are you going to have?"

"I usually order the *ris de veau*. The chef does them beautifully," said Michel.

"Oh! They have *volaille de Bresse,*" she exclaimed.

"Yes, the famous French chicken from Bresse," said Michel. "It is considered the best chicken in the world. There is no other flavor like it. You must have it if you like."

The waiter returned to the table with their aperitifs, setting them down quietly.

"Okay, I know what I'm going to have!" exclaimed Roberta enthusiastically, closing her menu with determination.

"*Sehr gut*. What can I get for you?" asked the waiter.

"I'll start with *soupe à l'oseille* and then the *volaille de Bresse*," she said handing him the menu.

"And I will have the *pâté de campagne* and then the *ris de veau*," said Michel. "And a carafe of the house wine."

"*Dankeschön*," said the waiter, writing the order on his pad, and walking quietly away from the table.

Roberta took a sip of her Lillet from the small and delicate etched-crystal glass. The sweet yellow liquid went down smoothly and was as good as she remembered it. The last time she had had the apéritif was with her aunt and uncle in Dijon so many years ago. It was a favorite of Aunt Germaine, who took a small glass each day. Her heart grew heavy for a brief moment as the memory came flooding back, clear and vivid as if it were yesterday. She steeled herself, forcing the memory out of her mind, and bringing her back to the present.

Michel watched her from across the table. He noticed the almost imperceptible change in her eyes, the brief and momentary sadness in her face, and then it was gone. She looked up at him and smiled.

"This is very good," she said, raising her glass. "Thank you for suggesting it."

"Mais oui!"

They sipped their drinks, watching the snow falling outside the window. "Enchanting isn't it?" said Roberta quietly.

"Yes," he said looking at her and not at the snow. "Tell me what are your impressions of the conference so far?" he asked, taking her mind away from the thought that had clouded it.

She frowned as she thought about what she had learned so far. She took another sip. "This will be a long, long process," she said, thinking about how weird it felt to be sitting on both sides of the issue at once, representing many of her clients who were the foes of an agreement and her personal commitment as a champion of an agreement. "I want to believe that the nations of the Earth can come together about this," she said, "I think the CO2 targets negotiated at Rio are not adequate enough. I found it telling that the small island nations most threatened by global warming and sea rise are on one side and the rapidly developing nations like India and China, who will produce more CO2 in the future than all the current industrialized nations combined do now, are on the other. How quickly the G77 got to the point the first day of asking to be relieved of inclusion in the reduction commitments," she said with a cynical smirk.

"India, China, Latin America and eventually all of Africa, have the chance to make a technological leap into the future by by-passing fossil fuels altogether, and going directly to alternative, clean-energy sources to fuel their growth," he lamented. "Yet, the needs of their people, and the rapid development they pursue to create economic growth does not allow for a slow progression. Their needs grow faster than the alternatives can be implemented. They will take the fastest, easiest route to economic growth, which means corruption, graft, pollution, deforestation, exploitation and the resulting environmental disasters yet to happen. Old enemies become trading partners, their leaders paid handsomely in order to foster the expansion of oil producing nations into poor developing economies."

There was a momentary pause in the conversation as each took a sip of their drinks.

"Monsieur Clinton is much more disappointing than environmentalists expected him to be," said Michel, continuing their previous conversation. "Tomorrow, tomorrow, tomorrow is the plan of your country."

"The Clinton administration has set low expectations for this conference on purpose so that any small amount of progress can be hailed as a victory," concurred Roberta. "They are committed to helping the former Soviet Union develop a market economy to foster democracy. That is their first priority. The oil lobby is very unhappy with any progress made on setting limits on CO_2 emissions."

"Although I hate the oil companies, they have a point," said Michel. "Developed nations are forced to comply, while the big polluters like China and India are left to continue unabated.

Roberta started to say that she knew exactly how the oil companies felt, but bit her tongue. Her firm was closely associated with the Global Climate Coalition, the lobbying group that represented the big American oil companies, and through her father's efforts, had registered their strong disapproval of the climate conference negotiations at Rio. She was having a lovely time and did not want to open up that can of worms.

"The Global Climate Coalition has made it their aim, with the backing of billionaire industrialists like Volk Industries and American Mining Coalition and others, to generate negative stories about climate change, and the science behind it. They call it a fraud. The GCC grew out of an organization called SPACE, have you heard of them?" asked Michel innocently.

Roberta looked at Michel to detect whether he was being facetious or honestly didn't know that her father had started the anti-climate change science organization. But why would he? RPR's name was nowhere to be found in any of the press releases or background information about the organization and its true purpose. She felt a prick of conscience as she thought of this, and wondered if she had done the right thing in keeping the oil companies as clients.

"Someone suggested to me today that climate change should be included in US foreign policy planning," she said, changing the subject. "Arguing that it is as much a national security threat as was the Cold War and nuclear weapons. Newt Gingrich and the Republicans want to reduce our foreign involvement and devote all of our resources to solving problems at home," she said as her soup and Michel's pâté arrived. "The President is having a very bad day at the office, so to speak," she snickered. "Fending off the up swell of isolationism in the Contract for America he cannot make any promises right now. He won't get any cooperation from Congress, and because of that I fear that things will get much worse before they can get better."

She dipped the large soupspoon into the bowl and tasted the creamy soup. The sorrel's distinctive flavor was lemony, and balanced expertly with cream and butter. Small orzo pasta had been added to give the soup a telltale bite.

Michel placed a slice of his pâté onto a small toasted slice of crusty bread, and added a small dot of French mustard to the top. He reached across the table and placed it on Roberta's bread plate. "Try this," he said. *"C'est très bon.* The chef has balanced the spices and brandy in the mixture perfectly."

She popped the morsel into her mouth and chewed appreciatively. *"Oui. Magnifique!"*

"Tell me about your friend Summer Sparrow. Such an enchanting name," he mused, changing the subject to something more pleasant for their digestion than the arguments between nations.

"Summer is my best friend. I've known her since college. She grew up on a commune and they grew all their own vegetables and lived off the land. Now, she has two famous restaurants in California," she explained.

"*Qu'est-ce-que c'est* commune?" he asked.

"Commune? I'm surprised you don't know it. It was a popular form of communal living in the 1960's, getting back to the land and growing food organically. It was part of the hippie movement, the experimentation with alternative living arrangements. People would live together in one big melded family, usually on a farm, and share the work, expenses, and upkeep. Men and women shared the child-rearing duties and the farm work, and oftentimes, each other. There was a good deal of "free love" going on at the time. I think that's why they didn't work out for the long haul. The reinvention of society without boundaries is anarchy, and only anarchists like anarchy. I think humans need structure and rules to co-exist peacefully. It's actually very hard to live off the land, and the free love thing really only benefits the men. The women still get stuck having babies."

"Only about three percent of animals in nature are monogamous," said Michel. "Swans, the albatross, Sandhill cranes, the Greylag goose. The only primate that we know of is the Lar Gibbon. And there's some evidence that the beaver is monogamous too. There may be a genetic predisposition in men's predilection to procreate with many females. A way of insuring his DNA will survive."

"How convenient for all those philandering husbands out there," she said contemptuously.

"Females have a reason to want to be monogamous. They are responsible for children. It does put them at somewhat of a disadvantage," he admitted. "Tell me more about Summer and the commune."

"Summer's parents lived on a farm in Vermont and theirs was a very serious venture. They had rabbits, chickens, goats, sheep, a dairy cow, and grew vegetables. They spun wool and wove cloth. Everything they ate was fresh, and the way Summer tells it, absolutely delicious. She started cooking at a young age. It was only natural that she would eventually open a restaurant."

The waiter took their dirty dishes away, and poured them each a glass of the house wine from the carafe. Additional waiters placed their beautifully arranged dinner servings in front of them. Michel didn't take his eyes off of Roberta, barely noticing the waiters.

"Bon appétit," he said genially, lifting his wine glass to her.

"Bon appétit," she concurred lifting her glass to him.

She dug into the famous French chicken. They had been slow poached and were as tender as butter. The chef had prepared a light lemon cream sauce with morel mushrooms and the first bite melted in her mouth. They ate in silence for several minutes. Michel placed a small forkful of his *ris de veau* on her bread plate, and she offered him a small bite of her *volaille.*

"You promised to tell me the story of how I became your source of inspiration," he said finally, refilling her wine glass.

"Yes, I did, didn't I?" She delicately patted her mouth with her napkin, picked up her wine glass, and sat back in her chair. "It all started on a trip across America after I graduated from college. Summer was there, my friend Evan Manning, who is now my CFO, and his little brother Steven."

"The Steven Manning? From the band A Higher Calling?"

"Yes, *that* Steven Manning," she answered.

"So she must be the Summer from their first hit song?" he asked.

"Yup! He wrote it while we were sitting around a campfire. Anyway, we were all together, driving across the country. Evan had borrowed his uncle's VW van, and we drove during the day, and camped under the stars at night. Steven had just graduated from high school. He kept us entertained with his guitar, and Summer made delicious meals on the campfire each night."

"Sounds very *romantique*," said Michel.

"We were all just friends, but really good friends. You know, people you can count on when you're in a jam. I'm glad to say we still are."

"Go on."

"Well, we had stopped somewhere, I don't remember, Idaho or Wyoming. We were at a grocery store picking up the groceries for dinner, and I saw your picture on the cover of Life magazine. You were young, just a couple of years older than I was, and it seemed like you had already done so much with your life. The caption read, 'French Photojournalist Michel Manon. His life's work is a higher calling.' You were staring back at me from that magazine cover, and I was ashamed that I had accomplished so little."

"I remember that article," he said, leaning in to hear more of her story.

"We were on our way to Oregon, and when we got there, we stayed with Summer's cousin, who was an environmental-activist/protest-organizer/college-dropout. There were a bunch of people there, friends of his from the university, and we got into a heated discussion about activism, and whether working inside or outside the system to foster change was best. They were going up to a logging camp to protest the logging practices by a company called American Pride. They challenged me to come along to prove my commitment to environmental causes."

"Why did you have to prove your commitment?"

"Because American Pride was a client of my father's public relations firm. The firm I now run. It was a big risk for me to chain myself to a tree that was going to be cut down by a company my father did business with," she said hesitantly.

"Ah," said Michel, a realization dawning. "You are the daughter of Robert Reed?"

"Yes," she answered quietly, feeling suddenly very naked. "And because of you, I went to that forest, and chained myself to that tree, and publicly humiliated my father on national television."

"And that is how your environmental fervor was born?"

"Yes. I went on to get a master's in environmental science, and then went to work with environmental agencies and foundations to further the cause of environmentalism and conservation. My father and I barely spoke to each other after Oregon. He died a year ago. He totally surprised everyone by bequeathing his shares and his title in the company to me. The last time I was at the UN conference in Rio, I was with *Environmental Action*. Now, I am here as the CEO of Reed Public Relations."

"There is no such thing as 'environmental public relations'. It is an illusion, an oxymoron, a purposeful deceit," he said contemptuously, clearly conveying his disappointment in this new revelation about Roberta.

"I think there is. My challenge to American Pride in 1984 for sustainable development was considered radical at the time, but they now have millions of acres of renewable forestland that they harvest," she said defensively. "I think that's progress."

"Yes, maybe, but I doubt their motives are pure. It is the financial advantage they see in it rather than the reverence for nature that motivates them. I guess as long as they get to the same conclusion, regardless of the motive, then it is progress of a sort. The reality is that they still clear cut the forests, which still damages the natural eco-system that their trees provide."

"I have made it my mission to educate my father's clients, my clients, about their responsibility to the planet, and the financial gain they derive from being truly green, and not just making it up, like my father did. I know he came from a different generation, but I intend to change all that," she declared. "I've already made a good deal of progress."

"I admire your dedication, but I think you will be disappointed. I am not sure that the most egregious polluters of the planet care about the environment. You will find you are beating your head against the wall with some of them."

"That's what Evan says, but I have to give them all the chance to come around, don't I? Don't they all deserve the chance to see the vision too?"

"Roberta," he said, with exasperation in his voice, as if he were speaking to a child, "you are terribly naïve if you think that the oil companies or chemical companies or mining companies care one little bit about the blatant abuse and destruction they cause to the environment. Look at the mounting evidence that coal ash released into the atmosphere from power plants produces acid rain, and the slag heaps left behind from coal mining releases heavy metals into ground water, causing human diseases like cancer, yet coal mining companies have no intention of cleaning up their mess unless they are forced to do it. Despite all of that evidence, the American government still continues to debate giving mining companies coal leases to public land. Land set aside purposely to preserve its natural beauty. Government regulation and vigilant oversight to insure compliance is the only thing that keeps them from turning our air, land and water into a smog-filled, chemical-saturated, oil-slicked mess!" said Michel heatedly.

Roberta sat back and sipped her wine. Michel's rebuke stung and she could think of nothing to say in defense. She suddenly felt very depressed.

Seeing the look of dejection on her face, he reached across the table and offered his hand to her. She leaned in and took hold of it. His anger instantly melted away as she placed her small hand inside of his, and he again felt that little electric shock that came from touching her skin.

"I do admire your commitment," he reassured her. "And I am flattered that it was an article about me that inspired you," he smiled and squeezed her hand. "I hope you turn out to be right. I hope that there will be corporations that come around to your way of thinking, and recognize their responsibility to the planet."

She smiled thinly and looked into his eyes, an unsettling black stab of doubt in the back of her mind.

Interlude

Tenzin Wangchuk climbed the open meadow at mid-morning, feeling the burn of his leg muscles and the growl of his empty stomach as he climbed higher in the thin air. He could see the traveler's hut along the banks of the stream. His yaks grazed contentedly on tender grasses and drank from the stream, the result of melting run off from mountain snow. The hut, a humble structure intended to decompose back to the Earth leaving no trace of its lowly existence, was made of stacked rough timbers. A simple door in the middle of the timbers allowed entry. Its roof was supported by hand-cut timber poles, and consisted of overlapping hand-hewn wood slats sloping downward from the gentle pitch of its peak to the timber walls, covering the modest dirt floor. It had stood in its location next to the clear running stream for generations, offering shelter to anyone that needed it, built and maintained by monks who have visited in earlier years.

Inside the hut, a small cast iron stove sat at the back corner, its chimney snaking up through the roof to carry smoke on the wind. A kettle, some kindling and matches were already there on a shelf next to the stove. Tenzin started a fire, placing the shards of kindling inside the belly of the stove and lighting them with the matches. He watched as the kindling catches fire, its smoke rising up the chimney.

"All that we are arises with our thoughts. With our thoughts, we make the world," he says aloud.

He picks up the kettle and walks to the stream to fetch water for his tea.

As he walks to the stream, he can hear the bells on his yaks tinkling in the distance. To make sure they do not stray too far, he whistles and calls their names. He shields his eyes from the sun with his hand and scans the hillsides, looking for his yaks. He sees a family of foragers from the village and he waves, momentarily disturbed by the sight of them. The family, an increasingly common sight on the mountains in recent years, is foraging for a caterpillar infected by a fungus believed by herbalists in Chinese medicine to be a remedy for cancer. They crawl through the meadow grasses on their hands and knees, each with a small pick ax combing through the loam looking for the telltale stalk no larger than a match stick protruding from the ground. They pick the mountainsides clean. The stalk they seek is the germinated fungus that emerges from the mummified body of the larval caterpillar of the ghost moth. Tenzin watches the family slowly crawl along the meadows. He feels compassion for the Earth as they dig with their small axes, and he traces their path with his eyes. In the past, he has found cigarette butts left behind by the foragers, and reflects on the irony and disrespect to the Earth of people looking for a homeopathic cure for cancer while using products that cause it. *They are so ignorant*, he thinks.

He checks his thinking, and calms the anger he feels growing in his heart. He says a prayer of enlightenment for them. He directs his words up the hillsides to them carried on the wind.

"Enlightenment is like the moon reflected on the water. The moon does not get wet nor is the water broken. Although its light is wide and great, the moon is reflected even in a puddle an inch wide. The whole moon and the entire sky are reflected in one dewdrop on the grass. May you find enlightenment in the drop of dew that you walk upon."

CHAPTER 21

Eventually, France Calls Everyone Back

GRABBING HER BAGS and shouting last minute instructions to her staff, Roberta ran out the door of her office and into the wood paneled elevator. Holly and Evan ran beside her as Roberta breathlessly rattled off new details of her trip. Her chauffeured limousine waited in the street below to take her to the airport. A leftover relic from her father's reign, it was one she had intended to change but had instead found invaluable in the whirlwind after her father's death three years before, and the endless client meetings and environmental crises that ensued.

The limousine was double-parked and the cars on New York Avenue were backed up for blocks, idling on the hot pavement waiting for the limo to move. Drivers honked and shouted obscenities in a rainbow of languages at Tu Hien, her neatly attired and unflappable Vietnamese driver, who supported a family of five on the salary she paid him. Owning a business had taught her many things. The most unexpected was that sometimes it was difficult to put her convictions ahead of the people that relied on her for their livelihoods.

Tu Hien opened the car door for her as she approached. He patiently made sure that she was inside before closing the door, and then slid swiftly into the driver's seat. He eased the sedan into the snarl of traffic and onto the George Washington Parkway on the way to Washington National Airport.

She had thrown herself into work. She soon found to her amazement that she loved it, and thought about the business 24/7/365. Her mission had taken her to the world's major cities to meet with her clients and visit RPR offices. Her role as the head of RPR was still new to her, and she cautiously moved forward each day with her plans. Her sterling reputation for environmental causes was well known. Once word got out that she had inherited her father's firm, many environmental organizations came calling too, asking for her help. She had not had a vacation in nearly twelve years, since that carefree June when she, Evan, Steven and Summer had taken the VW camper van across the country to Oregon. The year she spent in France afterward had been the worst year of her life.

Roberta winced with the emotional pain of the memories of that year in France with her Aunt Germaine and Uncle Pierre in Dijon. The deep secret that she and her mother shared had been kept locked away inside her heart all these years, and only Summer, who had come with her on that yearlong exile, knew of it. Even though Roberta had become depressed and anxious during their year in Dijon, Summer had flourished, taking cooking classes, learning about wine and tending to Uncle Pierre's huge vegetable garden. Summer came home and immediately moved to California where she opened two highly acclaimed restaurants. As luck would have it now, she was taking a working sabbatical from the restaurants. She would be in Lyon at the same time that Roberta would be in Provence, developing recipes and cooking with some of the best chefs in the region. Roberta had not been back to see her French relatives since that year. She and Summer had arranged to meet up with each other at Uncle Pierre's farmhouse in Dijon.

Tu Hien pulled into the drop off lane in front of the airport terminal. He looked at Roberta in the rearview mirror as she was about to open her door.

"You wait," he said in heavily accented English. "I open door."

Tu Hien raced around to the curbside of the car, and opened Roberta's door, reaching in to help her out of the car. He smiled warmly at her. "That right, it very important you let me do my job. It is privilege to always open door for you, Miss Roberta."

"Thank you, Tu Hien," she smiled, appreciating the warmth and respect he had always shown her. He took her suitcase from the trunk and walked with her to the curbside Skycap, handing him the bag and her first class ticket. The Skycap checked her in, and tagged her luggage before placing it onto the conveyer belt. In fifteen minutes she was on board the plane and in her seat on the Air France jumbo jet.

Roberta sat back in her seat and smiled inwardly at the twist of irony that this trip represented for her life. The butterflies in her stomach were multiplying. She ordered a glass of wine from the stewardess to calm her nerves.

Her work with the United Nations conference on climate change had brought she and Michel together the first time in Berlin, Germany the year after she took over at RPR. They had felt an instant attraction to each other, fueled by their mutual passion for environmental causes. Their paths crossed again at a fundraiser in Washington and then again at the World Economic Forum in Davos, Switzerland. They finally let down their defenses and consummated their growing desire for each other.

She had run into Steven Manning in Davos at a ski chalet. He was attending the Economic Forum promoting his environmental foundation. She had introduced him to Michel and they had hit it off immediately. Steven's star power and her high-visibility in the corridors of influence in Washington, had clinched it for Michel, and he had pursued her relentlessly afterward. Her work at RPR had consumed her existence and she repeatedly turned down his frequent invitations to spend two luscious weeks at his home in Provence in favor of her work. It took eight months of constant pursuit on his part until she finally gave in and made the travel plans, justifying the trip in her own mind by making it a working vacation. She could visit her Paris agency and meet with some of her European clients.

She had struggled with the decision to accept Michel's invitation not only because of all the work she was leaving behind, although that was the excuse she had used for too long, but because she and Michel had had a very rocky relationship fueled by Michel's angry emails and late night phone calls about her clients. As the head of the most successful environmental public relations firm in the world, she had had to instill her personal mission to her clients of their environmental awakening slowly, sometimes with mixed results. Michel did not always appreciate the delicate dilemma it put her in. Finally, here she was on her way to France, and a romantic rendezvous with her explosive and famous environmental activist lover, a man her father would have called "a member of the enemy camp".

She well appreciated the irony of it all. The bottom line was that because of the business she was in Michel did not totally trust her, and the irony of this trip, and her whole life in fact, was that she had had a rocky relationship with her father for the very same reason. She had not been able to trust him in their personal relationship because she had not been able to trust him in his business practices. She knew that if it had not been for her mother's interference, she and her father would have been completely estranged, because she herself had been "a member of the enemy camp".

Roberta looked up from her reverie to accept the cloth-covered tray of delectable French cuisine prepared by the Air France chefs. She took another sip from her glass of wine and thought about her father's life, and how different it was from her own. Growing up in her parents' home in Chevy Chase, environmental issues were discussed around the dinner table and while watching the evening news. Her opinions on the subject echoed those of her parents. She saw her father as a champion of the environment, a man who judiciously balanced environmental concerns with the needs of business, and she wanted to be just like him. As she grew older and became more involved in environmental causes, she found herself increasingly at odds with him. She finally realized he was no environmentalist, but was in reality a corporate propaganda machine responsible for the lies being told to congress and the public. Now that she looked back on it, her lifelong dream of working for environmental causes must have been her father's worst nightmare.

She dozed off in her reclined seat. She slept fitfully for only a few hours before the lights came back on in the cabin. The pilot announced their impending arrival into Nice airport. She eagerly drank two cups of strong French coffee offered by the flight attendant. She tried to rub the sleep from her eyes. She looked out the window at the faint ribbon of light on the horizon. A beautiful glow of pink and orange light faded upward from the Earth to the purple black sky dotted with stars and a silvery half-moon. She thought about Michel and his ruggedly handsome face and the butterflies in Roberta's stomach fluttered busily as the time of her arrival drew nearer. She got up out of her seat and reached into the overhead bin for her travel bag. She walked to the first class lavatory. She washed her face, brushed her teeth, reapplied her makeup, and then changed into a new summer dress. She walked back to her seat, feeling refreshed, and ready to handle whatever life had in store for her next.

CHAPTER 22

Summer Sparrow

THE YEAR THAT Summer spent in France with Roberta had been the single most important year of her life. As soon as she returned from France, she left her parents' home in Vermont and headed west to California. The trip to France had solidified what she knew was her purpose in life. Her experiences there had convinced her that cooking was the only thing she wanted to do and opening a restaurant was her goal.

Packing up her little Honda Civic with what few possessions she had, she crossed the country alone, a stack of cassette tapes piled into a box in the seat next to her. She drove with the windows rolled down the wind blowing her hair, singing to her favorite songs at the top of her voice. She made stops along the way to visit friends and relatives. Her parents worried about her, but they had given her a good foundation of love and support, and she had a good head on her shoulders. They had given her roots and wings. They knew that it was time for their little Sparrow to fly.

After four days driving across the country, she finally made her way to San Francisco. She quickly found an apartment and a job waitressing at a small café in Haight-Ashbury. It didn't take long to talk her way into the kitchen where she worked side-by-side with the owner, developing recipes and taking shifts. She soaked up every bit of information that little restaurant had to give. She learned the dos and don'ts of restaurant management, all the while honing in on the concept she was envisioning for her own restaurant.

She volunteered to take over the responsibility of placing the orders for the restaurant, and slowly began replacing the processed, pre-packaged foods from the restaurant supply companies to a few carefully selected organic items from local farmers. She had been talking to one of the farmers delivering an order one day, a shaggy young man in his late twenties dressed in overalls and flannel shirt. She had told him about her life growing up on a commune, her trip to France, and the epiphany she had experienced there. Everything in her life was pointing her to one thing; opening a restaurant of her own where all of the ingredients would be locally sourced, seasonally available, and organically and ethically grown. He had invited her to come up to his farm located about an hour north of San Francisco in the Sonoma Valley, and witness first hand how his food was grown.

He was the first of many farmers she would cultivate in the years to come. Their high quality produce and ethically raised meats would be featured prominently on her menus. She had opened her first restaurant, Summer's Bistro, in an old house in Berkeley with seed money from Steven Manning, Evan's little brother whose band had hit the big time with his single *Summer*. Four years later, she branched out with a second location, Chez Mes Amis, in the Sonoma Valley wine country. She was a pioneer in the farm-to-table movement and reservations at both of her restaurants were highly sought after. She regularly entertained movie stars, Presidents and tech titans eager to experience the *joie de vivre* she expressed in the food she served and the pride with which she served it.

It had been nearly twelve years since she had started on this food journey. Her restaurants could now run themselves. She took one last look at her pretty little bistro with the crisp white tablecloths and soothing summer colors, and then turned out the lights, locked the front door, and headed to the airport for a six week gastronomic pilgrimage with the food, wine and lovely people of France.

CHAPTER 23

The Problems Go Way Back

MICHEL MANON DROVE like a crazed madman through the streets of Nice, muttering obscenities under his breath at the other drivers as he honked and careened around the cars on the road. He wheeled his battered convertible to the curb adjacent to the airport entrance. He handed the gendarme 100 francs not to tow the car as he ran to the international terminal for arriving flights. He spotted Roberta waiting by the luggage carousel and took a moment to enjoy her beauty before he went up to her. Even with her back to him he would recognize her blonde curls, long legs and curvaceous form anywhere. He quietly crept up behind her and wrapped his arms around her waist.

"Bonjour, ma petite," he whispered into her hair.

She turned around to face him with his arms still locked around her waist and smiled up at him. Without saying a word, she melted into his body with a soft passionate kiss.

She stepped back and looked lovingly into his eyes, and then with a surprised look, said, "Oh! *Pardonnez moi, monsieur!* I thought you were someone else." She turned to walk away and he grabbed her hand and pulled her to him, throwing his head back in laughter. He had to wipe away the tears of joy in his eyes to see the bags she was pointing to on the carousel.

"I hope you are not very tired, *chérie,"* He grabbed her bags and motioned for her to follow him out the door, "We have an appointment in Monaco."

"We have an appointment?" she asked. "With whom?"

"With Jacques Cousteau at the Oceanographic Institute," He pointed to his car in the no parking zone.

"Really!" A smile leapt to her face and lit up her sleep-deprived eyes. "What are we going to do there?"

"Get in the car, and I'll explain on the way."

Roberta threw her carry on bags into the backseat of the little open topped car, noticing his European license plate that read **ENVIRO ACTIVE.**

The gendarme blew his whistle and stopped traffic to let Michel out. He waved his hand and smiled broadly at the helpful cop He looked at Roberta to make sure she had noticed.

"Wow!" she exclaimed. "Being with you is better than being with a rock star!"

Michel shrugged his shoulders and thought to himself, *a little grease in the palm doesn't hurt either.*

"I cannot believe that you are actually here!" He looked over at her and beamed a gorgeous smile while changing gears and negotiating the crazy drivers honking, waving or throwing the *bras d'honneur* as he cut across traffic, the French arm gesture known the world over. *"Ah, Didon!* Don't look at that *ma bichette.* It is very bad."

"And very typically French," she laughed, thinking of his many passionate and angry late night phone calls. "Quick to love and quick to anger."

"It took me a year to convince you to come," he said, putting a CD into the player. "I think that must be some kind of record!"

"I think it would be a record for you to have to wait five minutes!" she teased. "I'm sure women throw themselves at you all the time." There was no escaping the fact that this man was drop dead gorgeous.

"Ah, mon Dieu! Qu'est-ce-que tu pense de moi?"

"I think you are *incroyable.* But my French is very rusty, and I think we should try to keep our conversation in the international language of commerce. That would be English," she said teasingly, knowing it would infuriate him, "if you don't mind."

"Oh, such a loss to the world. The language of diplomacy and commerce should still be French. But alas, it will never be replaced as the language of love." He reached over to caress her face.

She closed her eyes and tilted her head against his caress. She felt the warmth of his hand against her skin. The opening notes of the French chanteuse Liane Foley came drifting from the stereo, her voice like smoke and warm honey, enveloping Roberta in all that is quintessentially French.

"You are the only woman I want, *ma minou*," he cooed.

He pulled his hand away from her face, but reached down to take hold of her hand, placing it on his thigh. "That's better."

Michel eased the little convertible onto the scenic coast highway between Nice and Monaco, and Roberta was awestruck by the magnificent view. The aqua-blue water of the Mediterranean Sea was juxtaposed against the jagged deep-red rocks along the hillsides that seemed to tumble headlong into the pristine water. The bright colors of the sun-splashed turquoise sea and red rocky hillsides were mirrored in the quaint villages that dotted the landscape. Money was evident all around in the luxurious harbor towns. Neat rows of elegantly appointed mega-yachts whose ownership was hidden in secret bank accounts and byzantine business connections, mingled among the unapologetically rich and infamous residents in their sprawling sea front mansions. Among them were the bloody despots who had raided donated aid money in their country's coffers, the forgotten monarchs who lived off the largesse of their subjects, and the drug kingpins who had made illegal fortunes on the addictions of innocent children. They all settled down in the quaint villages to a quiet life of ease in an atmosphere of chic snobbery where everyone looked the other way, and no one questioned where the money came from.

"Tell me about our meeting with Jacques Cousteau?" she asked.

"I have been asked to participate in a joint project with the Oceanographic Institute on cooperative efforts by the Mediterranean nations to improve anti-pollution measures." Michel's face grew serious as he began to explain the reason for their appointment. His eyes grew intense and his hands punctuated his words for emphasis. "We are tentatively scheduled to present it to the European Union in the fall. I'd like to have your opinion on what we have so far and especially your thoughts on how to best present it to gain public support."

"Oh, how exciting! I'd love to help if I can. Do you think there would be an opportunity for RPR to be officially involved?"

"We shall see. Right now, I would like you to meet Cousteau and let him make an evaluation. If you can get more permanently involved it would be welcome to have your advice and input. We in Europe are facing a great moment in our history. We have a chance to create cooperative, long-lasting environmental policy in a unified Europe. The Maastricht Treaty that created the union of European nations, and the central currency, has hit many roadblocks. The vote to ratify the treaty in France only passed with very narrow support, and the United Kingdom opted out of it altogether. Unification is so very difficult. We are not a collection of states with a common language and purpose, and there are still many issues confronting European nations associated with unification. The currency turmoil that resulted from the Danish and French referendums is still remembered by everyone, and many of the countries have taken an adversarial position."

"It sounds ambitious. How much opposition are you expecting?"

"We are not really sure yet. France is a leader in enacting strict environmental policy, but other Mediterranean countries are not as committed. Italy is sketchy, good in some areas and not in others. Spain and Portugal have severe economic hardships and would rather not risk losing a good relationship with a large company that employs thousands in order to force environmental compliance. In many of these countries, even when environmental laws are on the books, officials have been known to accept bribes to look the other way when industries pollute. Jacques and I will be presenting our scenario as a model for all Europe. The key will be to enlist the support of the public to pressure their leaders into making the necessary laws and then enforcing them."

Roberta's mind raced with ideas, and they spoke animatedly together as he told her the preliminary plans for the project. They pulled into the parking lot of the Oceanographic Institute, still engrossed in conversation.

The Institute, just a stone's throw from the royal palace, housed a research center and a museum, and sat directly on the cliff side coast of Monaco. In keeping with its' lavish surroundings, the museum boasted an imposing Baroque Revival architecture that befitted its' royal connections. The smaller research facility was located on a promontory jutting out over the sea. The comparatively low-key, coral-colored building built specifically to blend into its seaside surroundings. It's principal purpose was to bring research, knowledge and ideas together with the best minds in marine biology, and to educate the museum's visitors about the delicate ecosystems that form the intricate web of healthy marine life, and the threat caused by pollution on our water-borne planet.

Michel knew his way around the Institute like a regular. He led Roberta through the broad, windowed corridors. He stopped to talk to someone in the hallway and Roberta turned her attention to the ocean view beyond the cliffs. The splendor of the view stopped her in mid-stride, silent and awestruck at its beauty. A voice broke through the tranquil scene, speaking quietly behind her.

"There is no more beautiful place in all the world. It is *un paradis, non?*"

Roberta turned around to face the familiar voice that spoke to her. The famously weathered visage of Jacques Cousteau looked directly at her with a kind smile. His hawk-like nose and tanned skin as much a trademark as his famous Calypso diver. She was slightly taller than he was, and she smiled at him, offering her hand in introduction.

"Monsieur Cousteau, I am Roberta Reed."

"*Enchanté,*" he said, clasping her hand in a warm firm handshake. "I have heard many good things about you from Michel. It is my pleasure to meet you."

His charming nature shone through in his eyes and his smile. Roberta immediately decided that she wanted to work with him if she could. "I guess it goes without saying that I have heard good things about you, too!" she laughed.

He chuckled at the reference to his celebrity. "I am recognized everywhere I go. I think it must be my nose that gives me away." He tapped the side of his nose for emphasis.

Michel walked up to both of them, his arms outstretched. "I see you two have met. *Bonjour, Mon vieux,* it is good to see you again, Jacques." They embraced warmly, like father and son. "Shall we get started?"

"Oui! Allez!" Cousteau led them down the hall to his office. The interior was large with an expansive wall of windows leading out to a tiled terrace that faced the sea. The room was well organized. One wall was covered with row upon row of floor-to-ceiling shelves filled with books, videos, report binders, maps and photos. A replica of the Calypso research vessel stood in a corner of the room on a marble pedestal surrounded with framed artwork from school children and photos from his many expeditions. A young woman came into the office carrying papers and a file folder. She stood next to Jacques, quietly explaining the information in French. He finished his discussion with her and apologized for the interruption.

"I have been briefing Roberta on our preliminary plans," Michel began, "and she has had several very good suggestions to make. I'd like her to go over them with you, Jacques."

Roberta looked at Cousteau waiting for him to give her the go ahead.

"I would be very interested in hearing your ideas, Roberta, *s'il vous plais,*" he encouraged her.

Roberta walked over to the large white board on the other side of the room and drew three columns on the left side. In the middle, above the three columns she wrote and underlined the word GOALS. At the top of each column she wrote IMMEDIATE ISSUES, MID-TERM ISSUES, and LONG TERM ISSUES.

On the right side she drew there more columns and wrote at the top VOTERS, CONSUMERS, and POLICY MAKERS.

While Roberta set up her strategy on the white board, the young woman returned to the room with a tray filled with glasses, a bottle of sparkling water, and several canisters of flavored syrups with pretty botanical drawings on their labels. She set the tray on the table in front of

Cousteau and Michel and silently left the room. They continued to watch Roberta intently.

"I agree with Michel that it will take strong support from the public to accomplish your goal of achieving a unified approach to anti-pollution measures, but it will be necessary, in my opinion, to focus on small chunks of the overall issue to win their support. The approach we take with the public will be very different from the one with the policy makers. The first step is to define what the goals are, what a realistically achievable time frame should be, and whether those issues apply best to the voter, the consumer or the policy maker, and then tailor a campaign to focus on each of those demographics."

"Formidable!" exclaimed Cousteau. "I like it already."

For the next three and a half hours they filled in the columns on Roberta's plan. They discussed the best and worst case scenarios as they imagined them, and covered all the current hot buttons in European conservation and environmental effort. They identified the ones they could realistically hope to achieve in the near future while keeping an eye on their long-term goals. Cousteau was especially concerned with restoring the waters of the Mediterranean to a healthy and habitable bio-environment, and he focused their attention on all the pollution factors that affected that body of water.

"For centuries, the nations of the Mediterranean have used our sea as their private toilet," he explained. "Some areas now suffer severely with the loss of fish and plant life, and the coastal waters are choking with a layer of silt over three meters deep. The causes of pollution to the Mediterranean are the same as other bodies of water of industrialized nations. Effluent from untreated sewage and pesticide, herbicide, and chemical runoff that flow into the sea. Air-borne pollutants from power plants and manufacturing that fall in the form of precipitation. Crude oil washed from the inside of tankers. Warm chemical-laden water from power plants and the paper industry. Shipping and cruise line wastes, acid-heavy rain, and the catastrophic threat that is always lurking from the barge transportation of nuclear power waste and supertankers of crude oil that regularly use the Mediterranean shipping channels on their voyages from Russia or the Persian Gulf to the huge refinery at Rotterdam in The Netherlands," he concluded.

Together they came up with a realistic working plan to design several campaigns targeted at the three demographic groups in her list. She was pleased with their plan, and stood back to admire what she had done.

Michel stood up and walked out onto the terrace, stretching the stiffness out of his muscles. Roberta sat down at the table and poured herself a glass of water with a little strawberry syrup, a pretty botanical drawing of a strawberry plant on the label. The combination was light and refreshing. She drank thirstily.

Cousteau walked over to the board and read through the list again. "You know, Roberta," he said as he stared at the board, "this plan represents the culmination of my life's work. To be part of something that is good for this beautiful planet that I love so much, something that will last for generations to come, is what I have worked to achieve my entire life. I only wish that I were presenting it to all the nations of the world, instead of just the nations of Europe." He sighed deeply. "I have dedicated my life to educating people about the beauty of this blue planet. I have even lost a son to the cause that I have embraced. I am often discouraged. The destruction of the planet's living systems continues to grow unchecked and unabated. I know I must never give up hope, but in my darkest hours, I feel that the success of the human species was the worst thing to have happened here. It is one thing, perhaps a forgivable thing, to destroy out of ignorance. But for humans to have achieved the consciousness to understand the delicate balance of the world we live in and continue to destroy that balance nonetheless, even at the cost of our own species, is the ultimate hubris of our existence. No other species on the planet has that power. We alone have developed the power to see this paradise in its' entirety from space. We alone have developed the power to destroy paradise and we alone have the power to understand the consequences of that destruction."

Roberta sat in silence as she listened to this wise old man whose passion for the diversity of life had played out in such a publicly dedicated way. The changes she had begun to implement two years ago in the way RPR does business was an ongoing, long-term process of educating her clients, but to people like Michel and Cousteau, it was not just a game of winning and losing as it had been to her father, but a struggle for life itself. The mushroom theory led to the mushroom cloud, and the destruction of paradise.

"Roberta," Cousteau broke into her thoughts, "you are in a business which has a very negative history for environmentalism. Yet I feel hopeful by the plan that you have outlined. I feel perhaps that on this day we have turned a corner, and we are embarking on a new course together. The adversaries of old have joined forces to become the leaders of the revolution."

"What revolution?" she asked.

"The revolution in human thinking, in attitude, in commerce, and the stewardship of the planet. A revolution in human destiny and the hope of the new millennium and the return to paradise by the outcasts of Eden."

Roberta sat very still, hearing his words echo her own thoughts. The hope of a new millennium, the hope of her own vision for her firm and for the planet.

"You know, Roberta," he said quietly to her, "I knew your father." He paused to study her face. "He and I did not see eye-to-eye on anything. In fact, I cannot say that I liked him very much, but I see that he has raised an intelligent and sensitive daughter, and for that I am grateful. If I were him, I would be very proud."

Tears welled up in Roberta's eyes as he said this to her. Her feelings for her father were a confusing mix of loathing and love. She still had not come to understand him completely and his decision to turn his beloved business over to her. But she silently thanked him for doing it as her purpose in life came together with undeniable clarity.

Michel came in off of the terrace and Roberta excused herself to wipe her eyes and freshen her makeup. When she returned Michel took her hand. "Are you hungry?"

"Famished!"

"*Bon!* We go to have lunch. Jacques, will you give us the pleasure of joining us?"

"*Malheureusement, non,*" he said, shaking his head. "I have much work to finish, and at my age, who knows how long I will be here." He turned to Roberta and hugged her warmly, kissing her cheeks in the French fashion. "It has been a very great pleasure to meet you, Roberta. I look forward to working closely with you on this project. Please contact me in the next few days so that we may work out the details of our arrangement with your firm."

"Thank you," she said, shaking his hand in both of hers. "It has been a rare honor for me to meet you. I can't tell you how much this has meant to me."

"I think I know. " He regarded her with a twinkle in his eyes and she felt that he did understand her very well.

The young woman they had seen before came in to remind him of his next appointment. They said their final goodbyes and walked out into the sunshine hand in hand, slowly making their way to the car. All of a sudden Roberta felt very tired. She leaned on Michel's shoulder.

"Tu es magnifique, chérie, I am very proud of you."

"Jacques said the same thing to me. I guess I'm getting my fill of admiration today. I'm pretty proud of myself, too." She momentarily thought of Evan, and how much she wanted to share what she had accomplished for the firm today. *He'll be proud of me too,* she thought.

Michel leaned out to open the car door for her, and before she stepped in, took her in his arms and held her tight. "Jacques has been more than just a mentor for me, *chérie,* he has been like a father, and it was very important to me that he approve of you. This is a great accomplishment for us, darling. I am very happy, for many reasons."

Roberta thought of her vision and the words Jacques used to echo her very own private thoughts, *the hope of the new millennium, and the return to paradise of the outcasts of Eden.* The purpose of her life was clear and rang like a bell in her mind. She no longer felt at odds with her work, her father and the world. "I'm happy for many reasons, too."

CHAPTER 24

Why It's Easy To Fall In Love
With A Frenchman

ROBERTA AND MICHEL stopped at an outdoor café along the waterfront in Cagnes-sur-Mer for lunch. Michel ordered a carafe of wine and a bottle of sparkling water. They sat in the bright sun, dining in the extravagant atmosphere of the Cote d'Azur. She had not eaten anything since the light breakfast on the plane and she was ravenous. She had a superb potato-crusted salmon with a delicate and creamy wild sorrel sauce. Michel had a whole *dorade*, a small Mediterranean bream grilled whole over an open flame with Provencal herbs and olive oil. He expertly fileted the fish with his knife and fork, taking the bones and head off in one long unbroken piece. Every few bites, he would reach across the table to lovingly feed Roberta small forkfuls.

They watched the people saunter along the wide promenade that curved in an unbroken line for miles along the coast. The chic and stylish women walked with their little dogs on long leashes and she noticed that they all seemed healthy and trim. Beyond the promenade, the pristine beach beckoned with brightly colored umbrellas. Boats bobbed on the waves in the distance. Sun-worshipers were packed like sardines on the yellow sand. Many of the women were topless and Roberta winced at the thought of all those sunburned breasts. She turned her gaze to the other side of the wide avenue. She scanned the windows and balconies of the posh high-rise hotels that faced the sea. She wondered about the people staying there and what kind of deal they had struck with the devil to get there.

She looked back at Michel and sighed in contentment. She was very proud to be in the company of such a ruggedly handsome man. She studied his face and body as he leaned back with eyes closed, his face tilted up to the sun. His wavy hair brushed against his cheek in the light sea breeze and gleamed with golden highlights as it fluttered in the wind. His face was tanned with a coppery glow, and she thought affectionately of his bright blue eyes that danced with animation when he spoke. He had such a handsome face, at the same time boyish and strong. Roberta had caught herself feeling a pang of jealous ownership as the women going by openly flirted with him, catching his eye and commenting in their various languages on his robust, virile physique.

He felt her staring at him, and kept his eyes closed to the sun as he spoke. "What are you thinking about?"

"I'm thinking about how easy it would be to spoil you rotten. You're deliciously handsome, you know?"

"*Ah, oui?* Tell me, how does an American woman spoil her man?"

"Hmm? Like everyone else I guess. Although, if you watch American television you'd think we were all rotten little whores from Dallas. But the reality is that we are a complicated lot. When we are in love with a man we are lavish with our praise, loyal to a fault, and attentive to all his needs."

"But your divorce rate is so high. In France, divorce is not as common or easy to obtain."

"In France, you don't get married. You live out of wedlock and your taxes pay to keep your children healthy, clothed and educated. Besides, Catholic countries are notoriously hypocritical about divorce."

"*Touchée,*" he agreed.

"But American women can be dangerously neurotic. Ownership, equality and jealousy all walk hand in hand to the altar. It makes for a crowded marriage. We strive for equality, yet we still throw it away for the white picket fence and expect a fairytale ending. It's no wonder that we get divorced almost as fast as we get married. Honestly, I think the pace of the modern world causes us to get bored too easily. We've all lost the ability to endure the pain of boredom, men and women both. We've been brainwashed into thinking that love is some kind of drug and we have to maintain the high."

"Relationships between men and women have become very complicated in your country," mused Michel. "Perhaps, you think too much, and don't have enough fun with each other. The joy between men and women should not be lost in the striving to achieve success in life. Watching the animals as I photograph them has taught me to appreciate the joy of simplicity. The bird sings his joy of life each morning and the whale finds his mate by singing his own song of joy."

"Yes, we are a complicated nation of people. We have communicated so much that we can no longer hear what each other is saying."

"Do you know what pollution threatens the whale the most?"

"The whale? No, not exactly. Some kind of chemical or something?"

"Noise pollution," answered Michel, just as a motorcycle went by on the street.

"What?"

"Noise pollution. The whale finds his mate throughout the vast ocean world by a complicated sounding mechanism. The noise emitted by high-powered military sonar, huge ocean going vessels and seismic surveys conducted to find oil under the seabed, is louder than the loudest jet engine, and disrupts the whale's sonar ability. Many biologists believe it is the reason why they become disoriented and stranded en masse on beaches. The whale's song, and as an analogy, all the animal's songs, are being drowned out by our dominion over the planet. Other than natural disasters, it is only the human animal that disrupts and ultimately destroys other species."

A phrase came to her mind that she whispered quietly to herself. "Tread tiny through frantic whispers."

Michel looked at her, intrigued by the statement. "Yes, that is it exactly."

He leaned forward to look into her eyes. He kissed her mouth and brushed the hair out of her eyes. He took her hand and smiled tenderly at her. "I would look forward to being spoiled by you, *ma puce,* but you are here in my country, and it is my time to spoil you."

His liquid blue eyes burned with longing as he stared at her. She felt her legs turn to rubber heat. A moist ferocious longing hit hard between her legs and she was grateful to be sitting down. He could see the effect he was having on her and he snickered a little under his breath. He enjoyed having this power over her.

Suddenly, he stood up with a flourish shielding his eyes with one hand and pointing toward the Northwest like an explorer, and said, *"Allez!* We go to Cannes to shop for dinner."

They continued their drive along the coast to Cannes and the open-air farmers market there. The gothic-style structure took up an entire city block and Roberta was enthralled with row upon row of fresh flowers, vegetables, fruits, herbs, cheeses and meats. The varieties seemed endless. Roberta spent thirty minutes just looking through all the buckets of flowers. They picked a large bouquet of lavender and pink lilacs, and small delicate lilies of the valley and yellow sweetheart roses.

Immediately after the flower stands, came the fragrant fresh herbs. Michel would be grilling local lamb for dinner. He took large bunches of mint, basil and thyme. As they walked through the stands of fruits and vegetables, Roberta was amazed at the assortment, and she tried samples of produce from across Europe: juicy pink and orange melons and fragrant blood oranges from the sunny hillsides of Spain, truffle infused oils and glistening olives from Italy, huge red strawberries, tiny yellow raspberries and deep purple blackberries from Portugal, an endless variety of salads, tomatoes, beans, eggplant, and squash from Provence, and hundreds of brined and aged aromatic cheeses from across France. The large selection of foods on offer made her realize how limited the selections were in American grocery stores. She decided that although the French eat what would be considered a high-fat diet with rich artisanal cheeses, butter, and red meat, their diet was much more adventurous and included many varieties of fruits and vegetables. They ate very little fast food, and as a consequence they were thinner and they looked healthier.

Together, she and Michel chose large heads of buttery lettuce and wild salad greens to make up a salad, tiny sweet green beans that the vendor handed them to sample, wild shitake and oyster mushrooms plucked that morning from the surrounding hillsides, and two large artichokes the size of cantaloupes. As they passed through the meat section, Roberta saw fresh, skinned rabbits, plucked poultry with the feet and head still on, and organs and other parts of animal anatomy she had never seen before or was aware could be eaten. Michel picked out six lamb chops, and a large chicken for tomorrow night's meal. He asked the lady butcher to include several more chicken feet, that he would give to his neighbor Yvette for making fresh stock. Roberta was surprised to learn that Yvette's husband, Henri, ate the feet, crunching them up in his mouth like popcorn.

Roberta reflected on what a wonderful day she had had as they drove to Michel's home with their purchases piled in the back seat. The drive through winding country roads to Michel's home in the countryside north of the coast traversed some of the most beautiful landscape Roberta had ever seen. Although Michel's success would have allowed him to live any-where, he had settled in the little town of Le Bar Sur Loup because of the beauty of the landscape and the friendliness of the people. The small village had become an artists' colony without pretense, where hand blown glass, pottery, sculpture, ceramics, wrought iron and tapestries were creat-ed in limited quantities by dedicated local artisans. The sidewalks and ca-fés were full of people and many waved at Michel as he drove by. Writers, inventors and wealthy transplants from other countries including a large community of ex-pats from Britain, had made the village their home. All of these diverse and interesting people mingled in the neighborhood cafés at the end of the afternoon with local farmers and tradesmen to talk poli-tics and share a glass of pastis.

Michel turned off the winding road into the long driveway that led from the wrought iron entrance gate to the garage at the back of the house. The driveway was lined on both sides with double hedges of lavender and rose-mary, and she breathed deeply of the sweet piney fragrance as she exited the car. Michel's dogs met them at the front door, spinning in circles and jumping in the air to show how happy they were to see him. Michel went to the kitch-en to put their purchases away as she looked around his beautiful Provençal home.

The French name their houses in much the same way that American ranchers name their ranches. Michel's home was called *Mas Mon Rêve,* or House of My Dreams. Although it had started out as a small stone *mas,* or farmhouse, it was now quite magnificent since Michel had added to its' origi-nal structure. The home's interior was light and airy with pale yellow walls washed with coat after coat of watered down paint, giving the walls a light reflective translucence to display Michel's simply framed photographs. Hand painted, eighteen-inch square, cream and blue ceramic tiles from Italy covered the large expanse of floor, and the rooms flowed effortlessly without interrup-tion into one another. Billowy lengths of pale yellow linen curtains covered the floor to ceiling picture windows overlooking the hillsides beyond, and were tied at the top with cute bows onto wrought iron rods with smiling sun finials at each end, handmade, he informed her, by his neighbor, José.

Mediterranean fabrics of yellow and blue covered throw pillows, tables and soft fluffy cushions. They were scattered on the couch and along the floor where Michel had laid rugs of woven jute and colorful Kilims from Pakistan and Turkey, placed seductively in corners and nooks for private conversations. There were six large window doors on the far side of the immense living area with heavy wooden shutters that kept out the hot summer sun. These opened onto a grapevine covered terrace of flowers and gnarled olive trees that also connected to the kitchen for convenience in dining *al fresco* under the canopy of stars on warm summer nights. A kitchen garden of herbs, eggplant, peppers, onions and tomatoes lined up in neat rows along the far side of the terrace. Flowering fruit trees pirouetted across the flat, terraced hillsides over a carpet of tiny yellow and white marguerite daisies that exploded in a profusion of color.

Michel drew a hot bath for Roberta while she arranged her clothing in the antique armoire he had found at a local flea market. He had scattered rose petals from one of many jewel-colored jars of bath oils and salts on the ledge of the tub. She slipped into the steaming rose-scented water and sighed with pleasure. A Japanese garden with a waterfall and small pond filled with sun-dappled carp was on view outside the wall of windows that enveloped the tub, and a latticework privacy fence covered with thick flowering jasmine surrounded the little Japanese garden. The heady fragrance mingled seductively with the rose-scented water. She lay back in the steaming water letting her muscles unwind from the day. Michel sat on the ledge, talking quietly as he circulated the water a little with his hand, and then reached across her for the looffah to which he applied a fragrant soap.

He told her to sit up, and he gently scrubbed her back. When he was done, she lay back again and closed her eyes. She was exhausted from her trip, and the eventful day, and asked Michel if there was time for her to take a nap. He left her in peace to relax.

She dried herself off with a large white towel then crawled naked into the luxuriously soft, down-quilted bed. The heavy muslin sheets were cool and smelled of lilacs, and she snuggled deeply into the fluffy feather pillows with Michel's little white Bichon, Tedy, tucked in closely next to her body.

She awoke several hours later disoriented and groggy from heavy sleep. She looked around the room to try to figure out where she was. An antique crystal vase filled with lilies of the valley and small yellow roses sat next to her on the table, placed there by Michel while she slept, and the memories of the day came flooding back. She smiled warmly, and rolled over onto her side, closing her eyes again and sighing contentedly.

A heavenly fragrance was emanating from the kitchen and she could hear the faint strains of a harpsichord concerto in the background. Tedy licked her chin affectionately and she scratched his tiny head. She arose and put on her robe, following the smell to the kitchen where she stood in the doorway watching Michel add cream and butter to the bowl of a food processor. She kissed him and took some bread to dip into the concoction, a soup of wild mushrooms and basil.

"Mm," she said, savoring the flavors. She popped another piece of soaked bread into her mouth. "Wow! This is wonderful! Do you cater parties?"

"Only my own, and only for very special guests." He took her in his arms and gave her a long tender hug, swaying gently back and forth as he spoke softly in her ear. "It's so nice to have you here with me, Roberta, sleeping in my bed and sharing my home. I could get used to this life."

She melted against his body as he spoke, listening to the deep timbre of his voice and feeling the vibrations of his words against her chest. She did not say anything in response, but held him tighter. Finally, she whispered, "I could too. That's what I'm afraid of."

He took hold of her shoulders and gently pushed her away from him so he could look into her eyes. Her hair fell in loose curls and her face had a crease in it from where she had slept on the pillow. He leaned down and kissed the crease, and said, "Being afraid of loving someone is the first sign that you already do." He smiled down at her and his eyes twinkled in the fading evening light. "Now, let me get back to my soup," he said, slapping her on the butt as she walked away.

She walked out onto the terrace and turned around in a circle to view the entire scene in the golden evening light. The sun hung just above the hills to the west. A rose-gold light suffused the air, adding a rosy glow to the silver-green leaves of the olive trees, and the delicate pink and white blossoms of the fruit trees on the terraced hillside. As the sun went down the evening air chilled rapidly. She wrapped her arms around herself and shivered in the cool air.

Michel came out to start the fire for the lamb chops, placing fruitwood shards and real wood charcoal into the massive stone grill. Roberta watched the flames leap into existence, and felt a shudder run down her spine. An uneasy feeling came over her for a split second, but she quickly shook it away. She ran back inside to change into warmer clothing, Tedy nipping playfully at her heels. As she passed by the foyer on her way to the bedroom, she noticed the large, stunning arrangement in a Japanese urn that Michel had made with the lilacs they had bought, adding lavender and red and pink roses from his garden. She stopped to smell the sweet soft fragrance before going into the bedroom to change for dinner.

She pulled her clothes from the antique armoire, choosing a long copper-colored silk skirt slit high to her upper thigh, a light-brown short sleeved cashmere sweater that she left unbuttoned save for the three in the middle of her chest and sexy lace up espadrilles. She went to the mirror to freshen her make up, applying lipstick, rouge and mascara. She fluffed her loose curls with her fingers, and after taking one final look in the mirror, walked back out to the terrace.

Michel had prepared the lamb chops with a dry rub of mint, rosemary, thyme, sage, salt and pepper, and they sat on a platter next to the fire on the stone grill. He had placed two diagonally contrasting tablecloths on the table, the bottom a cheerful blue and yellow Mediterranean fabric, the top an antique lace, and he had sprinkled yellow rose petals haphazardly across the table. The table was arrayed with several small hand-painted blue and yellow bowls filled with olives, fresh radishes and sliced melon, and his wild mushroom soup gleamed creamy-gold in delicate double-handled white china bowls in the candlelight. A crystal carafe of wine sat on a silver tray, and matching crystal glasses sat in front of each bowl of soup. The fire added to the golden glow of the evening, and a dreamy enchantment settled onto the terrace.

Michel was waiting by her chair, and he pulled it out for her as she approached the table. He poured the wine into her glass and leaned down to kiss her cheek before he sat down. She reached across the table for his hand, and looked longingly into his eyes. Her skin glowed in the candlelight and she smiled softly.

"This is so beautiful, Michel. Thank you for giving me such a lovely day."

"You've inspired me, *chérie,*" he said, lifting his glass. *"Bon appétit!"*

"Bon appétit!"

She ate her soup gracefully, ladling each spoonful into her mouth and savoring the delicate flavors that mingled lavishly on her tongue. When they were finished, she nibbled on the olives and drank her wine as Michel grilled the lamb. Melodic strains from a flute concerto wafted through the open door. She swung around in her chair to face him as they spoke, and her skirt fell open at the slit, exposing long, shapely legs. She made no attempt to close off the view, and Michel gazed at her as she crossed her legs seductively.

Michel came back to the table with the lamb-laden platter and a covered bowl of steaming green beans. He refilled her wine glass and sat next to her. She couldn't remember when she had ever been so hungry, and she ate her entire meal without saying a word, periodically uttering a deeply satisfied *mmmmm* to indicate her appreciation. He was grateful that she had a healthy appetite. If there was one thing he hated, it was a woman who ate like a bird. He watched Roberta as she soaked up the last bit of juice on her plate with a crusty bite of bread. She took another swallow of her wine to wash down the bread, and grinned up at him as she licked the tips of her fingers.

"What's next?" she asked smiling.

Michel rose from the table, picking up their plates. He walked to the large stone grill where he laid their plates and picked up two small bowls of salad. "As you probably know, in France we eat the salad after the meal as a *digestif* and I have made a simple one to cleanse the palate."

"This is very pretty," commented Roberta. "Is this the butter lettuce we bought at the farmer's market?"

"Yes," answered Michel. "Aren't they wonderfully delicate little jewels? And it is dressed with just a light drizzle of walnut oil, lemon, salt and pepper. *C'est tous!*"

"Magnifique!"

Michel reached into her bowl and picked up a tiny tender leaf of lettuce gleaming with drops of lemon and walnut oil and light sprinklings of salt and pepper, and offered it to her on his fingertips as he sat down next to her. She took the proffered leaf and closed her eyes, concentrating her mind on detecting the flavors he had described. They made a delightful combination on her tongue. She opened her eyes and he was staring at her with a soft sweet smile on his face.

"Come over here, my darling." He pulled her onto his lap and she curled up in his arms with a light kiss. *"Regarde, chérie,"* he said, pointing up at the sliver of moon perched just above the hilltop. "It looks as if it is sitting on the hill." He sighed deeply and kissed her hair. "When you are back at home, we will both see the moon and think of this night. The moon will never appear quite the same to us again." He had already begun to anticipate their parting, and felt the familiar melancholy settle heavily in his heart.

She kissed him for a long moment, their lips locked in gentle rhythmic suckling, their breaths mingled and drawn together in ever-quicker succession. He lifted her up in his arms and carried her into the bedroom. He placed her gently on the bed, his strong arms easily maneuvering her light body. He slowly unbuttoned the three tiny pearl buttons of her sweater releasing her breasts from their confinement. He cupped them gently in his hands, and squeezed them together as he kissed them. Without a word he unfastened her skirt and slid it over her hips. Her silk panties were tied at the sides with pink satin ribbons, and he left them in their protective position as he slowly removed his own clothing.

His body was carved from years of outdoor adventures, his chest and arms finely chiseled in sinewy perfection. Roberta looked at him without hesitation or embarrassment, and their eyes locked in loving admiration as he stood by the side of the bed. He lay down beside her and caressed her face with the back of his hand, tracing the line of her chin with his finger, then across her lips and down her neck. Her skin was soft and downy, and she moaned softly as his fingers gently caressed the curves of her body. He untied the tiny, satin ribbons that kept her panties in place, and slowly brought her to the edge of ecstasy, waiting for her to reach that height herself before joining her on the journey. They reached the pinnacle together and jumped over the edge at the same moment, and fell asleep entwined in blessed love-spent exhaustion.

CHAPTER 25

Evan Holds Down the Fort

EVAN FINISHED PACKING his briefcase, placing files and documents inside. It was after seven o'clock, although the extended hours of summer sun from daylight saving time made it seem much earlier. He scanned his desk hurriedly, and walked briskly out the door. He was having dinner at home with Harry and Jackie and was running a little behind. Harry prided himself on his grilling skills, and since Evan had first moved into Jackie's guesthouse, he had a standing invitation to the weekly Friday night cookout.

He had had a very busy day, and had worked on a number of client accounts with the project teams. Evan was surprised by how much he was actually enjoying the public relations business. It was the perfect marriage of art and business, and gave him the chance to use both his brain and his heart all day long. Today he had worked on a project for a new natural household products company, Clean Living, and ironically, a new campaign for American Pride, who could now boast of owning nearly fifteen million acres of sustainable growth timberland in the U.S. and Canada. Roberta's Oregon incident twelve years earlier had eventually turned the tide of public opinion, and the company now embraced her challenge to plant renewable forestland for use in harvesting the timber for the paper and wood products they sold.

After taking a good look at RPR's financial situation when Roberta took over, he had initiated stricter cost controls and reorganized the departments according to their function. David, Patrick and Robert Reed had pretty much done whatever they wanted with the firm's money, and everyone from Vice Presidents to copy writers had been given an expense account. The company was raking in cash, and Robert Reed had rewarded his most loyal employees quite handsomely, paying for both their complicity and their silence.

David Reed had been right when he said that Robert Reed was a tyrant. In the last year of his life he had gone through eight assistants in ten months, the majority of them lasting less than a month, with only one staying for more than four months. Holly had informed him that the women Robert Reed hired were all young, attractive and variably competent. They were required to have skills in creative thinking, poise and diplomacy in his fast-paced, high-visibility executive office.

The assistant was in control of the planning and execution of Robert's extensive travel schedule, juggling his calendar appointments and preparing his speeches in large type so he didn't need reading glasses. He frequently had confidential client meetings with high-level executives where strategy ideas were hatched. The assistant was also required to strictly control access to his office by anyone in the company, and she had keys to his secret personal files where he kept handwritten notes about his meetings with trade associations and CEOs of the Fortune 500 companies they represented.

He was very demanding. Evan had learned from Holly that he threw fits of temper, as well as pencils, pens, paper clips, file folders, dry erase markers or anything else handy, at the girls if a letter had a typo, his calendar was overbooked, or a car wasn't there to pick him up when he arrived at the airport. Each girl had started out the job believing that they were joining a firm that supported environmental causes, but as Holly had succinctly put it, "soon learned he and his upper management team were in fact just making shit up."

Holly had confided everything to Evan and Roberta over drinks one night, shortly after they had fired all of Robert Reed's diabolical sycophants who helped him dream up the schemes that the company put out for public consumption. She had been working for Robert Reed for a little more than a month when she unwittingly made the mistake of arranging an interview for him with a reporter at National Public Radio. Robert had been taking a lot of heat from the media about his tactics and had been accused of fabricating most of his client's good environmental records. She convinced him that it was a good idea to tell his side of the story, and NPR was the place to do it.

The news report, however, had not been favorable and had made some very serious accusations about what the firm really did. Robert, his face red with anger and his voice loud enough for others outside the door to hear, had accused Holly of complicity with the interviewer. As he was telling her to pack her things, he clutched his chest and fell to the floor. He died of a heart attack right in front of her.

Despite the confusion she was feeling she sprang into action and called the ambulance. She called Jackie too. She stayed on after his death, helping David Reed, organizing company events, sending out the death notices to clients, answering questions, and helping Jackie with her correspondence. She laughingly confided to Roberta that she was sure that the first day she walked through the front door as CEO, would be Holly's last day at Reed Public Relations. Roberta assured her that she had been invaluable from the very first moment. After two years of working with Roberta, Holly had grown to love her and believed wholeheartedly in her cause.

Evan headed down to the building's underground parking and to the Jaguar that Jackie was letting him use. Jackie could not have been more kind and gracious to him, allowing him to live in her guesthouse and accepting him into her heart as if he were part of the family. She checked in on him at least twice a week. He had dinner over at the main house as often as he could, alternately laughing at Harry's rustic down home charm of fishing tales and jokes about his corn-cob smoking granny, and then marveling at the glimpse he would sometimes give Evan of the power he wielded in the Senate.

The temperature of the evening air was pleasant, the oppressive, choking heat of summer not yet upon the nation's capital. Evan drove to Chevy Chase with the top down and the radio tuned to a local jazz station, Boney James mellow sax helping to bring his weekend mood into alignment. He pulled into the driveway and parked the Jag in the six-car garage adjacent to the main house. The impeccably clean garage already had three cars neatly lined up in their stalls, Harry's ten-year old Lincoln Continental, Jackie's brand new Mercedes coupe, and a classic 1965 Ford Mustang convertible in mint condition. He could see Harry through the garage windows standing over the charcoal grill next to the flagstone pool. A chef's hat was cocked jauntily atop his head and he was in his favorite white apron emblazoned in red letters with "If you can't stand the heat, get out of the Senate" across the front. Jackie's elegant all-black standard poodle, Alphonse, stood at attention in front of Harry, deftly catching a tossed piece of cooked chicken or sausage in his mouth. Evan waved at Harry, and quickly crossed the brick pathway to the guesthouse where he changed into shorts, a T-shirt and sandals, and went back out to join Harry by the pool.

"Hey Harry," said Evan, as he popped the top off of a Heineken and took a seat in the comfy lounge chair. "Who's hide are you grilling today?"

Harry Markham was an irascible and irrepressible Southern senator whose career in the Senate had spanned more than thirty years. He had risen to a position of power and influence both feared and respected by his colleagues. A man of intelligence and patience mixed with raw, cunning ambition, he knew when to use the velvet glove and when to use the dagger. He had wrenched many Senate bills from the jaws of defeat as he walked the corridors of power talking to the newly elected and the old-timers alike, with a fatherly pat on the back or a firmly whispered threat of public exposure for a momentary indiscretion.

"Ha!" exclaimed Markham. "Today it's the new majority leader." He skewered the sausages on the grill with his long-handled fork, stabbing them as if he had a saber in his hand. "Since Bob Dole resigned the Senate to run for President the place is in turmoil while Trent Lott sets his agenda. Instead of Thad Cochran who would have brought some balance and thoughtful leadership to the institution, Lott wants to renegotiate everything we've done in the last year. He's aggressive and wants to curry favor with younger conservatives who were swept into office on the coattails of the Gingrich agenda. The House is full of nincompoops, and sometimes we forget that the Senate is supposed to be the adults in the room."

"I guess that means your bill that's stuck in committee gets killed," said Evan.

"He's an ideological baboon!" Markham flipped a slice of eggplant. "The country's going down the toilet and he spouts rhetoric!"

Jackie came out of the house looking her usual elegant self in a flowing aqua pantsuit and a matching chunky beaded necklace. Her high-heeled mules clicked against the brick walkway, as Min-Min, Roberta's cat for whom she was baby-sitting, followed closely behind her. She was carrying a large platter of rice pilaf and a summer salad in a hammered metal bowl. Alphonse, seeing Min-Min, looked momentarily unsure whether to chase the cat or stay next to Harry to catch another tossed piece of chicken. He cocked hi shead back and forth a couple of times from Jackie to Harry, the wheels in his little dog mind turning ferociously.

"Here, let me take that," offered Evan, jumping to his feet. He took the large platter, and turned around to place it on the outdoor dining table that Jackie had already set with plates, napkins, wine glasses and silverware. Alphonse made up his mind and chased the cat up a tree.

"*Ah, merci!* Hand that to Harry, please," she instructed him. "Harry, just arrange all the vegetables and meats on top of the rice, *s'il vous plais.*"

Harry did as he was instructed, artistically arranging the platter and carrying it to the table.

Alphonse barked at the cat at the top of the tree, his paws placed against the tree trunk to emphasize his threat to her. *"Alphonse! Viens ici! Laisse le chat tranquille!"* Alphonse obeyed and ran back to her side.

"Is there anything else we need?" asked Evan.

"I'll just go get the wine," answered Jackie.

"I'll get it," said Evan. "You sit down." He pulled out her chair for her.

Jackie stood still for a moment looking at Evan, as he waited for her to take her seat. "You are so thoughtful," she said, patting his cheek. "You'll make someone a very good husband one day."

Evan's eyes grew darker for just a split second as an image of Jane flashed into his mind, but his smile never left his face. "I would like that."

"The wine is on the counter in the kitchen," she said as he walked away. "He's such a good man," she said to Harry, as Evan walked into the house. "I wish Roberta could see that."

"Oh, deep down she already knows it. She just can't think of him as anything but just a friend. I just hope that when the day finally comes that she realizes how much she loves him, it won't be too late," he said. "You don't get many second chances at happiness," he added, looking lovingly at Jackie. "Now, hand me your plate and I'll dish some of this out. What would you like, my sweet little ladybird?"

"Just some rice and vegetables for me."

"Now Jackie, eat up, little darlin'. There's a nice piece of chicken here for you."

Evan came back with the wine in an acrylic cooler and placed it on the table. He picked up the bottle and filled Jackie's glass.

"Harry?" he asked, proffering the bottle.

"Yes, please, I'll take some of that. Help yourself to the sausage and vegetables," he said. "Hey, I heard a new joke today," he said with a twinkle in his eye.

"Yeah?" asked Evan, as Jackie looked on warily. "Tell me."

"Man goes to his doctor after having terrible headaches. The doctor can't find nothin' wrong with him, but tells him what he does when he gets a headache. "Whenever I get a headache," said the doctor, "I go home and lie down with my head between my wife's breasts and after twenty or thirty minutes my headache goes away. Try that. It always works for me." The guy tries it and goes back to the doctor, and says "Doc, that was amazing. I tried it and it works great." The doctor says, "I'm glad to hear it." And the guy says, "By the way, Doc, you've got a nice house." As he delivered the punch line, he drummed a familiar, bah-da-boom, on the table with his hands.

"Ha!" Evan laughed and Jackie rolled her eyes.

"Okay," Harry said agreeably to Jackie. "Here's one you'll like about my grandpappy. My Granny and Grampy were sittin' together on the big porch swing, holdin' hands and a-swingin' back and forth. Granny was puffin' on her pipe, and they was relaxin' after a round of golf. And Granny asks, "Pappy, do you think there's golf in heaven?" And Grand Pappy says, "I don't know, that's a good question. Let's make a pact. The first one of us that dies will come back and tell the other if there's golf in heaven." They agreed on it, and lo and behold, three weeks later, ol' Grampy goes and kicks the bucket! A couple days later, his ghost comes back and sits on the bed next to Granny in the bedroom. "Who's there?" says Granny. "It's your dearly departed husband. I've got some good news, and I've got some bad news. The good news is there is golf in heaven. The bad news is you've got a 1:00 tee time next Thursday." Harry laughed merrily at his joke, beaming at Evan and Jackie.

"Ugh," Evan groaned.

Jackie laughed good-naturedly. "Cute," said Jackie approvingly. "That one you could tell at a dinner party."

"Okay that's all I've got for now," said Harry. "The adults can talk about something else."

"What's going on at the office, Evan?" asked Jackie, relieved to change the subject.

"I was in meetings all day with our creative teams," answered Evan. "Roberta is really making headway with some of our clients, and her message is resonating."

"I was here that night when the shit hit the fan with American Pride, excuse my French, my love," said Harry. "I was surprised they actually stayed with RPR. That was one stupid stunt she pulled."

"I tried to talk her out of it," commented Evan, chuckling with the memory of their argument in Summer's cousin's kitchen, "but she was determined. As it turned out though, she was right on the mark with her sustainable development comment. I just had a meeting with American Pride today. They now have over 15 million acres of renewable timberland. Everything comes full circle doesn't it? We use it in their PR campaign now. She was just ahead of her time. Robert made a wise decision making her President of the firm."

"I guess we didn't see it at the time," said Harry. "Robert had a different attitude about it."

Evan was sure that Harry Markham knew full well what Robert had been doing. He and Roberta had found the files in the office that told the full story about the extent of his subterfuge in promoting his clients' internal agendas. Having a high-ranking member of the senate in Robert's pocket helped grease the wheels on Capital Hill.

"The thing is," continued Markham," when you think about it, it's the women who have moved us forward on conservation and environmental issues. Most people don't know it, but it was Maggie Thatcher that convinced Ronald Reagan that the science behind the ozone hole was real. Thatcher knew something about science. She had been a research chemist in her early life. It was because of her that he signed the Montreal Protocol that phased out CFC's. She believed in the science relating to climate change and he loved nothing more than to be outside chopping wood and riding horses. The man truly loved nature."

"Maybe it was his way of paying penance for appointing James Watt as Secretary of the Interior," said Evan with a snicker.

"The Reagan years were pretty much of a wash as far as his environmental legacy," said Markham. "The environmentalists feared he would dismantle regulations and give away public lands and resources, and industry hoped he would deregulate, paving the way to easier access to oil, coal and timber on Federal lands. As it turned out he did neither, pleasing nobody, but also, doing no further harm. He was one conflicted cat. He loved nature but didn't love government regulation. The proverbial rock and a hard place."

"I wonder where Roberta is right now?" asked Jackie. "Let's see, its well past midnight over in France."

"I spoke to her this morning. She called just as I was getting into the office. Michel took her to Monaco to meet Jacques Cousteau. They're working on a big project together for a presentation to the European Union. It sounds like she landed new business for the firm her very first day there!" Evan said with obvious pride.

"Jacques Cousteau, how wonderful!" exclaimed Jackie. "She just loved him when she was growing up, she never missed one of his programs on TV."

"Did you know that Summer is in Lyon at the same time that Roberta is in Provence? She's planning to meet up with Summer at your sister's farm in Dijon," he confirmed.

I haven't seen Summer in years," mused Jackie. "I keep hearing wonderful reviews of her restaurants. She's become something of a celebrity out there."

"Roberta hasn't seen her aunt and uncle since she and Summer spent the year there after Oregon," Evan said to Jackie.

Jackie looked at Evan for a moment, then said, "That should bring back memories for them both."

"I think my brother is in Barcelona with his band right now. Seems like everyone, but me, is in Europe."

"I guess somebody has to stay home and hold down the fort," said Jackie apologetically.

Evan thought he detected a look of worry in her eyes.

"It's alright Jackie. I don't mind," he said reassuringly.

"Oh, I know," she answered him, chasing the concern from her face with a smile. "Who wants more pilaf?"

CHAPTER 26

A Higher Calling

"THANK YOU! THANK you!" shouted Steven Manning into the microphone in front of him. He and his band mates stepped back and waved to the crowd of thousands tightly packed on the lawn of the concert venue in Barcelona. They walked off the stage and out to their limousines waiting at the security entrance behind the stage. The girls that followed the band from city to city waited by the door, hoping to be chosen by their dreamy favorite to accompany them back to their hotel. Tommy and Glen picked out two girls to join them in the limo, and several yelled out "Stevie! Stevie!" but Steven ignored them, uninterested in another one-night stand. He had a girlfriend now, and he was trying to be faithful to her.

Steven was the band's unelected leader. After they had cut their demo tape of his original songs when he returned from Oregon, including their first hit, *Summer,* that skyrocketed to Number One on the charts, they had eagerly allowed him to manage the band's direction. Before they submitted the tape to the record company executive, they had talked about the band's name and decided they liked the multiple meanings of A Higher Calling, and the name stuck. It said everything about the band, their music and their purpose.

It was not only Summer and Roberta who had had an epiphany in that old growth forest in Oregon, but Steven had also. He went back to Vermont with a vision of his band in his head, and what their music would stand for. Steven wrote songs about anything that hit his fancy, and he kept a stack of notebooks where he doodled lyrics, poems, sketches and ditties that rattled around in his very creative head. Anything could trigger a song lyric or melody. Their songs ran the gamut from high-energy, balls-to-the-walls rock and roll anthems to sweet acoustical guitar ballads about love and remorse. The one thing that was unique about A Higher Calling was their dedication to environmental causes. Steven's melodies incorporated the joyful songs and mournful cries of the Earth's animals and peoples as he told the stories of their lives and their struggles to survive in his music.

His fame and fortune had exploded overnight with chart topping hit after hit, selling millions of records. He flew on his private jet, splitting his time between London and New York where he owned luxurious apartments in the most sought after buildings in those cities. He owned a stone mansion in Sonoma County, California where he was a part owner of a vineyard with a Hollywood director, and his personal wine cellar there boasted thirty thousand bottles of the world's finest wines. He hobnobbed with the rich and famous and had become friends with some very smart people who had turned their ideas, and their companies, into tech industry titans.

Wherever Steven went he talked about the environment, and many of the industry leaders he befriended shared his concern. Together they had set up a charitable foundation that donated money and resources to build schools, protect habitat, conduct research, ship food, dig fresh water wells, donate seed and grain, teach conservation to local farmers, fund game reserves, fight poaching, stop mass deforestation for agricultural purposes, reduce carbon emissions, and protect the world's oceans from pollution and over-fishing. The band never said no to an invitation to play at an environmental fundraising event after a natural or man-made disaster, and they were the eagerly anticipated last act at their annual rock fundraising event, Green World Festival.

Steven would not have guessed that when he jokingly told the chick in the grocery store in Wyoming to watch the news for them in Oregon, it would have turned out to be prophetic. Before he met Summer's cousin, Dylan, Steven was unaware of the extent of the destruction being perpetrated each and every day on the planet's delicate balancing act. Dylan's challenge to Roberta to defy her father and prove her dedication to the movement had opened his eyes to the duplicity and callousness of the businesses that were willfully ignoring their destruction of the ecosystems that had thrived on the planet for millions of years. He was rooting for Roberta to succeed in her quest to educate her clients, but he doubted that for most of them, anything but the almighty dollar would ever be their guiding principle. A Higher Calling had been the object of their vitriolic criticisms many times when a revelation about a company's unethical or illegal environmental practices had hit the news. The band used their power to influence their fans to boycott the offending company. Many of these same companies would make large cash donations to his eco-foundation, and distribute the press release with their picture taken with Steven and the band to promote their products as Earth friendly. Steven took their money, but never trusted their intentions, and just hoped that the money would do some good in a remote part of the world where it was needed.

Steven got into his own limo, leaving the boys in the band to their usual after concert party. They needed to decompress after the energy of a live show, and they would head back to the five-star hotel where they were staying to order room service and drink some hundred-year-old Napoleon brandy. And, of course, the girls would help them release all that pent up energy. Steven mentally crossed his fingers and hoped that he wouldn't read about a drunken orgy of destruction in the news tomorrow.

The limo pulled out of the back entrance to the stadium and the local police waving his driver through. The limo would be taking him to his personal jet, and back to London for a little time off to chill and work on new songs for the next album. As he was boarding his jet his cell phone rang. Very few people had his personal cell phone number. He answered it right away.

"Hello?"

"Steven, hey! It's Summer."

"Hey chef! What's cookin'!" said Steven with genuine enthusiasm.

Steven had called her chef since their trip to Oregon, and it always made her laugh. He was one of her best friends, and he had always believed in her. From the very first time they had walked down that grocery aisle together he had been one of her most ardent supporters and her first investor. "I was wondering if you had any free time during the next six weeks?" asked Summer.

"As a matter of fact, I do. I'm just about to take some time off. I'm on my way back to London from Barcelona now. Why?"

"Perfect timing! How would you like to surprise Roberta, and meet me in France?"

"Awesome! I haven't seen Roberta since Davos. When and where?"

"Next weekend in Dijon. I'll pick you up at the train station."

"Fantastic! I'll be there!"

CHAPTER 27

Raison d'Etre

MICHEL SNUGGLED UP close to Roberta, lifting himself up on his elbow so he could watch her as she slept. He watched intently for several minutes as she breathed rhythmically in and out in a blissful, safe slumber. Her hair fell in gentle gold curls on the pillow and her mouth formed a tiny relaxed 'o'. She was beautiful and intelligent, and he knew he was deeply and helplessly in love with her.

He sighed and lay back on his pillow, gazing for a moment out the window at the moon. A star hung just to the bottom right of the Earth's only rotating celestial body. They were both fortunate, he thought. Even the moon had a companion tonight to keep it company as it traveled the night sky.

Michel gently rose from the bed, trying not to awaken Roberta. He would not be able to sleep yet, and he had some work to do. He quietly walked out of the room, closing the door softly behind him, and went to his office at the other end of the hall.

He sat down at his computer and opened his email folder. He had 217 new messages, and he scanned the messages looking for anything marked urgent. He sent off a couple of replies to environmental research organizations asking him to be a part of future projects. Unlike his well-paid expeditions with National Geographic or Cousteau, whose books and magazines were always big sellers, the research projects that were associated with universities almost always had limited funding, and Michel's deals with them usually involved no charge to the project sponsor, but he would maintain sole proprietary ownership of his photographs which would later be included in a book or article, or sold to galleries, private collectors or nature groups. When deciding on accepting a project, he had to weigh the potential income against the risk or popularity of the subject being studied. There had been times when he had taken projects simply because he himself was interested in the subject or location, even though its economic value was limited.

The philosophies that Roberta and Michel embraced were in some way very similar although they worked from opposing ends of the debate. Roberta came to the table with the philosophical dictum that said if you are not part of the solution you are part of the problem. She had dedicated herself to teaching corporations about the benefits of becoming truly green. She believed, and had documented proof to back up her claim, that businessmen and women could be taught to marry reverence for the Earth with a culture motivated by profit. Her hope was that her clients would see that keeping a business viable over the long-term would weigh heavier than short-term profits. As responsible corporate citizens, she was sure they would see the devastating implications of using up natural resources faster than they can be replaced if it were presented to them in an intelligent and informed way that showed the benefits to the bottom line.

Michel went to the kitchen for a glass of wine as he pondered the difference between he and Roberta. Michel's view was that business would never do anything that would interfere with short-term profit as long as they were financially beholden to shareholders and board members. He believed, and had evidence to prove it, that the only time real change was effected was when governments forced industry and business to comply with regulations limiting pollutants, and set up agencies to watchdog compliance with those regulations. He was even more adamant that the regulations didn't go far enough. He truly mourned the loss of species while useless debates raged about the true extent of the damage or the cost to shareholders, taxpayers or property owners associated with change.

Michel's distrust of corporate environmental public relations campaigns were well founded, based in the unpleasant reality that disinformation is information nonetheless and will influence public opinion. He knew that spreading disinformation, challenging scientific data and creating a desire for a product despite its' environmental impact was a trademark of the corporate pubic relations game. While big business made the consuming public feel warm and fuzzy with nice headlines about recycling paper products, aluminum cans in the lunchroom and toner cartridges in the copy room, the real polluting of the environment was going on behind the public's back, or frequently, right before their eyes.

The wide-ranging environmental policies, or lack thereof, that governments around the world adopted kept people like Roberta and Michel juggling balls of expectation and disappointment. Governments in Africa, South and Central America, Asia and parts of Eastern Europe had no comprehensive environmental policies, and played a dangerous game of catch-up and cleanup one step ahead of apocalyptic catastrophes. The catastrophes involved an almost incomprehensibly long list of industries, and new potential disasters raised red flags each day in one or another part of the globe.

Accidents at decayed and aging nuclear power plants in the former Soviet Union, such as the one at Chernobyl, threatened the populace of Northern and Eastern Europe and the clear cool waters and beautiful fjords of Scandinavia. American fast food companies paid the indigenous people of South and Central America to clear cut rain forests so cattle could be raised to produce cheap beef to satisfy the fast food addiction of people in the United States and around the world. The result was the corruption of the ancient culture of indigenous people, wiping out unknown numbers of exotic, unstudied species, as well as the loss of oxygen-producing forests for the planet.

Michel was enraged at the human stupidity, foolish superstition and ego-fueled arrogance behind the widespread poaching and killing of exotic and threatened animals in unspoiled areas of Africa and Asia. Local trackers were paid by intermediaries to satisfy the twisted lust of wealthy men for the exotic. Endangered mountain gorillas were hunted and killed, their large human-like hands embalmed and turned into table ornaments for their human owner's amusement. Or because of foolish superstitions, as in the ancient belief that certain animal organs have healing properties or act as enhancements for male sexual performance, and threaten the very existence of rare and treasured creatures. Michel despaired to think that a rare Bengal tiger would be sacrificed so that his penis could be dried and brewed into a tea because of some man's misguided belief that it will increase virility or cure impotence. Or when, because of long-standing practices attributed to cultural heritage, certain countries with otherwise peaceful and loving people brutally hunted whales, dolphins and sharks, sometimes to the brink of extinction.

But Michel's most explosive anger was reserved for the most egregious offenders, the oil companies whose financial power and political clout in countries around the world dwarfed all other industries combined. Oil companies held governments around the globe in their grip because of the essential nature of the commodity they sold. Armies moved on oil, industry produced and distributed goods and services on oil, and emerging markets fueled growth in their economies on oil. Poor African nations run by megalomaniacal despots lined their pockets and turned over large swaths of unspoiled land to oil companies whose derricks pumped the black liquid from deep below the surface, giving none of the financial gain to the people of those nations who so desperately needed it. The seabed was punctured with miles of drilling equipment, snaking it's way to the Earth's caverns engorged with the vital energy-giving substance, and pipes carried the black lifeblood of world economies to holding tanks and shipping tankers in every corner of the world. The governments of western nations struck covert deals with repressive Arab partners to buy the precious commodity in exchange for peace and stability in the region while native Arab people suffered at the hands of brutal dictatorships. Pipes burst, tankers crashed and drilling rigs exploded, killing workers and spilling millions of gallons of the toxic substance onto the land and into oceans and harbors. The power that oil producing nations held over the countries who were net importers of oil led to shifting allegiances and catastrophic wars fought over drilling rights between neighboring Arab countries, sending oil prices into the stratosphere and always ultimately enriching the cartel of exporting countries. Military forces set fire to oil wells in Kuwait sending billowing plumes of toxic fumes into the Earth's atmosphere, and blew up the main terminal at the Persian Gulf, spilling tens of millions of barrels into the gulf waters. While European and Asian nations invested heavily in alternative energy sources to try to break the grip of oil's dominance in their countries, in the U.S. oil remained the dominant energy fuel of choice, and was granted unprecedented subsidies by it's oil-financed leaders in the White House and Congress.

Michel took another sip of his wine and sighed. The lack of serious attention given to so many environmental crises looming just over the horizon was a constant reminder to him that he must work harder. The one thing that Roberta and Michel did agree on was that education was the most enduring and powerful tool for effecting real change. Third world countries were using up their own natural resources at an alarming rate to fuel the insatiable demands of first world countries. It was in mostly third world countries where the planet's untouched eco-systems suffered real, irreversible damage. In industrialized nations, education had to be done at the consumer level, and especially with the children, the future consumers of tomorrow, to educate them about the impact of the choices they made each day. Though government regulations and corporate greening were necessary, without the full support of the consumer to use less of everything, waste little of what they use, and to support clean, truly green products and businesses, and support their governments efforts to enforce new and existing environmental regulations, the work being done to curtail the loss of critical habitats in third world countries would fail.

Despite its standing as a beacon of hope to most of the world, America was not always the leader in environmental practice or legislation, and people like Roberta's father had fostered a critical confusion in the American public that bordered on lunacy. Michel sometimes felt like giving up on Americans, unable to fathom their utterly nonsensical conflation of bad information with their "don't tread on me" independence. He hoped that the children of America would be different, and become future consumers who would vote with their lifestyles, their wallets and at the ballot box to support their leaders in government enforcement. If the consumer led the demand for higher fuel efficiency in cars, less plastic packaging on products, better energy efficiency in homes and buildings, and availability of alternative energy infrastructure to reduce oil consumption it would lead to the break of oil's deadly destructive grip on the world.

CHAPTER 28

The Edenists

MICHEL REFILLED HIS wine glass and continued scanning through his emails. He stopped on a message from Gustavo Perretti, an Italian artist that he had befriended in Palermo. Gustavo spoke no French and Michel spoke no Italian, so they communicated in English. Gustavo was still working on the nuances of the language, and had had Michel in stitches the night they sat in the palazzo getting drunk on grappa and making fools of themselves with the women that walked by. He eagerly opened the message.

'Buongiorno, Michel. I hope you safe and warm in arms of beautiful woman tonight. I still are laughing from your description to me of the expedition in Central Africa which you find yourself face to face with amorous female gorilla in mountainous jungles. Even to animals you are irresistible, amico mio. I am not touch another drop of grappa since that night in Palermo, and maybe never drink again. I love the Internet. Thank you for showing me. I run across interesting place you maybe like, environmental chat room on World Wide Web. Let me know when I see you again. I maybe drink a toast to you then. Ciao!'

Michel replied. *'Allo Gustavo! I am indeed in the company of a beautiful woman and she's no gorilla. She was in my arms earlier but I seem to have put her to sleep. Maybe I need to work on my technique. I'll check out the chat room, sounds interesting. I don't know when I'll get back to Palermo. How about you, any chance of you coming to the French Riviera? You Sylvester Stallone types are always welcomed by the ladies. Aloha, my friend!'*

Michel typed in the web address that Gustavo had provided in the email and entered the chat room. He sat back to evaluate the room's interest to him. The conversation was in full swing.

gang green: the only way to bring the world back to a natural state is to eliminate the humans. I say nuke 'em.

Sloe Munk: that's stupid. Have you invented some kind of selective nuking? You can nuke people but not nuke animals and plants?

gang green: after several million years they'll all be back to normal. Let evolution take its' course.

Sloe Munk: yeah, and in the process you've altered the genetic composition of the very thing you wanted to preserve, and then you've got a bunch of mutant animals running around. Who knows what that would produce? That's no way to get back to Eden.

Anti-tec: technology is the problem. We've let our inventions rule our society and rule our ethics. We no longer have any connection to the things we need to survive, so we have no respect for their existence. If we personally had to raise and kill the chicken before we ate it, we'd give thanks to the chicken or the chicken god for sustaining us. We go to the grocery store to buy a chicken wrapped in plastic, and never think about the deplorable conditions the poultry farmer has subjected it to. We put gas in our cars and never think twice about our dependence on fossil fuels and its' effect on the environment. We flip on a light switch and never think about the coal plant or nuclear power plant that's at the other end of the wire. We flush the toilet and don't know where the waste goes. We are disconnected from our own survival, from our very selves in fact. Technology has turned us into cyber-creatures, alienated from our own humanity.

gang green: and here you sit using technology to bash technology. Get real!

Anti-tec: I can use technology to further my cause. I bash technology because it divorces us from our humanity. We pave over the Earth we once walked upon. We drive on roads enclosed in a technological cocoon at speeds that don't allow us to connect with the world around us. We walk through city streets with plugs in our ears, tuned in and yet tuned out from each other. Someday, while the real world around us burns, we'll be watching a virtual reality world of our own making. Technology is the new drug that allows us to turn on, tune in and drop out.

Dr dino: I agree that certain technologies have had a negative effect on the planet but technology and science have also had a positive effect, and may ultimately be the very thing that frees us to get back to Eden. The Internet carries information to all parts of the world and eliminates the need to use a car, a plane, a train or a ship to deliver it, thereby saving fossil fuel and the planet's atmosphere. Telecommuting instead of driving to the office will be the way of the future. We'll print less paper sending emails, and we'll communicate using our watches like Dick Tracy.

keer-ka-guard: you'll never get people to not utilize technology. They won't stop driving cars, they won't stop flying in airplanes, they won't stop using energy that comes from sources that pollute, they won't stop destroying habitats or overfishing or cutting down forests or polluting the planet's atmosphere unless you make it very easy for them because people are lazy. We're not going to go back to living in grass huts and carrying spears. The simplicity movement isn't a movement at all. It's just a fad. We've come too far. I can't live without air conditioning.

Sloe Munk: maybe the answer isn't to stop using technology but to focus our big brains to create technology that is benign to the environment, that has no effect or as little as possible. Look at all the alternative energies that we don't utilize because of the power of the petroleum industry. Why aren't we all driving electric cars? Why aren't we all using windmills and solar energy? Why aren't we taking electric trains instead of jets to cross our country?

Why are we so dependent on fossil fuels? Because the auto industry and the petroleum industry got together thirty years ago to make sure we didn't have access to that technology by buying up all the patents. I'd love to look in their vaults. There must be a wealth of inventive genius locked up for the sake of their profits.

gang green: The US is the hand puppet of the oil industry. To paraphrase Shakespeare: first, nuke all the humans; let the Earth go back to the animals.

Joan of Arc: technology is not the problem. Gang green's tongue in cheek comment about nuking the humans aside, I agree that humans ARE the problem. Science has contributed to the demise of species and the lack of reverence for life because of its insistence that we cannot attribute human characteristics and emotions to animal behavior, thus disallowing empathy to guide and inform the discovery process. American biological and behavioral sciences made their first critical mistake by adopting Morgan's Canon as their gospel. For 100 years we have all gone along with this idea that we must never attribute behavior in animals to similar behavior in humans. We can never make the connection or we are accused of bad science. Instead, science reduced animal behavior to the concept of "instinct". Behaviorists, and their lab and field biology followers, have attributed animal behavior to a lack of mind, a lack of intelligence, a lack of emotions, and a lack of conscious CHOICE, and have shut the door on studying the most interesting and worthwhile questions possible. While purporting to unemotionally seek answers to scientific questions, science has furthered the denigration of loftier goals in human interactions because we are not allowed to see ourselves in other animals, and instead science has advanced the baser instincts of behavior as natural, giving carte blanche to American-style business to justify their bad acts putting personal interest over societal benefit.

adam: I agree with Joan. The three opposed yet intertwined facets of human endeavor and exploration, that of science, business and religion, have agreed on only one thing throughout history, that animals and nature exist on a lower order, and were put on Earth for man's use and domination. Each of them, in their own twisted and distorted way, sees nothing sacred or wonderful or humbling in the interconnectedness of all life on the planet.

Dr dino: just because you study something dispassionately does not mean you are complicit in their demise, abuse or misuse. You must separate anecdote from fact. There is a good reason to abhor human-based interpretations of animal behavior.

gang green: Anyone who has taken a high school science class knows what anthropomorphism is because it has been drilled into everyone that the cardinal crime in either lab or field study is to use empathy to explain animal behavior, and oh, guess what? At the same time religions have drilled it into everyone that animals have no souls. And business conveniently exploits both of these conditions to march unimpeded across the landscape destroying habitats and ecosystems. The cohorts of science and religion, who purport to be diametrically opposed and on opposite sides of knowledge and superstition, have both placed humans at the top of the pyramid for their own reasons, while denying the part of the pyramid underneath from which the humans sprang and depend. As humans we delight in seeing the behavior of the animals around us, whether in the wild, at the zoo, or in our living rooms and comparing their behavior to our own, yet we cannot feel empathy for them if it impedes our progress. At the same time that science was building a foundation for evolutionary biology that humans evolved from common roots, they were telling us that it was okay to cause animal suffering in the quest for knowledge because they do not possess minds nor emotions. The central ethical fallacy of this is that if the animals that were used to model the human experience of pain, fear, depression, anxiety, and helplessness do not experience these conditions themselves, then their use as models is scientifically unjustified, and if they do experience these states then their use is morally and ethically unjustified. And that is why my gang has repeatedly broken into labs and released caged animals being used for inhumane experimentation.

Joan of Arc: the closer we get to the knowledge of all things, of good and evil, the knowledge of God as described in Genesis, the more we need the Earth and its wonders to remind us that despite the fact that we have uncovered the biological processes that make us work, we still have the capacity to love, to hope, to nurture and to do something altruistic. We need a belief system that puts the planet and its inhabitants on an equal, revered level with humans. The Scala Naturae, the hierarchical ladder that science has always used to categorize organisms from simple to complex with humans at the top, should also have a second level called Scala Humanae; a scale categorizing human beings from the enlightened at the top to the Earth destroyers at the bottom.

keer-ka-guard: lovely irony, there. Because with enlightenment comes humility, which brings human beings on the same level as other sentient creatures.

Dr dino: as long as the primary human impulse is survival and as long as we are motivated by individual greed rather than altruistic good, humans will poach wild animals, cut down trees and steal inventions to safeguard their existence or their power. Our culture reflects who we are, and finds little that is interesting about goodness nor does it celebrate the greater good over personal interest. In business, politics and media we celebrate vice and denigrate virtue. We are saturated with it. On the Scala Humanae, it's the wealthiest and most powerful at the top. They are the ones in all societies, both developed and developing, that are viewed as successful.

Joan of Arc: Modern human culture reflects the baser instincts of our nature because that is what we have been brainwashed to believe! Everything is relative; your truth is not my truth so there is no truth! This is the bullshit that the holy troika of science, religion and business has foisted on the world and this mantra has now permeated our courts, our politics, our very way of life. What shared values can we truly say we hold? We can no longer say that we believe in any absolute truths because everyone speaks from their own selfish perspective. We think by rejecting everything we are exhibiting independence and free will, but in reality we are all so twisted by relativism we cannot make a decision on basic ideas of right and wrong.

Annran: the only way to ensure a return to Eden, and inspire man to utilize only environmentally benign technology is by changing the factors that motivate human behavior. There will be no change in the future of the planet unless there is a vast and deep change in human nature. We must elevate human social systems to reflect a strong immutable desire for moral self-governance. All of our religions, philosophical and political systems must result and emanate from the collective soul that is guided by individually strict moral self-governance, and to achieve personal fulfillment from ethical behavior, not for self-reward or financial reward, but ethical behavior as the reward in and of itself. And the only way to do that is to educate the people of the planet that their choices have consequences, and each and every one of us must govern our own actions accordingly. Love thy neighbor or the Golden Rule, or whatever you want to call it, must be seen to apply universally to corporations, governments, and individuals alike, and indeed, must emanate to every living thing on the planet. The bird in the tree, and the tree itself, are our neighbors and we must treat them with respect and accord them the right to their existence.

High-zen-burg: no matter what we do on the planet, it will affect the planet's eco-system. You can't build a home, lay a road, mow your lawn, walk your dog, own a poultry farm or graze your cattle without it having an effect. Based on Edward Lorenz theory of deterministic chaos, under the right dynamical properties, the turbulence in the atmosphere created by a butterflies wing beats in North America grows like ripples on a pond into a typhoon in China. Everything is interconnected and overlapping and unified. You cannot live in the world without altering it in some way. It is impossible. Even if we got back to a simpler existence, got back to the authentic self, Eden as you call it, we can't divorce ourselves from the effect we have on our environment.

Sloe Munk: but that doesn't mean we shouldn't make an effort to limit the impact we make. I like what Annran had to say, it has to emanate from the individual, from individual moral self-governance. If moral self-governance ruled all individuals; the people who run the companies, the individuals who own the shares, the companies that manufacture the goods, the people who consume the products, the ones who do the research, then we are all in harmony. Then we are all in sync. Then we can be sure that we're always doing the right thing.

keer-ka-guard: so who's going to determine what's moral and what's not. What replaces capitalism and democracy? What replaces the profit motive?

adam: it isn't a matter of replacing profit necessarily, but using compassionate consumerism, or maybe a better way of explaining it would be enlightened consumerism, to guide it.

Annran: moral self-governance is both integral to and beyond social systems, and touches the moral center of each individual's inner conscience, inner god as it were. It is not a matter of letting go of the profit motive, but asking how much profit is necessary before you begin doing more harm than good. As long as we are producing and consuming environmentally benign products, there will always be supply and demand, and there will always be profit.

keer-ka-guard: but compassionate consumerism will only go so far. The problem with that idea is that it requires altruism as a means of governance to benefit the group as a whole, and is contrary to the selfishness manifest in our DNA. As long as greed and jealousy plague and inspire human endeavor, you will never reach the inner god of self-governing moral behavior in everyone. If altruism ever existed, other than as a means of self-preservation, it would have shown up in industries and businesses at some time in the past. The pharmaceutical industry is a perfect example. Where would altruism have been better applied than to that industry? Yet we know altruism is not the reward they seek.

adam: this is a serious problem in many industries. We as consumers should make decisions on where we spend our dollars based on the level of greed or altruism of the company manufacturing the product or selling the service. If you are a pharmaceutical company that pays its CEO $300,000 instead of $30 million, and you plow your profits not only into new research, but equally into benefiting poor, underserved populations, than you have a company I will gladly spend my money with. Hell, even if you charged more for your drugs than your competitor, I would tell the pharmacist I want your drugs.

gang green: but you will never know the truth behind the companies that manufacture the products you buy because they are masters of deceit. How will the consumer ever know the truth about the practices behind the lumber they buy to build their deck, or the company that manufactures their computer, or their pharmaceuticals, or their clothing? Consumerism is the culprit that fuels unwarranted growth and imbalances in power. We need to stop buying stuff. Use less, recycle what we use, waste nothing.

Dr. dino: if contacting the inner god, as Annran states it, were possible, this would work. But I'm not sure everyone has it universally or to the same degree. And there would still have to be some way of enforcing shared morals against those that don't comply. Who determines to what extent ethics and moral behavior outweighs profit, or exactly what moral is?

Annran: ethics review boards are used currently in application of technologies that confront our notions of humanity. In the same way that we evaluate the use of technology in biological and medical ethics, we could empanel a board of directors from a cross section of cultures to give input, and a world wide governing body could be elected to oversee the application of the moral code that results from the boards findings. My guess is they would start with certain basic tenets found in every major religion on Earth.

keer-ka-guard: Sorry to burst your bubble, but that'll never fly. It would be feared to be the first step to world government.

Annran: not world government, planetary cooperation. National borders are not lost.

Dr. dino: but even if we were to get back to Eden, can the lion really lay down with the lamb? Was there really ever a time when there were no meat eaters on the planet? Carnivores have existed for millions of years.

Sloe Munk: I don't think we're actually saying that all creatures would live in harmony together that way, in some kind of paradise of creation. When we talk about getting back to Eden, we're talking about our own role as stewards of the planet, and reverence for the diversity of life. Living in harmony with nature, making a smaller impact, and using our brains to create technology that is benign in its impact to the planet. These seem like very worthy goals. Many animals use the resources from their environment to survive; birds build nests with material from their environment, primates use twigs to snag termites and use leaves to build foundations for sleeping in trees, but man is the only animal that uses the Earth's resources beyond its' capacity to regenerate those resources, and he is the only animal that fully understands that he is doing it and can wrap his brain around the consequences of it.

High-zen-burg: it sounds like you're creating some kind of new movement that incorporates environmentalism with religion or moral action.

Annran: religion as we know it has divorced god from the human being, making it outside of the individual rather than within. This sets up the current state of our cultures where immoral and unethical actions have no consequences because there is no inner attachment or connection to the thing that gives us our humanity in the first place, our conscience. And biological science has compounded it by denying any god or conscience, positing that morality or altruism or social cooperation, whatever you want to call it, is not fundamental to human survival, but rather a veneer laid over a foundation of brutality. Biologists that advocate for the selfish gene theory of behavior are flat out wrong in my view, and provide justification for selfishness, perhaps even their own, by saying that we are simply following nature, thereby giving humans an excuse for behavior that results in bad consequences for the future of human society. It is wrong, and it makes no sense.

High-zen-burg: well, except that your scenario doesn't effectively deal with the presence of true evil, with amoral or antisocial behavior and whether or not we can all touch the god within us.

Annran: on the contrary, it frees us to humanely and compassionately research, study, and eliminate evil from our presence, because it will no longer be associated with religious concepts like the devil, but with brain function, physiology and environmental influence. And if true evil really does exist, we will have the clear thinking to see it, the moral courage to stand up to it, and the inner peace to eliminate it. We won't be manipulated by evil because our inner moral compass will always point us in the right direction.

Joan of Arc: so what do we call ourselves, the people of this new movement?

adam: We should call ourselves Edenists.

Annran: Yes, Edenists. I like it.

Joan of Arc: me too.

gang green: Yeah, I'll go along with that.

Sloe Munk: The Edenists. That's beautiful.

Michel sat in front of the screen transfixed by what he had just witnessed. He hit the print key on his computer and stood up to retrieve the pages when his phone rang. He looked at the clock on his desk. It was 3:30 in the morning. Nothing good ever comes from a call at 3:30 in the morning.

"Allo?"

"Michel, it's Justine Chuchote," said the caller. Justine was a reporter for the international news agency, *La Voix de France,* and a long time friend of Michel's.

"Justine, you sound out of breath. What's the matter?"

"We've got a big news story breaking down here at the coast guard station in Nice. There's been a terrible accident at sea! You need to get down here right away!"

CHAPTER 29

They're All Just People Doing Their Job

Captain Sergei Ivonovich made his final rounds on the *Ileana Star* just before midnight and then collapsed on his bunk for some shuteye. His first officer had taken over the helm, and the Russian tanker sped through the black water at full throttle, cutting the thick fog that had settled over the surface of the Mediterranean Sea. The tanker was running behind schedule, having left Novorossiysk, Russia on the Black Sea seven days late due to a freak summer storm that had knocked down power and phone lines and left the port without electricity for three days. The tanker's holding compartments were filled with crude from the Tengiz oil fields in Kazakhstan, one of the fifteen independent republics that emerged from the collapse of the Soviet Union, eager to exploit its hidden wealth deep underground. The crude had made its way through a politically complicated and geographically circuitous route from the northwestern Kazakhstan oil field, under the Caspian Sea, and via pipeline through war-torn parts of Chechnya to the Russian port city on the Black Sea, where it would make its way to European and American markets. Millions of dollars, both legal and illegal, had changed hands, and the parties to the transaction had been handsomely compensated via several Swiss bank accounts.

The freak summer storm had put them behind schedule, and the crew had rushed through its' pre-launch checklist inspection before the behemoth embarked on its' voyage, paying off port authority inspectors to look the other way as the crew skipped over sections of the checklist, and rushed through the cleaning and preparation. The crude oil spilled into the cargo tanks quickly, openly discharging the toxic vapors that built up in the tanks into the air above. As each tank was topped off, crude spilled onto the deck and into the harbor from the flexible hoses. The Russian port used outdated equipment, and opening and closing the valves that connected the transfer hoses was a dirty and risky job.

The tanker's cargo had come out of the ground and across the geographic landscape via a jointly owned project between the Russian oil giant, RUSoil, acquired by Vladimir Dvorkovsky through the scheme of share loan privatization after the fall of the Soviet Union, and Purity Oil of America. The joint venture had been sanctioned by the U.S. government and fostered by the U.S. Department of State to help kick start the economy of the struggling Russian republic after the dual programs of perestroika and glasnost led to the collapse of the Soviet Union. President Clinton was eager to help the nascent democracies of the former American enemy, and encouraged large US businesses to work with Boris Yeltsin's new Russia, and especially its former republics of Kazakhstan, Uzbekistan, and Azerbaijan, to develop oil and gas fields, open up trade, promote democracy and foster a free enterprise system to help the formerly communist countries and their people. The US oil companies offered expertise in finance, pipelines, seismic analysis, and drilling technology. The US government had restructured Russia's massive debt and provided an additional $1.6 billion in aid to clear the way for grain exports to resume in Russia. Clinton's pledge of aid to Russia, was in addition to the nearly $12 billion already disbursed under his predecessor, George H. W. Bush. President Clinton had asked Vice President Gore to work with his Russian counterpart on a joint US-Russian Commission on Technological Cooperation to give energy development the same priority previously accorded to arms negotiations in the past.

The Russians proved to be adept students of American capitalism, and quickly became important players in the world's dependence on oil. The *Ileana Star* and her sister ship, the *Ileana Sun*, sailed the Earth's waters under an ownership regime purposely intended to create a murky trail of jurisdiction to follow in maritime law. The tanker had been built in 1982 by a Japanese shipbuilding company, and was registered in the Bahamas by a Liberian listed Russian shell company, and had been chartered by RUSoil under a separate company it owned based in Switzerland. The ship's Russian crew were hired and paid by a Greek company, Island Maritime. The responsibility for the tanker and its upkeep in this mud of international ownership was anyone's guess. The secretive Russian owners used layers of obfuscating businesses to mask its ties to RUSoil, and in adopting the economic philosophy of free enterprise profit over communist central planning ideology, were always looking for ways to keep their costs down and profits up, which made life on the ship very difficult. Sergei feared that the company's policy of cutting costs would one day lead to disaster, and he prayed that it wouldn't be on his ship or during his watch.

As supertankers go, the *Ileana Star* and the *Ileana Sun* were small by comparison to newer behemoths. Measuring 335 meters, long enough for some of her crew to ride bicycles over her long, flat deck, they each carried 225,000 tons of crude fully loaded. The *Ileana Star* was an older vessel and she did not have a double hull design, her interior oil storage tanks were fixed to the outer hull. The size of the twin tankers was thought at the time of their construction to be the maximum standard size achievable due to the amount of draught they required to run fully loaded, and they barely squeezed through the Suez Canal in ballast. Since their construction, deadweight tonnage had increased to over 300,000 with some as large as 500,000. The half-million ton tankers could scarcely find enough depth of water in the approaches to many terminals and were required to transfer some or all of their cargo to specially designed ships prior to entering a terminal port.

The *Ileana Star* traveled throughout the Earth's mighty oceans and in good sea conditions and engines running full throttle she could maintain a cruising speed of nearly 12 knots. Sergei always found something interesting and different in the world outside of Russia, and on his last trip to Japan, he had watched a game from America on television called basketball, and went to an English-only theater to watch an American movie called *Lethal Weapon*.

He returned to the ship carrying a hoop, a basketball and a poster of Michael Jordan, and instead of his usual calm directive from the bridge of "Full Speed Ahead", like Mel Gibson in the movie he told his crew to "Haul Ass!" when he wanted to increase speed.

The crew had attached the basketball hoop onto the deck, putting the poster directly underneath the basket for inspiration, and although none of them knew how to play the game, they had tremendous fun making up the rules as they went. They had to be reminded to take the basket down each time they entered their homeport at Novorossiysk. The inspector still had not noticed the holes in the wall where the hoop was put up each time they left, and they held their collective breath every time he walked past the spot.

Sergei had a nagging feeling that in the rush to leave Novorossiysk after the storm the crew had overlooked something important in their inspection of the ship's systems. The ship had had a brief interruption of electrical power fifty miles outside of Athens and all of the console lights and the navigation system had momentarily gone black. The blackout had lasted no more than a minute when the power came back on, not even long enough for the automatic back-up generator to kick in. Although the crew had searched throughout the ship for the possible cause of the problem, they had not been able to locate it, and it was assumed that a water leak or a crafty mouse had briefly shorted out a connection somewhere in the massive engine room. Sergei went to sleep in his bunk with an uneasy feeling, and resolved to ask the company to schedule a complete inspection of the ship when they reached Novorossiysk again.

The tanker's final destination, the refinery at Berre, just west of Marseille, France on the Mediterranean coast, was still four days away. It had already been two months since Sergei had seen his wife and daughter in Stavropol, and it would be another two months for the return voyage and some time off to spend with his family. His daughter, Ekaterina, would be celebrating her sixth birthday tomorrow, and he had hoped to be in port to place the call wishing her a happy birthday. He could place the call from the ship, but it would be against regulations, and he already had many infractions on his record.

Most of the infractions were minor, and involved ways of keeping up the morale of his crew. He was respected and admired by his men, and he went out of his way to do little things for them. He understood how hard it was for them to be away from their families and loved ones, and he had thrown parties and allowed radio to be used for personal calls on a wedding anniversary or at the birth of a child. He felt strongly that paying a little attention to the crew's comfort and morale went a long way in eliminating errors in judgment and lax attention to detail when the monotony and boredom set in. Despite the repeated violations of company policy and the notations in his personnel file, he continued to support this belief in any way he could.

The crew sometimes took advantage of his generous spirit. Aleksei, the engine mechanic, had secretly smuggled a small cat onto the ship that he had found on the streets in Novorossiysk. When the crewmembers found out, they threatened to tell the captain, but he argued that the cat would keep the mice population under control, which had become a serious problem on the ship. Despite their reservations, he won their complicity in not telling the captain, and the little cat became his bunkmate.

Aleksei laid on his bunk, leafing through a copy of Zaftra, the anti-Yeltsin newspaper. The newspaper's backer, Aleksandr Prokhanov, accused Yeltsin of representing the ideals of the West and blamed Yeltsin for the growing gulf between the rich and poor. The paper accused Yeltsin of ignoring the needs of ordinary citizens, and promoting cronyism in the loans for shares scheme he had cooked up for privatization of industries that was handled between the banks and Yeltsin's well-connected businessmen friends in Russia. He had sold out the country, the paper claimed, and Aleksandr Prokhanov's numerous screeds against the joint ventures with Western oil companies were vitriolic and racist, claiming Jewish bankers in the West were feasting on the energy of the Russian nation. Aleksei wasn't sure what to think about all of the posturing going on before the election. Zaftra was promoting a return to communism, and supporting Gannadi Zyuganov, the Communist Party leader, for the presidency. The election had heightened the tensions on the ship, and arguments regularly broke out between the men. All Aleksei knew was that the changes being brought about by privatization and the joint ventures with the West had gotten him this job, and he felt that he would probably vote for Yeltsin again in the upcoming election.

Aleksei rolled over and turned out the light above his bunk, and his cat jumped down from the bed. He had been right in assuming the cat would control the mice population. The cunning nocturnal animal had quickly found a hole in the wall under the bunk and would sneak out of the crew cabin each night. He had been stalking and exploring the ship for two weeks, and ventured out a little further each time, bringing back the mice he would catch, dropping them in front of the bunk where Aleksei slept, like a gift.

This night the cat had followed a particularly crafty little creature into the engine room, but had lost it when he ran into a hole in the wall too small for the cat to go into. He pawed at the hole to try to enlarge it, but soon gave that up, and crouched down low to wait, sniffing at the air once in a while to make sure that the little mouse was still inside.

This was the same little mouse that had previously caused the ship to go black. His fondness for the taste of plastic wire would go forever unnoticed, and he continued to chew on the plastic casings of the electrical lines leading from the electric generator to the ship's navigational console.

The bridge lights flickered on and off and Lieutenant Lebed considered calling the captain in his cabin. It lasted only a moment and he decided not to wake him. Five minutes later the entre ship went black for several seconds and the engines coughed and sputtered. The Lieutenant reached for the receiver to phone the captain just as the console again lit up in full array and the engines came back to life.

The little mouse had gotten tangled in the wires and struggled to free himself. The cat could hear his frantic movements and meowed with anticipation outside the little hole. The more the mouse struggled to be free, the more tangled it became, until it dangled helplessly, exhausting itself in the effort to be free. It gathered its strength and gave one final violent wriggle, and freed itself as the wires pulled from their loose connections at the junction box. The mouse dropped to the floor with a thump, and scampered past the startled cat as the entire ship went black.

CHAPTER 30

A Terrible Tragedy

FIRST OFFICER ERMAL Desai looked up from the console on the bridge of the 32,000-ton, 1,056-passenger luxury cruise liner *Heavenly Seas* and blinked to clear his eyesight. He thought he had seen lights ahead through the heavy fog, but now they were gone. He stared into the distance and slowed the engines down while he searched the horizon. The fog was thick but patchy, alternately heavy then clear. Just ahead of him the fog was thick, yet if he turned to face left, he could still make out the lights from the coastline of France to the north. He still could not see any lights ahead of him, and he resumed his cruising speed. It was then that he saw the dull gray hull of the tanker about 150 meters ahead of him, as the emergency generator of the giant ship kicked in and the thing lit up like a Christmas tree in front of his eyes. He shouted and slammed the engines of the luxury liner into reverse, turning the wheel hard to starboard.

The point of the bow rammed the side of the tanker at an angle to the hull, breaking the outer hull and ripping a hole into it the size of a one-story building, lodging the bow of the liner in the hull of the tanker. Desai was thrown forward with the force of the collision, and was knocked unconscious against the gleaming brass railing along the console, and lay helpless on the floor of the bridge.

The tanker's cargo of crude oil was spilling out of the hole in the tanker's hull, the only thing keeping the oil from spilling more rapidly and the water from entering more quickly was the cruise liner's bow stuck in the hull blocking the huge gaping hole. Diesel fuel from the tanker's engines spilled onto the floor of the engine room, and the wires the little mouse had freed itself from danced and sparked their way across the room as they came in contact with each other and ignited the fuel. The emergency generator continued to roar and sputter for several minutes, and then went dead as water came rushing in from everywhere.

The emergency claxon on the *Heavenly Seas* wailed with ferocity and urgency, as the crew directed passengers down the stairs and into the lifeboats, urging those already in the boats to quickly row away from the ship's hull. The captain was on deck, and screamed orders to his crew as the ship's passengers streamed onto the outside decks.

On the tanker, Captain Ivonovich jumped out of his bunk and opened the door of his cabin, stepping into the hallway. The entire ship was pitch black, and he felt water running under his feet. He quickly ran through the hallway and up the stairs to the top deck to see what was going on. Men were running everywhere, and he heard an emergency siren and people shouting and women screaming. *Women?* He turned and saw the cruise liner for the first time sticking out of the hull of the mammoth tanker and saw the flicker of fire on the water, and the passengers of the cruise liner screaming as they dropped into the black water in the little boats that would take them to safety. His heart sank to his stomach, and he ran to the fire alarm and pulled the lever. The horns bellowed their warning and he called out the names of several of his crew who were releasing the lifeboats from their locked positions to follow him. He opened the glass panels along the deck to hand out fire extinguishers. "You've got to get that fire put out," he shouted above the noise, "or all the lifeboats will go up in flames!" He handed the crewmen the extinguishers and said, "Aleksai, come with me to the engine room. The rest of you, get to the water level and put out the flames on the water. Be careful, the ship will go down fast when it sinks. Go! Hurry, hurry!"

Aleksai followed the captain through the corridors in the darkness. "Wait. Let me get a flashlight out of the locker," said Captain Ivonovich. He opened the door next to him and fished around with this hand, over the broom and mop, and spare blankets until he found what he was looking for. He found two flashlights and handed one to Aleksai. The hallway became illuminated with a narrow beam of light and they continued toward the stairs that would take them down to the engine room. They released the hatch door at the engine room and Aleksai pushed against it. It resisted his effort and water trickled through the tiny crack as the door opened slightly. The smell of diesel fuel gagged in their throats. They hesitated a moment, and then they pushed against the door together. It opened about a foot and the diesel-laden water rushed against their legs, quickly covering their ankles. A burning object came through the opening, and Aleksai jumped out of its way and watched in horror as he saw his dead cat floating by.

Captain Ivonovich looked up from the burning cat in terror and shouted, "Close the door!" but it was too late. The wave of fire came crashing around them through the doorway, igniting their diesel soaked clothing and engulfing them in flames.

The fire made its way through the hallways of the ship, quickly igniting the highly flammable oil leaking out of the tanker's compartmentalized hull. Just then the ship let out a loud cracking moan, and lurched lower in the water. The tanker lurched again as the sea continued to enter and expand inside the hull, breaking it apart. The bow of the cruse liner was still stuck inside the hull of the tanker, and as the weight of the tanker continued to sink further into the sea the bow of the cruise liner tilted downward, the aft deck tilting upward, pointing the luxury liner toward the bottom of the ocean.

The cruise liner's passengers rushed up the stairs of the ship to the upper deck as alarms bellowed throughout the hallways. The captain and his crew quickly readied lifeboats for the passengers, and they trampled over one another to reach the deck. The captain tried to impose calm, and prayed silently, hoping First Officer Desai had followed protocol and radioed a MAYDAY from the bridge. He sniffed the air with alarm, and smelled the acrid choking odor of his worst fears. Oil! At least half the passengers were still on deck waiting to be lowered into the remaining lifeboats.

Desai came to from the blow to his head. He stood up on wobbly legs and wiped the blood from his eyes with the back of his shirtsleeve. His head swam and he had a slight headache as he attempted to think clearly. He looked up and saw the massive tanker's hull through the windows of the bridge and in a sudden realization of what was happening, he reached over the console and threw the engines in full reverse in a frantic attempt to free the cruise liner from the hull of the tanker. The liner backed up and began to break free of the tanker with a horrific high-pitched sound of ripping and bending metal; the backward motion dragging the tanker along until the liner finally broke free of the behemoth. As they broke free the tanker narrowly missed rolling over on top of the liner and dragging them to the ocean floor. Desai slowed the engines but continued moving backward to be free from the sinking tanker. The backward movement of the ocean liner created a large oil-slicked wake that swamped the tiny lifeboats. The passengers and crew paddled furiously against the ocean waves created by the wake in an attempt to put as much distance between them and the ocean liner as they could.

The fire on the tanker swept rapidly through the hallways and onto the upper deck, sending plumes of thick smoke and flames into the sky. Small fires burned on top of the water, and two of the 10 lifeboats already in the water caught fire, the passengers within them screaming in agony as their oil and diesel soaked clothing caught fire too. Several jumped overboard to escape the flames, trying desperately to swim away to the relative safety of open water, only to find that they quickly became too heavy to float above the surface.

The tanker exploded, sending the aft wheelhouse into the air, blowing a hole in the upper hull, and the tanker listed to port, taking on flaming gulps of water in its gaping holes, causing it to sink further beneath the surface. Still rolled over onto its port side, the aft deck slid under, and oil spilled out of the gaping hole made by the ocean liner in a gigantic cascade. The ocean sucked the tanker downward, as men and women screamed and the sirens blared. The tiny boats paddled furiously, racing away from the vortex created by the tanker entering its watery grave, making a giant sucking sound as if the angry Earth were eating them alive. In a matter of seconds the huge Goliath of man's creation had sunk beneath the surface, the water all around roiling and bubbling black and thick, as the giant tanker gulped in the seawater and exhaled its final breath.

CHAPTER 31

Next Stop Paris

MICHEL HAD IMMEDIATELY awakened Roberta and they had raced down country roads in the middle of the night to the SNSM station in Nice, the voluntary maritime rescue organization in France, which had dispatched a search and rescue mission to pick up survivors. The drive to Nice took Michel just over an hour, his emergency lights flashing and laying on his horn behind any drivers in his way. Michel's press credentials got him and Roberta into the cordoned off area at the station, and her heart sank when she learned that it was her client, Purity Oil, a joint-owner in the oil tanker, that was involved in the accident. Her first call was to Evan Manning, who called David Reed. Her second call was to Charles Conway at Purity Oil, and they had agreed to meet at her office in Paris. Evan would be staying back in D.C., at least temporarily, to handle operations from there.

Roberta caught the first direct train to Paris from Nice station, and the superfast TGV arrived at the Gare de Lyon in a little over five hours. By the time Roberta reached her Paris office, the accident was the number one news item of the day, and details of the tragedy were being broadcast continually on French and American news channels. Helicopters circled above the accident site, where pieces of wreckage and oil-slicked debris hundreds of miles wide floated on the waves. The oil was already beginning to wash ashore along the Mediterranean coastline from Monaco to Marseille, and volunteers had set up washing stations for birds and wildlife caught in the massive spill. Protests had sprung up on the beach in Nice, and outside of the Purity Oil offices in Paris, New York, and Houston, Texas, calling for an end to oil drilling and transport of fossil fuels, and a new group calling itself The Edenists, had begun running commercials using footage of the disaster, and encouraging action on the part of citizens around the world. Interviews with survivors from the tanker and the cruise liner were already taking place, and the news organizations were trying to figure out how the joint US and Russian partnership worked, and how maritime law would apply to the Liberian registration of the ship. America's CNN and France's TV5 producers quickly found experts in maritime law to help explain how flags of convenience worked, and how monetary damages would be handled, and which country's laws would apply.

The receptionist waited at the door of the modern and light-filled RPR Paris office for Roberta's arrival, and quickly led her to the conference room where her team was already assembled and working. The RPR office was located on the left bank in the 7th Arrondissement, and the glass enclosed 6th floor conference room offered a breathtaking panoramic view overlooking the River Seine, from the Pont de la Concorde to the Pont des Arts, and the Tuileries gardens across the river on the right bank.

Roberta sat down at the table, and someone handed her a cup of espresso. Her cell phone rang and she glanced at the screen. It was Michel and she shut off the ringer. The only call she would take at the moment was from Charles Conway.

"So tell me where we are?" asked Roberta, taking a sip of coffee and looking around the table.

"We were just discussing the response we should craft for Charles Conway. We don't know who was at fault," said Alain Bertrand, the head of the Paris office. "We are not sure if we should issue an apology yet."

"Well, we definitely must craft a message of condolence for him, and it needs to go out immediately," answered Roberta. "For now, it should only include condolences to the family and loved ones of both the tanker and the cruise liner." Roberta stood up. "Who's keeping the notes from this meeting?"

"I am," said a young girl, shyly raising her hand. "Sandrine Girot."

Roberta walked to the flip chart in the corner and began writing.

"We need to be prepared to set up a press conference for Charles Conway outside their Paris office. I want a draft of a condolence statement in ten minutes. We assign no blame, nor take any responsibility. We express sincere sorrow for the victims, and reassure the public that we are working with all the authorities to find out what happened. We implore the press and the world to give us time for the investigation."

"I think we should discuss beach clean up, and how Purity Oil should respond," offered Alain. "The news footage of seabirds and wildlife covered with oil is not pretty. Purity Oil should have its own contingent of volunteers from the company to help with the beach clean up. And some press reports are indicating that the joint venture with Russia will complicate the issue of assigning blame. The trail of ownership and registration of the ship is going to make it difficult."

Just then, a young man at the conference table jumped up and walked quickly to the TV at the end of the room. *"Merde!"* he exclaimed.

He turned up the volume and everyone turned to watch. The captain of the *Heavenly Seas* stepped up to a podium lined with news reporters.

"We want to offer our deepest condolences to the family of the victims of this terrible tragedy. As Captain of the Heavenly Seas, my heart goes out to everyone who has been affected, and our thoughts and prayers are with you all. We also want to say a sincere 'Merci!' to the French authorities and all the brave volunteers who helped with the search and rescue operation. Without their valiant efforts, the loss of life would have been even greater. *Nous sommes sincèrement reconnaissants,"* he said charmingly.

"Wow!" said Roberta. "Nice touch!"

"Can you tell us what happened?" asked a reporter.

"At approximately 0300 hours, my First Officer Ermal Desai, was piloting our ship in heavy fog. The tanker, Ileana Star, had lost power at some point during the night and was completely black and without emergency lights. As you know, there was heavy fog that had settled over the water last night. The Heavenly Seas did not detect the tanker in their path until it was too late, and ran into the tanker, piercing the hull."

"Where were you at the time of the accident?" shouted a reporter.

"I was in my quarters, I had turned in about an hour earlier. Although First Officer Desai was knocked unconscious by the force of the accident, he managed to come to and dislodge the Heavenly Seas by backing out of its hull. His actions saved the lives of hundreds of people."

"What would cause the tanker to go dark?" asked a reporter.

"I can't speculate on that," answered the Captain. "I can tell you that I have worked with Cruise Corporation for twenty years, and we are diligent and rigorous in making sure our vessels are safe and seaworthy, and go through laborious preparations and frequent inspections. Who knows what they do in Russia? We'll have to wait for the results of the investigation."

"Has Charles Conway, or anyone from Purity Oil, been in contact with you, or anyone from Cruise Corporation?" asked a reporter.

"No, not that I am aware of. But I would like to add that Cruise Corporation takes our responsibility to the environment very seriously. Our very livelihood is dependent on the beautiful beaches and sea life that our ships take cruise passengers to explore. In light of this commitment, we have a team of volunteers already in place at the shoreline helping to clean sea birds and wildlife caught in this devastating disaster."

"Merde! This is not good," said Alain.

"No, it's not," said Roberta, shaking her head, a sinking feeling in the pit of her stomach.

"It makes us look like we are just ignoring the situation," said Alain. "Is there anyone else from Purity Oil that can act as spokesman until Conway shows up? What about someone from the Paris office?"

"His instructions were that only he would face the media. We just have to wait," said Roberta. "C'mon everybody. Let's get back to work. Conway will be here tomorrow and we need to be prepared."

CHAPTER 32

Blame the Russians

DAVID REED BOARDED the Purity Oil private jet at the Landmark Aviation Terminal at Dulles International Airport. Besides Charles Conway, Purity Oil's CEO, the team that had been scrambled to go to France included the head of media relations, Jim Hathaway, Conway's executive assistant, Crystal Cox, and Purity Oil's in-house legal counsel, Buddy Durant. Charles Conway's young wife, Katya, had wheedled her way along too. He had met the Russian bombshell on one of his many trips to Russia during negotiations with RUSoil, and fallen head over heels for her. He had quickly divorced his second wife to marry her, and had been beguiled by her exotic charms for the first year of their marriage, spending lavishly on her and taking her everywhere with him. She was insatiable in the sack and for a year he lusted after her all day, but now, after three years he had become bored with her and was fed up with her antics. She spent his money freely, and she was so dumb she could be outwitted by a three year old. She had insisted on coming with him to Paris so she could go shopping and see her friends. He had tried to talk her out of it but she threw a fit in his office, and he had reluctantly agreed just to shut her up. He had hoped to have some alone time with Crystal, who he was hoping would be his next mistress. He knew once they got to Paris, Katya would be off with her fag friends and he would see neither hide nor hair of her. After a week, he'd send her back home on a commercial flight, and he and Crystal could have some fun.

The pilot was under way in a matter of minutes, and the passengers were free to move around. Drinks were flowing freely. Mrs. Conway sat at the back of the plane with her husband's young assistant, chatting away excitedly about all the things she would do in Paris, a flute of champagne in hand while she leafed through a fashion magazine.

"Fucking Russians!" Charles Conway fumed.

No one said anything for several minutes, while Conway ranted. They all knew it was best to let him blow his top for a while before they tried to get down to the business at hand.

"That fucking tanker hadn't been in for repairs or maintenance in over two years, yet somehow passed inspections at every port" he said. "The fucking penny-pinching bastards!" He swallowed his drink, and poured himself another. "Those fucking Russians! I should have never gotten in bed with those fucking cunts!"

After a minute or so of silence, David Reed spoke up. "We have to have a game plan, Charles. We need to discuss how we want to handle this. The news reports are not good, and the footage of the wreckage and miles of oil along the beaches of St. Tropez will not sit well with the Europeans," he insisted.

"You think I don't fucking know that already?" he snapped back at David.

"The Cruise Corporation has already issued a press release, and the captain of the liner held a press conference beachside in Nice this afternoon," said Jim Hathaway, Purity's head of media relations. "We need to get out ahead of this."

"Right now, until we know what actually happened out there, my recommendation is we say nothing," said Buddy Durant, Purity's in-house legal counsel.

"I disagree," said Jim. "We can't let the cruise line take the high road while we sit silently by saying nothing or we'll be skewered in the press and in the court of public opinion. We have to issue an apology and be sincere in our condolences."

"Issue an apology? No fucking way!" exclaimed Conway. "What the fuck's wrong with you? Issuing an apology is tantamount to an admission of guilt, and would add another billion dollars onto the settlement. We're already screwed by public opinion, and it doesn't matter what the public thinks because they have no alternative. Oil is the lifeblood of the planet."

David Reed sat back and listened. He knew enough to keep his mouth shut while they argued back and forth about the strategy.

"What do you think, David?" asked Jim, pulling David reluctantly into the conversation.

"I agree with Charles," he answered. "I don't think an apology at this time is a good idea."

The pansy prick, Jim thought, glowering at him. "I'm just saying that if we look like we don't care that our tanker was involved in a major accident, with loss of human life, and the habitat destruction it will cause, no matter whose fault it was, we are going to pay in the long run," insisted Jim.

"We'll issue a company statement to the press offering our condolences to the families, but we will not issue an apology," said Conway. "You should get started on it now," he said to Jim. "I want it ready to go when we land."

"Why don't we wait to see what Roberta has to say?" asked Jim.

"No, we're going to be working through David on this," said Conway.

David did his best to hide the smile of satisfaction threatening to break out on his face as Jim stood up to go to the back of the jet to start working on the press release.

David got up and poured himself and Conway another drink. As he sat back down, he spoke in a low whisper to Conway and Buddy Durant. "My advice? Stay cool, look defiant, blame the Russians, and end up with a bigger slice of the pie," he hissed under his breath.

CHAPTER 33

Blame the Americans

VLADIMIR DVORKOVSKY WALKED the halls of the Kremlin with ease. His office at RUSoil was close by, and his friendship with, and political support of President Boris Yeltsin, gave him unfettered access to the richest and most powerful men in Russia, he being one of them. The oil assets that Yeltsin had inherited from the sloppy and inefficiently run planned economy of the former Soviet Union, had been sold off to a handful of bidders in a rigged auction that allowed Dvorkovsky to purchase RUSoil at a fraction of the true cost, and with little or no taxes assessed or paid. The Russian state was in shambles, financially weakened beyond recognition, and Yeltsin had been badly in need of support from powerful, well-placed friends to win the election. Dvorkovsky thanked his lucky stars that he had been in the right place, at the right time, at the right moment in the history of the Motherland.

Yeltsin was currently out of sight on one of his legendary benders. The man had a penchant for drink, and used it as a form of therapy to unwind from the strain of his job. Dvorkovsky found the man and his weakness for drink reprehensible. He was a walking bloody-eyed corpse, and stunk of alcohol that seeped out of his pasty skin, his clothes, and his rancid breath. He frequently checked himself into a sanitarium for a month to dry out. It was a disgusting sign of the man's weakness.

He did have historic, monumental problems though. As the first elected leader after the fall of the former Soviet Union, he was faced with seemingly insurmountable social and economic problems. He was continually skewered at home in the opposition press for selling out to the West, and then damned in the West for throwing out reformers in order to appease the apparatchik wolves constantly biting at his heels. Virtually no one could be trusted, and potential assassins, both verbal and actual, lurked around every corner. No wonder the man drank himself into oblivion.

Dvorkovsky had been called to the Kremlin by the Deputy Prime Minister about the accident in the Mediterranean with the RUSoil tanker, *Ileana Star*. The French ambassador had made it clear that the French government expected RUSoil to pay to clean up the mess, along with their joint-venture partners, the Americans. This would be a sticky situation. The American company's portion of the deal was only 20%. The tanker was part of the deal, but was operated and maintained exclusively by separate companies owned by RUSoil. Charles Conway was a son-of-a-bitch, and Dvorkovsky knew that getting the Americans to fork over any money to help in the clean up and to compensate victims would be next to impossible without taking them to court. He did not want to sour the relationship with Purity Oil. He still needed their technical expertise and equipment, and would continue to need it, for many years to come.

What a clean up would cost, as well as the financial reparations that would have to be made for lost revenue from the commercial fishing ventures was unknown and hard to estimate at this early stage, but everyone would have their hands out. In addition to their P&I insurance which had a limit of $28 million, Russia was a participant in the International Oil Pollution Compensation fund that had been set up in 1971 to compensate victims damaged by tanker oil spills, but the fund was woefully inadequate for most spills with a liability limit of $50 million, and only applied to tanker owners, not the drillers or suppliers. Tanker ownership and registration involved scams and schemes designed to purposely avoid direct responsibility.

How jurisdiction of international law courts would apply to Russia was another question he would need to discuss with his lawyers. The French government would certainly bring suit against RUSoil in the French courts to pay for environmental damage and civil penalties above and beyond what was covered by the IOPC fund, and possibly also in the court of the EU in Brussels, the new headquarters of the EU. If the spill reached the shores of Spain, Monaco or Italy, each of those countries would also bring suit for compensation. Russia was not part of the EU, and overtly and covertly opposed entry into it by any of the former Soviet-bloc countries. The European Union was seen by Russia as an economic version of NATO, and any block of nations that colluded against others for benefits in trade and commerce was vehemently opposed, unless of course, it was the block that supported Russia's aims. The Russians demanded special status among the former Soviet countries using blackmail and favors to keep the former satellites in line, even while opening up trade with the United States. Oil had been a major part of that trade opening, and the Americans had eagerly jumped on board the gravy train, seeing a new chance to satisfy the insatiable appetite for oil in America while throwing their Middle East suppliers, with whom they had long-standing backdoor arrangements, on the scrapheap. The Americans' eagerness and largesse had personally earned Dvorkovsky a massive fortune.

The oil in the cargo tanks of the *Ileana Star* had come from Kazakhstan, but had crossed miles of disputed territory that Russia still claimed as its own. Millions of dollars in bribes, necessary to do business with Russia, had been paid to government operatives, consultants, and innumerable intermediaries and family members in Russia and Kazakhstan by Purity Oil and the American government to kick-start the faltering economies. Former American government officials now worked as well-paid consultants and lobbyists on behalf of the Russians and the American oil companies, and the money changing hands or wired to Swiss accounts, was astronomical, and paid for the little baubles of furs, diamonds, speedboats and luxury homes needed to keep the Russian tycoons, and their predilections for kinky adventures, afloat.

Knowing what to do in this situation would be difficult and fraught with consequences. Diplomats from every country at the highest levels of government would be involved. Russian oligarchs from every sector of the economy, and their teams of lawyers, would be watching the outcome of this situation with bated breath, and the Americans, the French, the marine industries and the environmental activists, each with teams of lawyers to advise them, would be picking apart the nuances of this situation for years to come. It would be well into the next century before the courts finally decreed who was guilty. He had bought off everyone else; he could buy off a judge too, when the time comes.

Right now, his biggest problem was Charles Conway. Since he had no stick to compel the Americans to take his side in this battle, he would have to offer a carrot. Just how much that carrot would cost him, and his company, was anyone's guess.

CHAPTER 34

The Free Press

La Voix de France

Oil Tanker and Cruise Liner in Horrific Accident at Sea, Lives Lost

By Justine Chuchote

NICE, FRANCE, JUNE 28, 1996 – French coastal communities are preparing for widespread oil contamination in the coming weeks after a horrific collision at sea between a cruise liner and a giant oil supertanker holding more oil than was aboard the Exxon Valdez. The collision between the luxury cruise liner, Heavenly Seas, and the oil tanker, Ileana Star, occurred during the night, in the heavy fog off the coast of France in the Mediterranean Sea.

Oil soaked seabirds including pelicans, gulls, and cormorants began floating to shore within hours of the accident. Environmental organizations from across Europe have descended on Nice, organizing washing stations with citizen volunteers for those birds still alive, while wildlife conservation and zoological parks were seen carting off the cleaned animals in cages, taken to vans and buses to be transported and housed at wildlife sanctuaries while the oil clean up begins. The Oceanographic Institute in Monaco, in a statement, said that soon other sea life such as ospreys, eagles, seals, dolphins, sea turtles, and harbor porpoises would begin rolling ashore and they called on European nations to speed up the requirements currently under consideration to require sturdier tanker designs with double hulls that would reduce the risk of big spills. The environmental rights group, The Edenists, issued a press statement asking people of the world to support clean energy alternatives in their daily lives. "People should stop and think every time they drive their car or buy a product that uses petroleum," said an anonymous spokesman for the group.

The oil continues to spill from the tanker's split hull about 100 miles from the coast and in water a mile deep. Estimates ranged from as little as 20 million to as much as 100 million gallons already released into the Mediterranean Sea. The oil slick, seen spreading in dark rainbow-hued reflection in aerial photographs, covers roughly 100 square miles.

The cruise liner, Heavenly Seas, which ran into the tanker due to a catastrophic loss of power in the tanker's engines and electrical system which had rendered the tanker black and helpless in the thick fog, limped back to port under its own power, accompanied by tugboats and French Navy cruisers, its Captain and First Officer being hailed as heroes for their efforts to save lives and free the liner from the hull of the tanker. All survivors have been accounted for, and all but one of the tanker's crew of eight were lost. The Heavenly Seas managed to get all of their 1,056 passengers into lifeboats, but two caught fire, and three passengers lost their lives trying to swim away from the fire. Of the 200 crewmembers aboard the cruise liner, three were lost.

European and American weather service forecasters are keeping the French government and oil-spill experts updated with regular weather reports. Although the fog has lifted and the morning dawned bright and clear, forecasters are warning that a heavy weather front was heading northwest, with winds in excess of 50 miles per hour and directly in the path of the giant oil slick. The direction of the storm would spread the oil into the territorial waters of Spain and Portugal. Although the slick had not reached the shoreline yet, aerial photography had tracked its path offshore and in six hours it had already spread out hundreds of miles.

The tanker's load came from new oil fields in Kazakhstan, and is particularly thick and waxy, and does not break up readily. The tanker, sitting at the bottom of the sea, may be in water cold enough to freeze the oil, however once it reaches warmer waters nearer the coast it will undoubtedly liquefy on the surface of the water.

How much oil is still left in the single hull tanker is unknown, and if the ship broke apart as it hit the sea floor, all of the oil will eventually seep out and make its way to the surface, finding its way to the pristine beaches of the Cote d'Azur and neighboring communities.

CHAPTER 35

Your Father Was A Genius At Pubic Relations

CHARLES CONWAY AND his team arrived by limousine from the Paris airport at RPR's Paris offices the next morning. They had slept fitfully on the jet, and their nerves were rough-edged with the effects of too much coffee, too little sleep and the adrenalin rush created by the threat of the situation at hand. Conway had spoken to Dvorkovsky from the jet, and they would be meeting in Paris to discuss the situation.

David Reed was anxious to get the latest news about the spill, and the actions that had been taken by the Paris team. He had continued to stoke the fire with Conway, cozying up to the man with snide comments about Roberta and her environmentalist ilk, and a backslapping camaraderie meant to impart a sense of us-against-them loyalty and trust. He walked into the office and stopped at the reception desk to introduce himself. He had never been to the Paris office, and was impressed with the European-style chicness of the space and the people. The women were dressed elegantly but with a simplicity that he could not describe. Understated yet fashionable was what came to mind. He immediately understood the descriptions he had always heard about women in Paris, and saw with increased clarity why his uncle Robert had married Jackie.

The receptionist showed them to the conference room, where Roberta's team was busily organizing the upcoming activities.

"Charles," said Roberta, shaking his hand and smiling a warm greeting. "We have a lot to show you. Let me introduce you to the team and bring you up to speed on what we've done so far." Roberta made the introductions and everyone took a seat.

"We have a draft press release ready to go, and are ready to set up a press conference for you at Purity headquarters later this morning," said Roberta, as she handed Conway and his team red binders they had put together overnight, tabbed and organized with the plan she and her team had devised. "As we discuss each topic associated with the spill, and its consequences to Purity Oil, we will add to the binder so that we have a living document that tracks our progress and process."

Conway briefly scanned the press release, and closed the binder dismissively. "We won't be doing a press conference," said Conway flatly. Everyone fell silent for a moment. "Jim has a statement for the press that I approved. Right now, we're going to stay mum until the Russians come forward with a plan," Conway continued.

Jim stood up awkwardly, feeling torn between his personal opinions about the way the company was handling this, and the decision that Conway had made to offer only a brief statement of condolence. He walked over to Roberta at the head of the table and handed her a hand-written note torn from a yellow legal pad. Roberta read the two line press release and gasped.

"Charles, I really don't think this is good enough. This makes you and your company sound less than compassionate about any of the damage the oil will assuredly cause. I really must counsel you against such a terse first response," she said, her eyes wide with disbelief. "It will surely have negative consequences."

Conway turned his face to Roberta with a look of such stern disapproval that her breath caught in her throat, and her heart skipped a couple of beats while she waited for him to speak.

"The ramifications of this oil spill to my company may be enormous, and I will not hand my enemies the rope with which to hang me. I am responsible to nothing, including the fucking planet, and to no one, but my shareholders and my partners. You have missed the point of your role as my public relations firm. You are here to serve me, and not the environmental agenda you espouse. Your father was a genius at pubic relations and I am disappointed that you have not grasped the reason why I pay you," he said.

The room fell silent, the mood of shared effort and common cause from the day before vanished. Jim and Roberta blinked bewilderedly, and several people squirmed uncomfortably in their chairs.

"Why don't we take a five minute break," said David standing up, breaking the pall Conway had cast over the room. "We'll come back to this after we take a break."

Conway stood up and walked with David out of the room. They stood huddled outside the door, whispering into each other's ears.

Roberta looked at Jim still standing next to her. Her heart felt like a stone in her chest. The rest of the staff began milling around the room, getting coffee and checking emails, talking in chastened, hushed tones, trying to process the public dressing down that had just happened in the room.

Jim sat down next to Roberta, and whispered, "I have to warn you. There's more at stake here than just this oil spill. Conway made it clear on the jet that he wants to work through David, not you. He walked in here with plans to cut you, and your agenda, out."

Roberta immediately stood up and walked out the glass door to the landing where David and Conway were standing. Everyone in the glass enclosed conference room silently watched her move in, exchanging heated words. Then the three of them walked down the stairs and into her office, and she closed the door.

CHAPTER 36

Roberta Thinks She's Making Headway

"Look Charles, I know that you see me as the enemy but honestly, I'm not. We shouldn't look at this as if one side is against the other, enemies shooting at each other. I think that Purity Oil can be both profitable and environmentally sensitive," said Roberta, taking a seat across from David and Conway. "You are already fighting an uphill battle in the press and with public opinion, and the worst thing you can do is come out with a statement like that! You must be sensitive and brutally honest about the damage your product causes, and you can take steps to limit the damage."

"You just don't get it, do you?" said Conway. "This is a global business that, literally, fuels the world. We don't have to do anything until we are forced to do it. And even when we are, we have teams of high-priced lawyers to figure out ways to circumvent whatever they throw at us. You are naïve, Roberta, in the worst way. What are you doing in this business?" he asked sarcastically.

"I'm in this business to try to enlighten you and the rest of your generation that good environmental stewardship is not mutually exclusive to making money. Think of the mountains of positive press that you would get if you took steps to reduce or eliminate the pollution you cause before anyone else did? Think of how much that would mean to your bottom line?"

"I have partners, Roberta! Russian partners who call the shots. The US government looks the other way while we help the Russians and their fellow communist comrades set up a free enterprise economic system. We have a lot of capital at risk. We don't want to be fettered with more expense and increased regulations, and the government isn't going to do anything to hinder us," said Conway with exasperation. "Do you *not* get that?"

"But Charles, this is Europe!" exclaimed Roberta, as the face of Jacques Cousteau flashed in her mind. "American-style business is not rewarded here. Think of where you are. The beaches where oil soaked birds are washing ashore is in Nice! Do you really think they are going to let you just do business as usual? You will be pilloried here."

"We can withstand it," he said.

David had been sitting silently, unable to find a good place to jump into the heated conversation. He didn't want to let Roberta gain any traction with Conway, but he had to play it cool.

"So what are you proposing?" asked Conway, after a long silence.

"We are proposing that you do a press conference and offer heartfelt condolences to the families of those that lost their lives. That part is a no-brainer, but you must, as honestly as possible and without divulging any secrets or putting your partnership with the Russians in jeopardy, answer questions about your ownership in the tanker, the oil, where it came from, and put out some information about helping with the beach clean up, the economic consequences, whatever we can say to show that you *care*. It must be done," concluded Roberta emphatically.

"David, what do you think?" asked Conway.

"I think it's stupid," said David without hesitation, betting that Conway was not going to like Roberta's idea. "I agree with the part about the condolences, and maybe, just *maybe* the bit about the environmental clean up, but I disagree completely with the idea that you say anything about your ownership in the tanker, your partnership with the Russians, or anything at all about your business interests. We have a major investigation to get through, and we have potential liability from every country on the Mediterranean coast that oil washes up on, the cruise line company, the fishing and tourism industries, and the environmentalists. Hell! The whole world will be coming down around our ears!"

Conway sat quietly for a moment. "Okay," he finally said. "I'll do a press conference *after* I talk to the Russians this afternoon, and only to give my condolences to the families and to express my dismay at the environmental damage the oil may cause. Period. Get me the talking points on the environmental stuff. Schedule the press conference for 7:00 this evening. That way everybody back in the states will be asleep when I put my ugly mug in front of the cameras."

David smiled inwardly at his little bit of successful maneuvering. Roberta, on the other hand, was worried.

CHAPTER 37

—— ᗤ ——

Their Surprise Is Ruined

"I GUESS YOU'VE been following the news about the oil spill?" asked Summer.

She and Steven Manning were driving at a leisurely pace along the back roads of Dijon in Uncle Pierre's old Citroën 2CV on their way to the farmhouse. Uncle Pierre had helped Summer open the leather ripple bonnet before she left for the train station to pick up Steven, and the hot summer sun shone down through the open top from an imperial blue sky. The air was redolent with the intoxicating fragrance from the fields of lavender and mustard flowers that they passed along their way as the sounds of thousands of bees and the songs of hundreds of birds mingled with the air that rushed in through the open windows of the little vehicle.

"Yes," answered Steven, breathing deep to smell the air. "It's going to be devastating to the beaches and sea life all along the coastline."

"Did you know that Purity Oil is Roberta's client?" asked Summer.

"No!" answered Steven.

"She's in Paris, trying to help them come up with a game plan for the response. I talked to her last night. Needless to say she won't be meeting us in Dijon any time soon," explained Summer.

"Oh, I'm sorry to hear that. The last time I talked to Evan, he was worried that something like this would happen. He wanted her to divest some of her clients, the oil and chemical companies and their lies her father had built the firm on. Although he would never say it, I'm sure he's thinking, 'I told you so', right now," said Steven. "The band and I are looking into doing a benefit concert somewhere in the south of France to help the victims. Our manager is looking for a venue."

"How long will you be able to stay?" asked Summer.

"At least three or four days. I had hoped to stay at least a week, and I was looking forward to seeing Roberta again, but I have to draw attention to the situation if I can," he said, looking over at Summer. "It's my mission in life, you know?"

"I know. I'm just sorry it has to be Roberta's reputation that's at stake. It's eating her up inside."

"What about you? How long were you planning to stay?" asked Steven.

"Roberta and I were supposed to spend the week together. It would have been so nice for her to take some time to reconnect with her family," said Summer. "Her aunt and uncle are disappointed. I know they were looking forward to seeing her too."

Summer slowed the car and pulled off the road onto a dirt lane between rows of neatly tied and tended grape vines. A small, elegant stone sign at the road, read, 'Les Deux Frères Vignoble de Bourgogne'.

"I didn't know Roberta's aunt and uncle have a vineyard," said Steven.

"They don't. They lease the land to two brothers, the renegade sons of one of the more famous vintners in the area," said Summer. "It's a family saga that's been in the papers for nearly ten years. The boys wanted to run things their own way and the father wouldn't let them, so they started their own brand. About every six months the father says something to the local press about the swill the boys are producing, and tempers flare, feelings get hurt, and the tit-for-tat that the French are so good at, riles everyone up. To make things worse, Uncle Pierre and the father have been friends since grade school, and he gets dragged into the conflict, but the boys make a good product, and they keep Aunt Germaine and Uncle Pierre in free wine. I've even arranged to have twenty cases shipped to my restaurants to add to the wine list. I think you're going to like it. You might want to add some to your wine cellar."

Summer drove along the rutted dirt road slowly, weaving around the bigger potholes in the surface to avoid any damage to the old Citroën. "The boys are supposed to grade the road again soon. We've had some heavy rain lately and the road has suffered. And according to the boys, so have the grapes. They need the rest of the summer to be dry and hot."

The rutted road finally ended and led to a clearing at the top of a gentle slope, and the large stone farmhouse covered in trailing vines and surrounded by flowers and shrubs could be seen. A pack of dogs came bounding up to the car, large and small, to greet them.

"I'll make introductions," said Summer to Steven, pointing and petting each one as she did. "This hairy oaf, " she said as a huge dog jumped up to lick her face, "is Whiskey, he's a Briard," she said, pushing him off of her. "These two are Babette and Sugar," she said, pointing to two black and white spotted hounds that were licking Steven's hands. "They're something called a Braque d'Auvergne. And this little piece of glorious happy sunshine with the fluffy tail and enormous ears is Louis XIV, a Papillion, the sweetest little creature that ever walked on four legs," she said, smiling and scooping him into her arms. She held him close to her and he licked her face and neck.

Summer put Louis XIV down on the ground, and they walked toward the house, the dogs barking, rubbing against their hands and legs, and circling around them as they walked. As they approached the vine-covered portico, the large dogs went off in search of something fun to chase just as the front door opened, and out walked the portly figure of Uncle Pierre, pipe in hand, a beret on his head, his merry eyes and jovial face full of smiles. Louis XIV trotted happily past him into the house.

"Bonjour!" cried Pierre. "Welcome to our home." He reached out and shook Steven's hand warmly. "We are so happy you have come to visit us," he said, leading them through the door.

As soon as Steven walked in he was hit with the most tantalizing aroma of something wonderful cooking, and his stomach growled in response. The entryway was large and airy, with whitewashed walls and solid stone cornices over wide polished wood doors. A large flower arrangement in a Mille fleur Chinese vase sat atop an antique table in the foyer, and a small needlepoint settee sat off to the side of the room atop gleaming wide-plank floors. Bronze wall sconces in the delicate shape of a woman's hand held hand blown glass shades, emanating a warm golden light against the bright white walls. The room, and the feeling of cleanliness and simple elegance it imparted, enchanted Steven.

Aunt Germaine came into the hallway from behind a door, wiping her hands on her apron. Steven could see the large modern kitchen beyond the open door and realized it was from there those enticing aromas had originated. She approached him with open arms, and kissed both his cheeks in the French fashion.

"Welcome Steven," she exclaimed, a soft smile on her face. He could see her resemblance to Roberta's mother, Jackie, with the same lovely bone structure and facial features as her sister. "We are so glad you come," she said in broken English and lovely French accent. "I have made a *déjeuner superbe.* I hope you are hungry!"

"Starved actually. It smells heavenly, I can tell you that!" said Steven.

"Come, you and Pierre will take your place *sur la Terrace* for the apéritif, and Summer and I will finish in the kitchen," said Germaine. "Pierre has a little plum brandy for you that we make here on the farm."

Steven followed Pierre to the back of the house through high, wide glass doors that led out to the terraced patio, where a large wrought-iron table was covered with a white tablecloth with pale blue striped edging, and a large bouquet of blue and white hydrangeas had been placed in a clear glass pitcher in the middle. Several bottles of wine, with the Deux Frères label, sat on either side of the bouquet. Pierre motioned for Steven to sit down on one of the comfortable rattan chairs on the other side of the terrace, where two small apéritif glasses and a long necked bottle with no label had been placed on a coffee table. Pierre pulled the corked stopper and poured the purple brandy into the glasses. As he poured the liquid, Steven noticed there was a hand-carved wooden figure inside the bottle of a man climbing a ladder, and he briefly wondered how they got the figure inside the bottle. In the tiny, delicate crystal apéritif glasses, the brandy was a pale reddish-purple, gleaming iridescent in the light of the Sun.

"*A votre santé!*" said Pierre, clicking Steven's glass. "To your health!"

"To your health," answered Steven, taking a swallow of the brandy. It was smooth and sweet, and slid across his tongue and down his throat like silk.

Summer came out with a load of plates, flatware and napkins in her arms, followed by Germaine, carrying a tray. Summer distributed the place settings around the table, as Germaine placed small bowls of olives, radishes and melons down on the table. They turned and smiled cheerfully at the men and then turned around and walked arm-in-arm back into the kitchen.

Steven sat sipping his brandy and gazed at the view. The house sat atop the hill surrounded by fragrant white flowered hedges, fenced gardens, landscaped pathways, and a variety of fruit trees, the old branches on some spreading wide and held up with notched wood poles. Several sheds and outbuildings dotted the area, and Steven could see a pear tree in the distance with what appeared to be bottles tied to some of its branches glinting in the sunlight. The large flagstone patio sat next to a rock lined swimming pool where the dogs lazed in the shade, periodically stepping into the cool water in the hot afternoon sun. Beyond the landscaped gardens, the terrace looked out over the vineyards, which fanned out in even, measured rows from all sides of the house and across the rolling hills for what seemed like miles.

"Do you own all of this land?" asked Steven, gesturing with his arm to take in the sweeping view.

"We do," answered Pierre. "We have 240 acres. I am too old to farm, so we lease the land to the Gillet brothers. They produce small quantities of Viognier, Chardonnay and a Mourvedre/Grenache blend. They are quite good, and are making a name for themselves in the world of wine. We will have some with lunch."

"I look forward to it," said Steven, sipping his brandy.

"My ancestors built this farmhouse in 1776, the year your American war for independence ended. The original structure was half the size it is now, and succeeding generations have added to either the house or the land. We have managed to keep the house and land throughout a bloody history of wars, revolutions, confiscations and beheadings," he said solemnly, "and it will pass to my son when I am gone."

"Does your son live here or does he work in the city?" asked Steven.

"Oh, yes, he lives here. He is at summer camp in the mountains. He is a good boy, and very smart. He loves American baseball," said Pierre with a smile.

Steven was surprised that Pierre had a son in summer camp. He knew that Pierre was over sixty years old. "How old is your son?" he asked.

"He just turned eleven last March. He will be home in a few days. I hope you can meet him," said Pierre with an odd look in his eye.

A late life baby, thought Steven. Germaine would have been nearly fifty years old when she had him.

"Was your father a vintner?" asked Steven.

"No, my father was a *fruitier*. He grew pears, plums, apples, apricots and cherries. We still have a few fruit trees left, and I turn them into liqueurs like this one," he said, gesturing with his glass.

"Ah, so the little man in the bottle on the ladder is picking the fruit?" asked Steven.

"Oui, c'est ça!"

Summer came out of the kitchen and walked to the table with a large covered dish that she set on a tiled trivet. Germaine was right behind her with a large salad, and two crusty loaves of bread.

"Pierre, nous somme prêts, mon amour," said Germaine.

"Lunch is ready," said Pierre to Steven. They finished their brandies, and took their places at the table. Steven had never before felt so luxuriant as he

did now in the presence of such expertly prepared dishes and the beautiful surroundings despite having dined at some of the world's finest restaurants. The
afternoon slid sensuously by, the lavender scented breeze and warm summer
sun, the wine, the food, the laughter and conversation combining in magical
splendor, breaking down, as it had done for millennia, the barriers of culture,
language and experiences between humans.

CHAPTER 38

The Russians Strike a Deal

Vladimir Dvorkovsky sat silently at a tiny bistro around the corner from his hotel, watching the door as giddy lovers and chic shoppers came in for *un verre*. Charles Conway was late, and Vladimir sipped his vodka rocks with growing anger.

He had been rehearsing what he would say to the prick, hoping that he had planned for a big enough carrot to entice the man to be agreeable. He needed Charles Conway more than Charles Conway needed him, and that could be problematic for him. He would open with a low offer, knowing that Conway would want a bigger slice of the pie, and hopefully, they could meet somewhere close to the middle.

Conway walked in behind a pair of star-struck lovers, and quickly spotted Vladimir sitting at the back of the bar.

"Vladimir," said Conway sitting down. Vladimir extended his hand but Charles didn't take it. "Let's just get this over with," he said, waving the waiter over.

"Oui, monsieur?"

"Double scotch and soda. Make it snappy," he said, handing the waiter fifty francs.

Conway sat back and eyed Dvorkovsky. "Looks like you've got yourself into quite a little pickle, Vladimir," he said finally.

"Yes, well, I guess you could say that," said Dvorkovsky cautiously.

"I warned you before about those tankers," said Conway.

Dvorkovsky said nothing and waited.

"So what do you want me to do about it?" asked Conway. "I've got nothing to do with those rusty buckets, and now my fucking oil is spilled all over the fucking French Riviera!"

"We need to deflect attention away from us," said Dvorkovsky.

"Well, I'm not going to take it for you," said Conway, taking a large swallow of his drink. "This is your ballgame, pal."

"No, I don't think you should," said Dvorkovsky. "But you could throw suspicion onto the cruise ship." Dvorkovsky eyed Conway warily, waiting to see his reaction.

"Yes, that's true," he said, circling the ice in his drink. He didn't look at Dvorkovsky. He took another swallow.

"What if you said that the cruise company was at fault?" asked Vladimir.

"I think it's quite evident that your tanker was at fault," he said. "No one will buy that."

"Yes, but what if you just sort of cast doubt about who is at fault for the time being?" asked Dvorkovsky.

"And what's in it for me?" asked Conway, leveling his bloodshot eyes on Dvorkovsky's for the first time.

"Another five percent," said Dvorkosky. His face was tense, his eyes imploring.

"Nah," said Conway, standing up to leave. "Putting the blame to the cruise liner would make me look like an absolutely heartless bastard in the press, what with the hero status their captain and first officer have attained. I'd be crucified."

"Wait," said Dvorkovsky, reaching out to stop Conway from walking away. "What would it take? Just to throw the suspicion on them, at the news conference. Just to say, we're waiting for the investigation to conclude who was at fault, and say, us or the cruise liner?"

Conway leaned over from the side of the table, "I think twenty-five percent would be sufficient," said Conway.

"Twenty-five!" said Dvorkovsky with a shock. "That's ridiculous!"

"That's my offer," said Conway.

Dvorkovsky licked his lips nervously. "I can't do twenty-five. I can do twenty," he said.

"Twenty it is," said Conway, walking away. "I'll have my office send over an amended contract." He paused, and reached out his hand to Dvorkovsky. "Nice doing business with you Vladimir. It was good to see you again. We'll have to get together with the wives very soon."

As Conway walked out the door, Dvorkovsky let out a sigh of relief and ordered another drink.

CHAPTER 39

Press Conference

HUNDREDS OF NEWS reporters jockeyed for position in front of Purity Oil's Paris headquarters while they waited for Charles Conway to appear. The news conference had been hastily called for 19:00 hours Paris time, and the reporters had been scrambling to arrive before the man took to the outdoor podium. The Paris police and Conway's private security team made a sweep of the area and rerouted traffic as a light drizzle of rain began to fall, and a small awning had been erected for Conway to stand under. The dolled up female reporters opened umbrellas and put on rain gear that they carried in large bags to keep their carefully coiffed hair from getting drenched. The male reporters slid on trench coats or jackets, allowing the light mist to have its way with their own close-cropped, unflappable hairdos.

The weather had changed as they left the RPR office, Roberta and Jim Hathaway in a taxi and David Reed in the limousine with Charles Conway, his assistant Crystal Cox, and Buddy Durant. As they drove across the Pont des Arts and out of central Paris to the Purity Oil office on Avenue Jean Jaurès in the modern, commercial district of the 19th Arrondissement, the weather grew increasingly cool and wet, as they got closer to Purity Oil. Roberta cautiously repeated to Jim her conversation behind closed doors with Conway and what he was going to say. Jim seemed to be in complete agreement with Roberta and the strategy of condolence and contrition she had recommended, and she listened carefully to his comments as they rode in the back of the taxi, weighing his words to make sure she could trust him. In the back of her mind she scolded herself for allowing David to ride alone with Conway. She knew that he could not be trusted, and she should have insisted that David ride in the taxi with Jim.

The limousine pulled around to the back of the building and drove into the private entrance of the underground parking garage. Roberta and Jim were dropped off a block away and waited under the awning by the podium for Charles Conway to come through the front door. She wondered what he and his Russian partner had agreed to. In a few moments, Roberta spotted them coming from the garage elevator into the lobby, an armed security guard on either side of Conway with David and Buddy walking behind him. Crystal was nowhere to be seen, and Roberta guessed she had gone up to the office to wait, out of the rain and in safety.

They came through the door and Conway stepped up to the microphones on the podium. Roberta and Jim stood on one side, and David and Buddy Durant on the other. Her cell phone buzzed in her pocket and she took it out to see who it was. Michel's number appeared on the screen and she let it go to voice mail. He had left several messages already, and they had only added to her anxiety. The security guards that had come out the door with Conway went around to the front of the podium, and stood with their hands folded in front of them and legs spread apart in a stance that unmistakably conveyed that no one would get past them. The rest of his security detail that had been sweeping the area for suspicious activity dispersed themselves among the crowd of reporters and the Paris police kept the street clear of vehicles and pedestrians.

"Thank you for coming," began Charles Conway, to the assembled group. Everyone grew quiet as they waited for him to continue. "On behalf of the Purity Oil family, and its almost 200,000 employees, I would like to express our deep condolences to the families and loved ones of those that lost their lives in the tragic accident at sea between the oil tanker, Ileana Star, and the cruise ship, Heavenly Seas." Conway paused for a moment as the cameras whirred and flashed. Roberta stood perfectly still, watching his face intently. He looked momentarily unsure, and then went on.

"As has already been reported, and many of you know, Purity Oil has a strategic partnership for oil and gas exploration with the Russian oil company RUSoil. Purity Oil provides RUSoil with technical know-how and expertise in the exploration and extraction of energy, and we are proud to help the people of the former Soviet Union attain economic freedoms that they have been denied for so long. But I am here today to make it perfectly clear," he said, pounding the podium with his finger, "that Purity Oil had no direct involvement in, nor responsibility for, the tanker Ileana Star, its maintenance or its upkeep."

Roberta looked perplexedly at Jim and he looked back at her with concern and confusion. She saw David out of the corner of her eye staring at her with a self-satisfied grin on his face. She looked at him straight on. His eyes were full of contempt and her stomach lurched as she realized she had been tricked. She turned her focus back to Charles Conway, anxiously hoping that he would stick to the agreement on his public statement that they had discussed.

"We willingly offer the French authorities our full cooperation in their investigation, though we have little we can add. We, like the rest of the world, will wait for the results of the investigation by the authorities, on who, whether it was the tanker or the cruise liner, was actually at fault in this terrible accident. Thank you."

Charles Conway stepped off the podium, brusquely pushing past Roberta and Jim Hathaway, and walked back through the lobby door, quickly followed by Buddy Durant and David Reed. Roberta stood dumbfounded as the security guards moved in to block any further access, including her own, to the lobby entrance of Purity Oil.

CHAPTER 40

One Step Too Far

MICHEL AND JUSTINE sat at a table in a small café, downloading images from his camera to her laptop. His poignant, graphic pictures of oil-soaked wildlife and the human volunteers, their faces streaked black as they scooped up shining pools of viscous oil that coated the yellow sand, said more than words ever could.

It was nearly midnight, and he and Justine had developed a daily rhythm, meeting up twice a day at the same small café, once in the morning to plan their day and then late at night to exchange the latest information they had obtained. Michel provided quotes and background to her from the dozens of government agencies and environmental organizations that he worked with. Together, they sent the news of the spill out to the world, hoping that the catastrophe would be a wake-up call to the planet that the reliance on oil-based energy carries catastrophic environmental hazards.

The events had taken on a momentum of their own, carrying Michel along in the fast-paced riptide they created. He had not spoken to Roberta since she had left for Paris three days ago, but they had exchanged heated emails and Michel had left several angry phone messages describing the horrific scene he was witnessing while she was meeting with Charles Conway.

While Justine typed out her article, he sent Roberta another email, attaching some of the photos of oil-slicked seabirds he had taken today. Her naiveté about Purity Oil's intentions astounded him, and he was having serious doubts about her moral convictions in the face of this disaster. He scolded her in capital letters in the email, telling her that she must sever her business relationship with Purity Oil, describing her as a complicit partner in their deceptions, comparing her to complacent citizens in Germany who also did nothing while Hitler's Nazis marched through German towns rounding up Jews. He felt a twinge of guilt as he typed out the message, but he wanted to make a point, and could think of nothing else so important, so relevant, to drive it home. He hit send, just as Justine did the same, sending her latest article and Michel's photos to her editor at La Voix de France in Paris.

CHAPTER 41

⎯⎯ ᦞ ⎯⎯

The Spill Spreads

La Voix de France

Spill Spreads, Threatens Fishing Grounds Amid Devastation and Distrust

By Justine Chuchote

NICE, FRANCE, JULY 1, 1996 – The tide of oil spilled by the sunken tanker Ileana Star continues to spread to the north and west 100 miles off the coast of France, threatening the richest fishing grounds in French territorial waters, as well as the coasts of Italy, Spain, and Portugal.

The French government issued a fishing ban for the Riviera Coast from Nice to Marseille, and warned their neighbors on both sides to prepare for the potential of oncoming oil to their shorelines. The three Mediterranean countries, Italy, Spain and France, have agreed to work together to prevent potentially hazardous tankers from traversing through Mediterranean waters, and are preparing to escort two such tankers to port.

Fishermen from Toulon to Nice, desperate to protect their livelihood, spent hours of backbreaking work dredging oil from the sea with rakes and homemade nets, and complained about the government response to the spill. Along the shoreline, volunteers scooped oil laden sand into dump trucks, and washed the gooey substance from rocks. More volunteers came to help wash the sea birds that walked with wobbly legs onto the beach like drunken sailors, their feathers and faces covered in oil. Many animals that washed up were already dead, and were scooped along with the sand into dump trucks to be disposed of.

The toxic sand was being carted off to an ancient ceramics factory in Provence, where it could be successfully burned in high heat kilns. "We can only take so much of this toxic sand," said Francois Hulot, the owner of Céramiques Provençal. "The government must find somewhere else to put all this."

The French environment minister put the cost of the cleanup at $45 million dollars and offered assurances that the majority of the oil would congeal on the bottom of the sea, but that estimate was quickly challenged by environmental agencies and local fishermen as far too low, and put the true cost at three times the government's estimate. A spokesman for the tanker's insurer in London, Ipswich Insurance, has indicated that the ship's liability insurance is as high as $25 million, a paltry sum in light of the extent of the devastation. The European Union has pledged $95 million to aid in the clean up.

The Ileana Star, whose ownership cannot be easily determined amid the maze of countries and companies involved, is loosely connected to the Russian oil giant RUSoil, in partnership with Purity Oil of America. Charles Conway, the CEO of Purity, in a press conference yesterday, did not take any responsibility for the maintenance of the tanker, and put the responsibility squarely on the Russians. He also questioned who was at fault in the accident, alluding to Cruise Corporation as a potential culprit. Cruise Corporation roundly rejects this theory, and they have provided their own explanation of events the night of the accident, describing a scene of horrors as the lights and engines of the ghostly tanker sputtered back to life a mere 150 yards in front of them. It may be years before the courts make a determination of who is at fault and why.

Theo Kourkoulos, a marine biologist with the Oceanographic Institute, said that even if the oil did solidify on the seabed, toxins would still leach into the water and enter the food chain. "This was an accident waiting to happen," he said. "A large shipment of oil carried by an aging oil tanker that had no business even being in the oil business." The organization is demanding a swift end to the use of single-hulled tankers like the Ileana Star, and demanding the world's governments speed up the transition to double-hulled ships, a reform that is not required to be completed until 2015. He also encouraged individuals and governments to consider switching to environmentally friendly power sources.

Right now all eyes are turned to the sea, as gale force winds in the southern Mediterranean push the oil slicks closer to the shores. One of the slicks was less than two miles offshore this afternoon, and pushing closer, where it would threaten a vital mussel industry west of Marseille. Still two others were more than 40 miles out, the normally white, foam-capped waves tainted brown, whipped up like a toxic café latte from the storm to the south.

CHAPTER 42

Blame Your Father

ROBERTA RODE IN the back of a hired limousine sedan with Evan Manning once again by her side, on the way to her office from Charles de Gaulle Airport. The moment she had returned to her office after Charles Conway's press conference she had called Evan, and asked him to board the next flight to Paris. She had a number of decisions to make, and would need Evan by her side, his expertise in business, his knowledge of her options and liabilities, and his cool and level-headed demeanor essential to making those decisions.

"I spoke to David this morning," she explained "He admitted that he sabotaged the press conference, and had convinced Charles Conway to change his statement to the press. I don't think it took much convincing though. Conway was already resistant to my strategy that he make sincere condolences for the lives lost and for the environmental damage. David convinced him in the limousine on the way to the press conference that doing it my way would be admitting guilt. He played to Conway's worst fears. I've left several messages, but Conway hasn't returned my phone calls. David threatened to leave RPR and take Purity Oil and a number of other clients with him, namely, the ones we gave him control of."

"Well, I think we knew that was coming," offered Evan. "To be honest, Roberta, I think that having David take Purity Oil and Stanton Chemical is a good thing for you. I think it was naïve of you to think that you could continue to take the moral high ground while representing the companies your father did business with. They made it clear they did not believe in your mission."

Evan's comment, though well-meaning, got Roberta's back up. It was the same thing that Michel had said to her at dinner the first night in Berlin, and in every exchange she had had with him ever since. She felt in her heart that Evan was probably right, but she had wanted to try to bring them into the twenty-first century with a different outlook. She hated the idea that the oil, chemical and mining companies had set themselves against the forces of environmentalism and conservation instead of showing themselves to be good stewards of the planet, and the natural resources it needed to function. *They could have been so much better*, she thought. They could have been honest and forward thinking. Instead, they took sides and demonized their opponents, and for decades have poured a massive amount of money into disputing everything that legitimate science said about the effects of their products on the environment and human health. It had led to a good versus evil scenario that she knew in the long run they could not win; yet they were now entrenched soldiers, locked in unending battle, unable to change course. They had adopted naked, self-serving greed over their humanity. How much money had been spent in this shameful pursuit? The world would never know, but she was sure that if it could be added up, it would be more than it would have cost to do the right thing in the first place. Ultimately, she blamed her father for this mess the planet was in, and it instantly brought tears to her eyes. She shook her head and took a deep breath to dispel the heaviness in her heart. *Think strategically, Roberta*, she thought to herself. *What's the next step?*

"Conway was supposed to be having dinner with his Russian partner, Vladimir Dvorkovsky, last night," she said after a moment, unable to think of anything important to say. She was tired, and her brain was not functioning well.

"What do you want to do?" asked Evan.

"I want to sock David Reed in the nose!" said Roberta, hitting her hand with her fist to demonstrate. "Actually, I would love to get rid of him. I'd like to force him out without a penny."

Evan thought for a minute. "What's the first rule of high school dating?"

"Um, geez Evan," she said with a quizzical look on her face, "I really don't know. Don't try to go after the most popular guy in school because he'll break your heart?"

Evan scrutinized her face, regarding her curiously. "There's probably a story in there somewhere, but no, it's always: be the dumper not the dumped. I say we fire him."

"Can we do that? He's a partner," she asked doubtfully.

"I think you have grounds, Roberta," said Evan. "His new partnership agreement, which I wrote after coming on board, makes it clear that he cannot put the firm in jeopardy nor do anything that reflects badly on you or on the firm, nor can he do anything that is injurious to the firm and its mission, and that is clearly what he has done for his own personal gain. I think his actions qualify. I say we go after him."

"How would we do that?" she asked, hope springing to her mind.

"We send him a cease and desist letter outlining the reasons, everything he's done to sabotage you and your relationship with the client, and we just tell him, he's fired," said Evan. "I can draft it, and have Stan Morris put his stamp of approval on it. We'll offer him enough of a severance package to hopefully go away without a fight, but my guess is he'll fight it, but his contract states that he can't take any RPR clients for five years if his partnership is terminated for cause."

"Wow! Could we do that?" she asked, wide-eyed.

"I don't see why not! We just need to get the jump on him. Quickly! We need to be the dumper, not the dumped," said Evan firmly.

"What about Charles Conway? How do we handle him? He hasn't returned my calls."

Evan paused and looked Roberta straight in the eye. "I am going to be brutally honest with you, Roberta. Based on what you told me that he said to you in the conference room, and Jim Hathaway's warning to you, he's made his position clear. He's a man without a conscience. I'm sorry Roberta, but you *have* to cut him loose, too."

Roberta thought about Evan's advice. Was Charles Conway really a man without conscience? He was a man in the mold of her father, for whom the word "truth" had a slippery definition depending on the circumstances. *I am responsible to nothing, including the fucking planet,* he had said. *You are here to serve me, and not the environmental agenda you espouse.*

A terrible feeling of defeat settled over her. The thought of giving up on Charles Conway made her feel like a failure. Unlike the bleak, broken-down dystopian future that many saw as the Earth's ultimate end at the hands of heartless humans, she had always had a vision in her mind of an Edenistic planet, a place of gentle humans who moved effortlessly through a clean and bright environment, leaving no trace of themselves behind and doing no harm, enlightened humans that always did the right thing for the right reasons, not because of Jesus or Allah or Krishna or Buddha, but for the love of the beautiful blue orb that they inhabited, and she wanted Charles Conway and all of those men like him to see that vision, too, and to embrace it. Her naiveté, in some instances a terrible disadvantage for her, nonetheless motivated her to the hopefulness that kept her fighting, and gave her a positive outlook for the future of humanity. Was the future really so bleak? Would the human race never adopt a broader, altruistic vision? Men like Charles Conway pay lip service to responsibility to their children and grandchildren, but history would show that they see only as far as their own personal interests, no matter the consequences to others, to their grandchildren or the planet. *I am responsible to nothing,* Charles

Conway had said to her. Perhaps Michel and those who believed like him were right. Perhaps selfishness was written in our DNA, and our planet was doomed to a scarred and black future at the hands of mankind.

For all of her life, her utopian vision had spurred her to wage an uphill battle against the enemies of environmentalism. Her father had called her a member of the enemy camp, and Charles Conway thought of her that way too. Their personal philosophy, her father, Charles Conway, Henry Mueller, David Reed, and all those who thought like them, did not espouse a belief in the common good, and in fact, could be construed as inherently evil. Was this it then? Was this the battle between good and evil? If so, she believed that she had been fighting on the front lines for most of her life on the side of good, and here she was again at that same crossroads just like that day in Oregon, but now she had a greater responsibility than ever, and a bigger pulpit from which to preach. She had to take a stand, but what was the stand she should take? Should she cut him loose or give him one more chance to see her vision and possibly change the course of history?

Evan waited, watching her intently, seeing the wheels turning in her mind. Finally he said, "Roberta, you have to cut him loose."

"Since he won't return my phone calls, I must conclude that he cannot be convinced to change his tactics," she said, looking intently at Evan, her mind made up. "I'll send him a letter, letting him know that we are terminating our contract with Purity Oil and will no longer represent them as their public relations firm."

"Atta girl!" said Evan enthusiastically.

She smiled at him and suddenly felt hopeful, and very relieved, as if she had just emerged from a dark cave into the sunlight.

"Let's get this done quickly," she said excitedly, as the sedan driver pulled in front of the Paris office. "Then we hop a train to Nice, and stand with the volunteers down there, cleaning up the mess Purity Oil has made!"

She stepped out of the car, more determined and re-energized to fight another day.

CHAPTER 43

—— ✍ ——

Human Stupidity Is Greater Than We Thought

La Voix de France

French Aquarium Threatened by Oil Spill; Clean Up Continues

By Justine Chuchote

NICE, FRANCE, JULY 4, 1996 – La Vie de Mer, a saltwater aquarium park in Saint-Yves-sur-Mer, just south of Toulon, is facing a poisonous black tide approaching with rapid speed. The smell of oil is in the air here, and the seals and sea lions that live at the park, already sensing a problem, have abandoned their contaminated seawater pools for the dry land of rocks and beaches built around it.

"We built the aquarium as an homage to the sea, in a place that has been hurt by oil pollution the most," said Jean-Marie Mingui, the director of the aquarium. "We hoped to offer a sea life center where people would fall in love with the ocean and never dare to harm it."

Oil from the Ileana Star threatens the saltwater pools that house hundreds of sea creatures here at the aquarium. Valves that bring in fresh seawater can only be opened at high tide, and probably not for long, as brown-foamed waves broke against the rocks around the aquarium walls. "We are in serious danger from the oil leaking out of the Ileana Star," said Mr. Mingui.

As the slick moves closer, Mr. Mingui is making emergency preparations to evacuate the animal life that he cherishes. The huge tanks of fish, coral, octopus, and sea mammals that reside at the aquarium delight visitors. The aquarium is home to 30,000 fish and 62 species of invertebrates, some of which would not survive a transfer.

Further to the east at Nice the clean up continues, and the French navy has taken over coordination of soldiers and volunteers. Dead sea life litters the beach, and the lifeless corpses of dolphins, seals, seabirds and fish are piling up on the once pristine beach. The soldiers are waging a battle here, one without guns or tanks, but a battle nonetheless, as they continue to scoop up blackened-gooey sand with bulldozers, and wash the rocks with power sprayers mixed with chemicals that disperse the oil. The use of dispersants on the beach and at sea is controversial, since it is not known what damage they cause to the eco-system. Entrepreneurs with new ideas have presented products to the director of the clean up, Colonel Gerard Bouvet, who said he is willing to test the most promising ones, including a pelletized sponge-like substance that absorbs oil and oil-trapping filters that would be spread out on the surface at the leading edge of the slick and block the oil from reaching the shore.

"Everything points to continuing leakages from the downed tanker," said Theo Kourkoulos of the Oceanographic Institute. The French government is watching the weather and plans to send down a French submarine to examine the wreck first hand when the weather to the south clears.

Attempts by this reporter to unlock the puzzle of ownership of the Ileana Star have been difficult. The tanker was registered in the Bahamas by a Liberian listed Russian company, and had been chartered by RUSoil under a separate company it owns that is based in Switzerland. That company has at least two American directors listed on its board with past ties to Purity Oil. The ship's Russian crew were hired and paid by a Greek company, Island Maritime.

"The oceans of this world are truly a Wild West of commerce and treachery, the last bastion of no-man's land where rule of law is hard to enact and enforce," said Mr. Kourkoulos "The sheriff, so to speak, patrolling the vast expanse of the world's oceans, is made up of too many jurisdictional parts, and lacks cooperation between nations, and is easily enticed by graft and corruption."

Mr. Mingui, of La Vie de Mer Aquarium, said that damage from previous wrecks and pollution from run off has had disastrous effects on the ecosystem, and has yet to fully recover. The area has been restocked with commercially valuable species a number of times, yet other creatures like sea urchins, starfish, seahorses, and certain mollusks have not returned to this stretch of coastline near Toulon.

The European Union has called for a vote next week to ratify the legislation calling for the end of single-hull tankers. The present legislation allows these tankers to move about the waters of Europe until 2015. The new legislation will move that deadline up 10 years, to 2005, still a long time for these oil-carrying behemoths to wander the oceans of the Earth.

Mr. Mingui fears that such measures will ultimately fail because the oil industry has more clout than the average citizen. "We had hoped that our facility would help educate people about oil pollution, but alas, human stupidity is greater than we thought."

CHAPTER 44

—— ⚬ ——

Use Your Power For Good

It took Roberta and Evan a day and a half to finish the letters to David Reed and Charles Conway. Roberta had alerted Arthur Clark, giving him a run down of everything that had happened, and he agreed with both decisions. David's letter included specifics about his separation from Reed Public Relations, the disposition of his shares in the company, which he was required to relinquish as per his contract, and spelled out the expectations regarding clients belonging to RPR. After tackling David's letter, they finished the letter to Charles Conway and framed their decision in more amicable terms than what had been used in David's letter, citing differences of opinion, and declaring their intention to halt their business relationship with Purity Oil, effective immediately, along with the return of any moneys owed from the substantial fees they paid the firm.

Evan faxed copies of the letters to attorney Stan Morris in DC. He had no changes to the Purity Oil letter, but he quickly added more forceful language to David's letter about the disposition of client relationships, physical files and any information owned by RPR, and giving him forty-eight hours to agree to and sign the agreement, after which, if not singed and returned, the severance offer would be rescinded, and they would consider him to be terminated without severance. When Roberta read over the changes she laughed, knowing that David would be livid, and that he was getting just what he deserved.

Roberta listened as Evan worked with Stan Morris to put the finishing touches to the letters, and she felt elated that she was severing ties with the polluters at Purity Oil, and wondered what else she could do once she arrived in Nice. She remembered the words that Jacques Cousteau had said to her after their meeting at his office. "The adversaries of old have joined forces to become the leaders of a revolution," he had said to her. "A revolution in human thinking, a revolution in attitude, in commerce and the stewardship of the planet, a revolution in human destiny and the hope of the new millennium; the return to paradise by the outcasts of Eden." She had relished those words and they rang again in her conscious mind like a bell.

She had finally come to the conclusion that she would never convince a man like Charles Conway to do the right thing on his own, but she thought, *she could bring her formidable talents to bear working against him.* An idea suddenly popped into her mind, and she placed a call to the CEO of Cruise Corporation at his office in Miami, Florida. He was in Nice, his secretary informed her, and she promised to immediately contact him and pass on Roberta's message to him, and he had called her back in less than 15 minutes.

Roberta opened up to him with total honesty, explaining the situation in Paris, the press conference and how events had unfolded, and then she offered to put the services of her firm at his disposal at no charge, and use this terrible tragedy and the worldwide focus on it to begin a public relations counter-assault that focused on environmentally friendly alternative energies. She offered to create a campaign for Cruise Corporation based on the clean, pro-environmental principles and processes they had put on board every ship, and in exchange, she asked him if he would be willing to team up with the Oceanographic Institute in Europe and the Marine Conservation Alliance in the US to help push for legislation requiring double-hulled tankers. He was impressed, and agreed to meet with her in Nice to discuss her idea further. Then she called Jacques Cousteau at the Oceanographic Institute, and made him the same offer. He congratulated her on her daring idea, and agreed without hesitation to co-sponsor a campaign.

They sent copies of the letters by courier to David Reed and Charles Conway at their Paris hotels, and Holly sent copies by overnight carrier to the Purity Oil headquarters in Houston and to David Reed's townhouse in Alexandria, Virginia. And with that first step in their plan behind them, Roberta and Evan set off to catch the train to Nice. They had missed the express that went between Paris and Nice direct, and would have to stop at the station in Lyon for an hour, before moving on to Nice. They would arrive in Nice by late afternoon ready to pitch in, and help out in any way they could.

The quiet and comfortable train raced south across the French countryside toward Lyon as Roberta ate a sandwich of ham and cheese on a crusty French baguette that she had bought at the station. She was amazed at how good it was, and wolfed it down in a matter of minutes. She sat back in her seat and sipped her café au lait and stared out the window.

"Have you spoken to Michel?" asked Evan, sitting in the seat across the table from her.

She winced at the question. In the whirlwind of activity in the two days since Evan had arrived, she had not had time to even think about Michel, which in truth, was a blessed respite from the outrage he had directed towards her. From the moment that she had learned about the disaster, and Charles Conway had stepped into the office in Paris, she had felt under siege from all sides. Michel's emails and phone messages had unnerved her, and she had stopped responding to them. She understood his passion and commitment, and truly appreciated it, but his anger too often turned personal. The beautiful day she had spent with Michel, meeting Jacques Cousteau, going shopping at the open air market, and the evening at his home in Le Bar Sur Loup under a star filled sky, seemed a hundred years ago. She suddenly felt sad. The aura of love and enchantment that she had felt was gone, and she missed it very much.

"No, I haven't," she answered cautiously, deciding not to reveal everything to Evan. "I should let him know that we're coming. At least I think he'll be happy that I've severed ties with the enemy." She smiled sardonically.

"He's probably a lot like your father in that way, only he's coming from the other side," commented Evan. "It's ironic, in a way."

"He's very much like my father," agreed Roberta. "But Michel's passion comes from a commitment to a cause, whereas my father only wanted power, money and prestige. I guess that's a cause, a deceitful one not worthy of human endeavor."

"I've been truly amazed by the rotten things we've discovered in some of those files at the office, especially some of your father's hand-written notes," said Evan. "You hear about things like that happening, but it always seems overblown or embellished. You and I are living it and the rumors, as they say, are true."

"I haven't even had one moment to sit back and reflect on everything that's happened since I arrived in France. I feel like I've lived a lifetime in less than a week," she mused. "You have been invaluable to me as usual, Evan. You really help me clarify my thoughts."

"You just sometimes need a fresh perspective, and I can take a step back and see the big picture. You've been caught up living the drama, and there's been a lot of drama! We make a good team, Roberta," he said, smiling earnestly and feeling a sudden stab in his heart of the unrequited love he felt for her.

"Yes, we certainly do. Bringing you into the firm was the best decision I ever made," she said looking out the window.

"Believe me, it saved me from a terrible situation at home," said Evan.

"How is Jane?" asked Roberta.

"With everything going on I didn't want to burden you, but I found out last week the cancer is back," said Evan sadly. "She's not sure she wants to go through the chemo again."

"Oh, Evan, I am really sorry," said Roberta sympathetically.

"Me too," said Evan. "We'll have to make new arrangements for Cassie. I want her to come and live with me in Washington. I hope Jane will agree. It was one thing for Jane to be sick while Cassie was a baby, but she's old enough now to be scarred by watching her mother die."

"Have you been up to see Cassie?"

"I was planning to go up this weekend. I'll probably fly into New York from Paris after we wrap everything up here," he said.

The train pulled into Lyon station, and Roberta took Evan's hand. "Listen Evan, if you need to go back home to be with Cassie, please don't hesitate, just go."

Evan looked at Roberta and smiled gratefully. "Thanks, I know," he said.

"Hey look, we're in Lyon," said Roberta.

"I think I remember your mother telling me that you have family somewhere around Lyon. It's too bad we won't have time to let you stop and see them," said Evan.

"I wish I could. The plan to meet up with Summer has gone out the window. She's there now, at the farm in Dijon. She sent me an email yesterday. She's having fun with Uncle Pierre and Aunt Germaine drinking good wine and cooking up a storm in Germaine's beautiful farmhouse kitchen. I would love to stop and see them, but we really don't have time. Maybe on the way back," she said. "Let me send Michel that email while we're stopped here."

Roberta opened her laptop and typed out an email, keeping an eye on the time. The stop in Lyon was supposed to be less than an hour. She finished the email, letting Michel know that she would be in Nice by late afternoon. She only gave him a sketchy outline of the news about Purity. She would wait until she saw him to give him the blow by blow. She told him she had an appointment at the Oceanographic Institute in three days and invited him to join her. She debated whether to close the note with 'I love you', but so much had happened since she had left him in Nice she wasn't sure what she felt for him. She decided to close with 'can't wait to see you' and sent the email. She closed the screen on her laptop, and she and Evan sat quietly together for several minutes looking out the window at the station platform, and then at the other trains in the station. Forty minutes had gone by and no one had boarded the train, and the station was eerily quiet. Out the window she could see uniformed conductors, ticket agents, baggage handlers and engineers walking out.

She looked around at the other passengers. *"Qu'est-ce-qui passé?"* she asked those around her. "What's happened?" she asked again in English.

The passenger in the seat behind her stood up, while speaking to someone on his phone. He began to grab his bags from the overhead compartment. "You may as well get off," he said. "The train operators are on strike."

"What?" asked Roberta.

"They just walked off the job. You'll have to get to your destination another way," he said as he walked off the train.

Roberta looked up at Evan. "What should we do?" asked Evan.

"I guess we'll be spending some time with my aunt and uncle in Dijon, after all!" she exclaimed.

CHAPTER 45

A Ghost From The Past

ROBERTA AND EVAN stood under the vine-covered portico and waited for someone to answer the door. She rang the bell again and knocked as loudly as she could.

"Such a beautiful place!" exclaimed Evan, patting the dogs and looking around the lush landscaped grounds and pathways. The wisteria vine surrounding the portico was in full bloom with hundreds of purple flowers hanging down all around them.

The door opened, and Aunt Germaine stood on the other side wiping her hands on her apron. Louis XIV ran past her and barked a happy greeting, jumping up on Roberta's legs.

"Bonjour Tante Germaine," said Roberta smiling.

Aunt Germaine's face registered complete surprise, and she rushed out the door to hug her niece. *"Roberta, ma petite! Qu'est-ce-que tu fais ici?"*

"Les trains sont en grève," she said hugging her aunt. "We were on our way to Nice when they walked off the job."

"Ah, Mon dieu! Viens, ma chérie. Entrez vous. I am so happy to see you," she said switching to English. Germaine caught her first glimpse of Evan and he thought he saw a look of shock and confusion register on her face.

"This is Evan Manning," Roberta said as they stepped into the foyer. "Evan is my CFO. Evan, this is my Aunt Germaine."

"Bienvenue, Evan," said Germaine casting her eyes upon Evan's face with a slight furrow in her brow as her smile fell from her face. Roberta detected a note of caution in Germaine's reaction to seeing Evan.

Evan extended his hand to shake, and she scolded him. *"Mais non!* We do it the French way," she said, regaining her comportment and reaching up to kiss him on both cheeks. Evan quickly adapted, feeling the warmth and charm of the practice. "Come! Everyone is outside." She motioned for them to follow her.

They followed Aunt Germaine down the hall to the kitchen where preparations were in progress for an evening meal. A cake studded with oranges sat on a cake stand on the counter next to loaves of bread beside a plate of cheese covered with a glass dome, and fresh lettuce from the garden was spread out on large kitchen towels, glistening with water from the bath they had just had in the huge ceramic sink. A large whole fish stuffed with fresh herbs was cradled in a roasting pan, and a heavenly sauce of tomatoes, capers and olives was bubbling away on the stove.

Germaine opened the kitchen door that led to the outdoor patio, and they walked together out the door. Summer looked up and saw Roberta. "Oh my God!" she said running up to them. She gave Roberta a big hug. "What are you two doing here?"

"The trains are on strike," said Roberta laughing. As they hugged, she saw Steven in the distance over Summer's shoulder, his guitar cradled in his lap, sitting in the sun at a table writing lyrics. "Steven? Is that Steven?"

"Yep! It's me!" he said turning around in his seat. "Oh, my God, Roberta and …Evan! Hey, big brother!" Steven said when he saw Evan, putting his guitar down. "What the hell are you doing here?" he asked, walking briskly toward them and smiling broadly. He hugged Roberta and Evan tightly, patting Evan repeatedly on the back. "What are you guys doing here?" He asked again, standing back but keeping his arm around Evan's shoulders.

"Me? What are you doing here?" asked Evan, equally as surprised as Steven was.

"I'm here to surprise Roberta," said Steven. "But what are you doing here?"

"The trains are on strike. We were on our way to Nice, and just as we got to Lyon the railroad workers went on strike," explained Evan laughing.

"That's great, but why are you *here,* in France?" asked Steven. "Does this have something to do with the oil spill?"

"Oh, we have so much to tell you!" said Roberta, as her Uncle Pierre walked up the path that led to the patio. He was carrying two bottles of liqueur with pears inside of them.

"Roberta! *Mon Dieu! Qu'est-ce-que tu fais ici?* Am I dreaming?" he said excitedly, putting down the two bottles in his hands and extending his arms to Roberta for a hug.

"Uncle Pierre! It is so wonderful to see you," said Roberta giving him a big hug and realizing, as she looked at his lined face, how much time had passed. "It has been too long."

"What are you doing here?" he asked, his eyes sparkling with love and joy.

Germaine interrupted the reunion. "Pierre, this is Roberta's friend, Evan," she said to Pierre with a concerned look on her face.

Evan extended his hand to Pierre, unsure if he was supposed to kiss him, too. "I'm Evan Manning," he said.

Pierre took Evan's hand and shook it warmly and then pulled Evan toward him and gave him a warm manly hug and said brightly, "Welcome Evan. Welcome to our home."

"*S'il vous plaît*, everyone sit down," said Germaine. "We will have some wine, and talk, and Roberta will tell us everything."

"*Oui!* Please, sit down, and tell us what has brought you here," said Uncle Pierre, motioning to the comfortable rattan chairs and sofa in the shade of the veranda. Steven retrieved his guitar and leaned it up against the wall next to him, and then sat down, the dogs lying next to him on the cool tile. "Germaine, bring wine and glasses," said Pierre.

"I'll help you," said Summer. She and Germaine went inside and quickly returned with an armload of glasses and two bottles of wine.

"Well, I don't know how much of the situation with the oil spill you've been following in the news," started Roberta, as she went on to relate the rapid turn of events in the five days since she had arrived in France. "And that's the story," she concluded.

"Well, I am proud of you for cutting Purity Oil loose," said Steven. "I watched the press conference and was shocked by their callously calculated response. I knew he was just hedging; making sure whatever he said laid the ground for his defense in the court of public opinion."

"Blame the Russians, that's always an effective strategy," added Summer.

"We knew that David Reed would eventually show his true colors, but I personally thought he'd do it behind our back. He learned his business ethics well from my father. His manipulation of the events in Paris was *so* my father's tactics," said Roberta, shaking her head with disgust.

"So, what's the plan?" asked Steven.

"I think Evan and I will rent a car and drive down to Nice tomorrow," said Roberta. "I sent Michel Manon an email from the train letting him know we were coming, and I have an appointment at the Oceanographic Institute in a couple of days to start working on the PR campaign for clean energy. The team from Cruise Corporation is meeting us there."

"The news reports and pictures have been so heartbreaking," said Uncle Pierre.

"I cry every time I see those oil-soaked birds trying to walk onto the beach. You can see it in their eyes, how much they're suffering," added Germaine.

"Such a scandal, and it will be a great loss of livelihood to the fishermen," said Pierre.

"My band's been scouting venues in and around Nice for a benefit concert for the fishermen and their families. We'll set up donation stations for environmental causes and the Red Cross to house and feed the volunteers helping with the clean up. Our manager found a location yesterday, and I was planning to head down there in a day or two myself," said Steven.

"Hey, what if we all went down together?" asked Evan.

"Road trip Part 2?" asked Steven smiling. "That could be fun. Déjà vu all over again!"

"But no sleeping in sleeping bags this time!" said Summer.

"And you won't have to cook either," said Evan.

"Can we be ready to leave by tomorrow?" asked Roberta.

"Hell yeah!" said Steven. "I'll get us a car," he said, standing up and punching buttons on his cell phone. They watched as Steven spoke quietly into his phone.

"Something like 5,000 fishermen and their families are affected by the ban on commercial fishing, and they were among the first volunteers out there scooping up oil with nets and homemade rakes. Their livelihood will be affected for years to come," said Summer as they waited for Steven to finish his conversation.

"It's all set," said Steven walking back to the group. "My manager has a car rented and has booked all four of us into the Hotel Negresco on the beach in Nice," said Steven. "Fortunately for us, the oil spill has caused dozens of cancellations at the hotel, and we've practically got the place to ourselves. My manager got my band mates and all of us rooms without a problem."

"Wow!" said Roberta. "Hotel Negresco? That's very posh!" she exclaimed.

"Don't worry, it's on me," said Steven.

"Maybe we'll run into Charles Conway while we're there," said Roberta sarcastically.

"Well," said Summer, raising her glass. "To road trip part 2 and déjà vu all over again!" she laughed.

"To déjà vu," they all said, clinking glasses.

As they took swallows of their wine a young boy's voice called from the kitchen with joyful exuberance and anticipation. *"Maman? Papi?"* he called. *"Ou êtes vous?"*

"Ici, sur la Terrace, chéri," called Germaine. She glanced at Pierre with a worried look.

As the boy came running out of the kitchen door onto the terrace, Roberta, Evan, Steven and Summer turned to view him. Roberta's heart skipped a beat and her breath caught in her throat. Steven had a flashback to his boyhood, and Summer turned to watch Roberta. Evan sat in stunned silence as he looked into the face of the spitting image of himself as a boy of 11.

CHAPTER 46

—— ⌢ ——

Whose Decision Is It?

THE BOY SPOKE to his parents in rapid happy French as the stunned group looked on. Uncle Pierre looked from Roberta to Evan, and Germaine shushed the boy, reminding him of his manners in front of guests.

"Roberta, this is our son Claude," said Uncle Pierre.

Roberta stood up and walked over to the boy. She bent down and looked directly into his beautiful hazel eyes. "I am happy to meet you, Claude," she said. She couldn't believe she was meeting her son now for only the second time in her life. She had left him as an infant with her beloved aunt and uncle, and her heart pounded in her chest as she stared at him. He was an exact replica of Evan, except he had Roberta's eyes. Tears flooded her vision and the boy's face began to swim in front of her. She turned around and looked at Evan, tears rolling down her cheeks. Evan looked back at her in stunned disbelief.

"Excuse me," said Roberta, walking rapidly away. Summer stood up and followed her into the house.

No one spoke for a moment. The boy looked at Evan and Steven, and then at his parents with confusion registering on his face, saying nothing. Steven stood up and broke the awkward silence.

"Hello Claude," he said smiling. "I'm Steven Manning."

The boy looked at Steven and recognized his famous face immediately. He looked at Pierre. *"Oui, Papa?"* he asked. *"C'est le* Steven Manning?"

"Mais oui!" said Pierre, shrugging his shoulders. *"C'est* le Steven Manning."

"Bonjour, Monsieur Manning," he said, shaking Steven's hand shyly and smiling from ear to ear.

"Parle en Anglais, Claude," said Germaine quietly, keeping a protective hand on the boy's shoulder.

"Hello," said Claude still smiling broadly at the famous rock star.

"And this is my brother, Evan," said Steven.

Evan stood up trying to regain his composure. "It's nice to meet you, Claude," said Evan. He extended his hand hesitantly to the boy, who took it enthusiastically. Evan inspected the boy's face intently, feeling overwhelmed with emotions, as if someone had kicked him in the gut.

"Eet eez vewy nice to meeting you," said Claude in halting English, smiling sweetly at Evan, his face blushing from embarrassment. His long dark lashes framed beautiful hazel blue eyes that flashed brightly with charming innocence, and his sun-kissed cheeks were sprinkled with tiny fawn-colored freckles.

"Yes," said Evan. He stood dumbly for a moment, unable to move, unsure what to do, what to think.

Steven tousled the boy's hair, as Evan stood quietly next to Claude, listening to him chatter on in halting English as he and Steven talked about rock music, their favorite bands, and the albums he liked the most from A Higher Calling. Steven picked up his guitar and the two of them sang snippets of songs together, and Evan watched the boy's expressive face as he spoke, mentally evaluating his mannerisms, his build, and his face. Tears came to his eyes.

"Excuse me," he said. "I, uh. I need to use the restroom," he said lamely, walking away.

Evan walked through the kitchen door and saw Roberta and Summer whispering at the small breakfast table. Roberta was dabbing at her eyes with a tissue.

"Roberta," said Evan from the doorway. "What the hell is going on?"

Roberta didn't answer right away as Evan sat down at the table. Summer excused herself and went outside.

"I don't understand, Roberta. Is that my son?" he demanded.

"Yes, Evan. He is your son," she said quietly. "Our son."

"But what happened? When did this happen?" he sputtered.

"I got pregnant on our road trip to Oregon. That night in Wyoming," she said.

"That one time, *the* one time?" asked Evan.

"Yes," said Roberta. "After the incident with American Pride, my mother sent me to stay with Pierre and Germaine while my father cooled off. I found out I was pregnant while I was staying here. Summer and I stayed for a year, and I came home after I had the baby."

"But why didn't you tell me?" demanded Evan angrily. "I have a son, Roberta!"

"Because this was the best solution, Evan. I wasn't ready to get married and raise a child," she said defensively. "My father would not let me come home as an unwed mother. He would have forced me to get married."

"But why wasn't I told? I should have had some say in what happened to him. He's mine too!" said Evan angrily.

"What would you have done that was any better?" she asked angrily. "You were a 22 year old college student. It would have been a terrible burden and it would have changed your entire future, all because of one night of your life, and mine. I couldn't do that to you. I knew that you would want me to bring him home and you would want to get married and I just wasn't ready. It was my decision to make."

"Did you know he was living here?" he asked.

"Yes, I knew. My aunt and uncle adopted him legally, but I haven't seen him since I left him as a baby. I know seeing him is a shock, Evan. I didn't know that he looks just like you, but he's their son, legally. He's had a very good life, and he is well looked after. My aunt and uncle love him more than anything in the world," she said. "He will inherit all of this," she said gesturing with her hands.

"And your mother knows about this too?" asked Evan, thinking about the times he had eaten at Jackie's table, and she had never said anything.

"Yes, of course. It was her idea. My father had practically disowned me," she explained. "At the time it seemed like the right thing, the only thing to do, and I still believe it was."

"Roberta," he said with tears in his eyes. "How could you do that to me? We have a son, Roberta. I have a son," he said, slowly shaking his head in wonderment. "Cassie has a brother," he said softly, his eyes closed, tears streaming down his face.

CHAPTER 47

Back to the Work at Hand

THE ROAD TRIP to Nice was nothing like the first road trip the four friends had taken in their carefree college days. The mood in the car was somber and Steven was doing the driving this time. He had rented a Mercedes Sedan, a luxurious counterpoint to the little VW van from the first trip. Evan sat next to him in the front seat, and Roberta and Summer sat together in the back, lost in their own thoughts, looking out the windows at the row upon row of vineyards and fields of lavender, the pretty church steeples peeking out from the hills in quaint medieval villages, and reading the signs on the highway directing visitors to monolithic stone castles in the distance as they sped south toward Nice. No one spoke.

Saying goodbye to Claude had been excruciatingly painful for both Roberta and Evan, as they stood in the foyer of the ancient farmhouse, shaking hands with the polite and smiling little boy as if he were a stranger. Evan blinked back tears in silence for the first hour, and he too, stared out the window at the scenery, thinking about the life the boy had here, among the vineyards and ancient villages, seeing his son's face in his mind. He tried to make sense of it, tried to understand Roberta's thoughts as a young 22-year-old girl and what she must have been going through. He thought of the trip to Oregon and the night she conceived. She had told him that more than anything, she wanted to make a statement with her life, and do something important. He had loved her from the first day he met her and knew that he would have done anything to make her happy, to work things out and be the boy's father. How would her life have been different if she had told him they had a son, if they had married and lived as a family? She had made this decision on her own, without him, and he felt betrayed and angry, and toyed with the idea of grabbing the first flight out of Nice back to the States. He couldn't believe that she and Summer had kept this secret from him for eleven years.

Finally, Steven broke the ice.

"Roberta," he said looking at her in his rear view mirror. "What would be the chance we could get Jacques Cousteau to say a few words at our concert?"

"I don't know," said Roberta, breaking out of her silent reverie, wiping a tear from her cheek. "I can ask him. Have you set a date and time?"

"This coming Saturday," said Steven. "Once word got out that we were doing this concert, everybody's been callin' wanting to help out. We're gonna' have some incredible surprise guests working with us. It's gonna be an awesome show!"

"I'm sure if he's available he would be happy to do it," she said. "I can ask him."

"Good, he can just speak to the crowd. He's free to say whatever he wants," said Steven. "I was also thinkin' we could use some of Michel's photographs during the show as a backdrop, so people don't forget why they're there. We want to make sure we collect lots of money."

The mention of Michel brought back memories of her conversation with him last night. After her email to him explaining her decision to drop Purity Oil as a client and do some pro bono work with Cruise Corporation and the Oceanographic Institute, he had called her at midnight, and they had talked for over an hour. He was back to his charming self, giving her a good description of the work being done at the beachfront cleanup, and whispering words of encouragement and love into her ear through the telephone, but she had listened half-heartedly, and said goodbye, feigning fatigue, and cried into her pillow. All she had been able to think about while he whispered in her ear was Evan and Claude, and the girl she had been, the time that had been lost and the choices she had made.

The Mercedes inched its way through the crowded streets of Nice to the exclusive Cote d'Azur beachfront boulevard, Avenue des Anglais, finally arriving at their beachfront hotel. Steven gave his keys to the valet at the hotel and the four of them hastily crossed the busy roadway and looked over the edge of the beach promenade. The acrid smell of crude oil hit them hard, making them gag and stinging their eyes, as they gazed in wonder at the beachside scene below. A beehive of activity stretched for miles in both directions and they struggled to take it all in. The French government had acted swiftly to take over the cleanup, and thousands of soldiers and volunteers worked together in a frenzy of organized chaos. Bulldozers marched up and down the beach, scooping up black gooey sand, and dumping it into gigantic construction skiffs or the hundreds of dump trucks lined up for miles waiting their turn. People in white biohazard suits cleaned rocks with power sprayers, and wildlife-washing stations under wide, open-air tents dotted the beachfront and parking lots. Out beyond the beach on the oil-slicked sea, boats bobbed on the waves, their crew pulling in and spreading out oil-capturing nets, and a huge Navy trawler and several research vessels headed further out to the site of the wreck.

"Let's get to work," said Roberta.

They made their way to a Red Cross tent and a sign above it that had the word VOLUNTEERS in several languages. As they approached the tent, Evan saw him first, and felt a sharp pang of jealousy, as Michel Manon ran to embrace Roberta in his arms, a loving smile on his ruggedly handsome face.

CHAPTER 48

The Birds Will Break Your Heart

"Roberta, *chérie!* I am so happy to see you!" he exclaimed, kissing her passionately on the lips. "I have missed you so much, *me belle chérie.*"

Roberta pulled away from Michel's passionate embrace, smiling with embarrassment at Evan. "Let me introduce you to everyone," she said. "This is Summer Sparrow, Evan Manning, and his brother Steven, whom you already know."

"Mademoiselle Summer, I have heard so much about you and your wonderful restaurants from Roberta. *Enchanté!*" he said, kissing her hand. "Steven, it is very good to see you again, thank you for coming to help," he said, clapping Steven on the back and shaking his hand. "And you are Evan?" he asked, sizing up the man he knew was his competition for Roberta's heart. "Roberta talks about you so often. It is nice to meet you finally," he said.

"So what can we do to help?" asked Roberta, breaking the awkwardness of the moment.

"I want to help wash the birds and animals," said Summer.

"Me, too," said Steven.

"*Bon!* Follow me," said Michel. He wrapped his arm around Roberta's waist and walked toward the nearest washing station. Evan fought down another pang of jealousy, and thought again about going back home.

Michel stopped abruptly and turned around to face everyone. "I have an idea," he said. "Would you allow me to get a picture of you, Steven, and you Summer, washing the birds to run in the paper?" asked Michel. "It would help to show such a big name rock star and celebrity restaurateur helping out."

"I have no objection," said Steven.

"I think that's a great idea," said Summer.

As they walked, Steven moved up next to Michel to talk about the benefit concert, and Roberta dropped back to walk with Evan and Summer. She still felt so awkward next to Evan, and missed the warmth and camaraderie they had always enjoyed. She had relied on him for advice and counsel for many years, and she felt such guilt and confusion about her decision to give up her baby. *Our baby,* she thought. She wanted so badly to reach out and take his hand, to say something to him, to apologize for hurting him, but all she could do was walk silently by his side.

They arrived at the tent where the birds were being washed and Roberta's heart instantly broke. There were so many oil-soaked birds waiting for attention, sitting in cages and draped in towels to keep them calm, their beaks taped to prevent them from preening. The volunteers struggled with the birds, which were frightened and stressed from their ordeal, and they flapped and struggled against their handlers while ornithological experts from various organizations instructed the volunteers on how to wash the birds. A line of plastic tubs had been set up on tables, where the birds were washed with soapy water, and then handed over, towel draped, to be caged again, and finally picked up by rescue organizations for transport to a facility where they would be cared for until they could be released.

"Justine," shouted Michel, motioning to someone. *"Viens ici,* Justine."

An attractive young woman in a leather jacket and tight jeans came up to them. She had short bleach blonde hair and multiple piercings on her ears. She kissed Michel on both cheeks in the French way and Roberta watched their interaction with interest.

"Justine, I would like you to meet some friends who are here to help. This is Steven Manning from the band A Higher Calling," he said, as Justine shook Steven's hand with a look of admiration on her face. "And this is Summer Sparrow, a famous restaurateur from California. And this is Steven's brother Evan, and Roberta Reed, the woman I told you about."

Justine shook hands all around, and paused when she got to Roberta. "You are Roberta," she said with a hint of contempt in her voice. "You have the firm that represents Purity Oil."

"Well," said Roberta defensively," not any more."

"Ah," said Justine, still eying Roberta suspiciously.

"Roberta has dropped Purity Oil as a client," said Michel proudly to Justine. "*Écoutes* Justine. I am going to take a picture of them in the bird-washing tent to run in your next article. Having Steven Manning and Summer in a photo will be a boon to the cause, *n'est-ce-pas?* And Steven's band is hosting a benefit concert this weekend, we can promote it too."

"*Bien sûr,*" said Justine, still eying Roberta suspiciously.

CHAPTER 49

Celebrities Do Their Part

La Voix de France

One Week After Spill, France, Italy and Spain Impose Strict Tanker Inspections; Celebrities Volunteer Time and Money To Environmental Cause

By Justine Chuchote

NICE, FRANCE, JULY 7, 1996 – In the wake of the accident at sea one week ago between the oil tanker Ileana Star and the cruise liner Heavenly Seas, France has led a coalition of Mediterranean countries to impose thorough inspections on tankers deemed to be dangerous to their territorial waters and coastline.

The three nations agreed today that single-hulled tankers carrying potentially dangerous cargo, whether oil, tar or chemicals, through waters controlled by each country, would be subject to tough inspections.

Under the new rules, tankers traveling through territorial economic zones of each country, which stretch 200 miles out to sea, will have to provide information about their cargo, destination, ownership, and registration to authorities. The new rules also give authorities the right to conduct spot inspections of ships far beyond the usual 12-mile limit allowed under international law.

Celebrity volunteers have been among the thousands who have descended on Nice, eager to add their considerable influence to the push for tougher environmental laws in the wake of this disaster. Steven Manning, the lead singer for the band, A Higher Calling, was on site yesterday to help with bird washing and transport. "It's important that we all pitch in, and do whatever we can to help," said Mr. Manning. He and his band have organized a concert to take place this weekend to benefit the fishermen who have lost their livelihood due to the oil spill. Commercial fishing and tourism in the region represent nearly 30,000 jobs and bring in about $1.5 billion a year. The loss of livelihood for many is expected to last for years.

There has been no further word from Charles Conway, the CEO of Purity Oil, or his partners, RUSoil, about the spill. Neither firm has responded to requests for interviews. Roberta Reed of Reed Public Relations, whose environmental public relations firm in the United States has represented Purity Oil for more than thirty years, has publicly severed ties with her former client, and has offered the services of her firm to Cruise Corporation in a joint effort to promote environmentally friendly energy alternatives.

The French government is sending down a submarine to inspect the damage to the tanker, and measure how much oil continues to spill from its hull. Estimates have varied from as little as 2 million gallons to as much as ten times that amount. Marine salvage companies have speculated that the 25-year-old tanker suffered from metal fatigue, allowing the cruise liners bow to break through the hull of the tanker and split it apart. "Had the tanker been free of rust and it's hull properly maintained, it's possible that the extent of the spill could have been averted," said one. "But the only real solution is requiring all tanker carriers to use compartmentalized double hull construction. There may not have been any oil spilled if the tanker had been double hulled."

CHAPTER 50

A Plea To The People of The World

THE BIG CONCERT was about to begin and Roberta, Evan and Summer waited in the front row for the first act to take the stage. Michel was off taking photographs, and Justine was interviewing the performers. The four days leading up to the night of the concert were very busy for Roberta and Evan. They had met with the team from Cruise Corporation in Monaco at the Oceanographic Institute where they sketched out the plans for the counter-assault.

David Reed and Charles Conway had both received their letters. David had called Arthur, his father, and Stan Morris ranting about how everything had been misconstrued, pleading for another chance, and then angrily threatening a lawsuit. Arthur suggested a vacation, his father Patrick said he had warned him before not to take Roberta lightly, and Stan Morris counseled that he didn't have a case for a suit, and that they were prepared to depose Charles Conway and Oliver Skeets if they needed. He quickly hired himself a lawyer who negotiated a better separation deal. He flew back to Washington depressed and angry, and took a long vacation in Florida to play golf with a shady real estate developer.

Charles Conway had called Roberta while she was washing birds the first day she arrived in Nice. She politely scolded him for his shortsightedness, and urged him to come down to help with the clean up, to show that he did indeed care. He repeated the same argument that he had used in her Paris office, bolstered by advice from his legal counsel that getting involved would be tantamount to admitting guilt. Roberta made it clear that she definitely did not see it that way at all, and argued forcefully that showing he cared would humanize him and Purity Oil to the public, and could be the first step to creating a new persona for his company that could change the face of his industry. "Not in my lifetime," he had answered emphatically, and they agreed to part on amicable terms. She hung up the call with him still feeling that, despite her best arguments, she had failed, and the feeling haunted her for several days.

The two opening acts, local bands that were only too happy to open for A Higher Calling, finished their sets and left the stage. The arena went completely black for several seconds, and the opening chords of *Summer* on an acoustic guitar filled the space. As the crowd roared with approval, a single spot shown down on Steven, sitting on a stool, guitar in hand, playing and singing solo through the first verse. The crowd of concertgoers sang along with him, and Summer took hold of Roberta's hand and then Evan's who were standing on either side of her, and they sang along, tears welling in their eyes, the memories of their trip to Oregon flooding back, and the feelings they had had then as young, idealistic college students with their whole lives ahead of them. They thought of Steven, his dimpled grin and shaggy hair, sitting in the back seat of the van, strumming out tunes on his ever-present guitar. They thought of the night by the campfire when he first sang this song to them, and they had laughed when he included the line about paella. And Roberta thought about Claude, and the spark of life that she and Evan had created that night with the people she now loved most in the world right there with her.

As Steven began the second verse, the lights came up on the stage and revealed the rest of the band, and they joined in, the signature intro on the drums that had been on the hit version of the song, leading to the chords from the electric guitar taking over for the acoustic guitar. The crowd went wild, clapping and singing at the top of their lungs until the song ended.

"Thank you!" said Steven. "Thank you everybody and welcome to the show!" He waited for the applause to die down a bit and then continued.

"Thank you for coming out tonight to help with this incredibly important and worthy cause. As most of you know, my band mates and I have dedicated our lives to environmental causes, and we are here to help the commercial fishermen whose livelihoods have been devastated by this disaster, and to bring to light our fight for better environmental protections and stricter penalties for companies that pollute our planet. So we hope you'll give to the cause and give generously! And volunteer to help clean up the beach and the birds."

The crowd cheered and clapped, and he went on.

"When word got out that we were planning this benefit concert, so many friends called to ask if they could join us and do their part to help out, and I welcomed them all! So you are in for an awesome show tonight! The first one to call me was my good friend and someone all of you know, Johnny Hallyday!"

Johnny Hallyday, the French rock superstar, clad in his signature black leather vest and skin-tight black leather pants, guitar in hand, launched into *Fool for the Blues*, with A Higher Calling playing the bluesy number as back up for Johnny, and he and Steven going head-to-head in dueling guitar solos. Johnny left the stage, waving to the crowd with his guitar above his head, and the stage went black again. After several seconds, a spot came down in the center of the stage and legendary blues guitarist B. B. King, sitting in a chair with his beloved guitar, Lucille, on his lap, began picking out the first chords of his famous song *When Love Came to Town,* his gravelly voice reaching out over the crowd like low rumbling thunder. The lights on the stage came back on, and Johnny Hallyday and Steven were back on the stage, playing opposite B. B. to finish out the song.

The band took a break, and Jacques Cousteau came out to the microphone to address the crowd, as photos of his long life in the sea and pictures of Earth from space flashed across huge screens around the arena.

"Thank you, thank you very much," he said to huge applause. "For those who do not already know me, I am Jacques Cousteau," he said smiling humbly, and they gave him a standing ovation. He bowed and waited for them to finish.

"As you know, I have dedicated my life to educating people about the beauty and delicate balance of this blue planet. I have even lost a son to the cause that I have dedicated my life to. The destruction of the planet's living systems continues to grow unchecked and unabated, and it is imperative that we recognize the peril of destruction of our own making that we face. If we humans, all of us that gather here today with our technology and our sophistication, we humans that inhabit the Earth across every continent, put our minds and our hearts together we could achieve wonders so far unheard of in the pursuit of clean, planet-friendly living, but instead what do we do? We wage wars, we destroy habitat, and we spill toxic oil in our seas and on the land, and we shrug our shoulders as if to say that we are powerless to do anything. We see the destruction before our eyes and yet we do nothing. It is one thing, perhaps a forgivable thing, to destroy our planet out of ignorance, but for humans to have achieved the consciousness to understand the delicate balance of the world we live in, and to continue to destroy that balance nonetheless, even at the cost of our own species, is the ultimate hubris of our existence. We alone as a species have the power to see this paradise in its' entirety from space, we alone have developed the power to destroy paradise, and we alone have the power to understand the consequences of that destruction. It is for this reason that I implore all of you to go back to your countries, become educated, become involved, and act with your money, with your work, and with your *votes*, to change this deadly course on which we are headed. Work for this as if your lives depended on it, because they do! Thank you!"

The crowd stood up in one simultaneous jump, clapping for the man who has inspired so many to take up the cause of the Earth. Though he walked with less spring in his step, his fervor had never waned. He waved and smiled one last time, throwing kisses to the crowd, and then walked off the stage.

Steven and the band came back out and sang two more sets. He introduced producer and composer Michel Legrand who took over at piano and accompanied Nana Mouskouri on his composition of *The Windmills of Your Mind,* and then another with Dusty Springfield and Steven on *Son of a Preacher Man.* All the guests and friends came on stage with A Higher Calling at the end for the big finale, *Whale Song.*

"Thank you all for coming tonight, and we'll see you on the beach again tomorrow!" shouted Steven into his microphone above the cheering of the crowd.

The line up of stars on the stage held hands and took a bow, then waved to the crowd as they walked off the stage together.

Roberta, Summer and Evan went backstage to meet up with Steven, and Michel and Justine.

"I will come to your hotel room as soon as Justine and I download my photos and finish up with her article for the newspaper," Michel said to Roberta, while walking away with Justine by his side. "Okay, *chérie?*"

Roberta regarded him, her face a mix of emotions. "Okay," she said quietly. "That will be fine."

CHAPTER 51

The End Is Also The Beginning

ROBERTA WENT BACK to the hotel with Evan, Summer and Steven, her mood serious, her mind full of doubts. She excused herself from an invitation for a nightcap in the hotel bar with her friends, and left them in the lobby. She had a lot of thinking to do.

Roberta had called her mother in tears from her aunt and uncle's home, after the emotional revelation with Evan and Claude. Her mother had offered both sympathy and good advice, telling her that Evan would come around, and his anger at her would eventually fade. "He's a good man," she told him. "He has a good heart."

The week of events since she had arrived in France had been life changing for Roberta. She had been forced to face her limitations with Charles Conway, and had had to turn to Evan to help her. During everything that unfolded he had been supportive and levelheaded, contrary to the over the top and impassioned words and messages that Michel had used to make his case. She did have much to thank him for. He had introduced her to Jacques Cousteau, and had helped her to expand her footprint to a new market, but when she needed him most, he had turned against her. He had never truly believed in her vision for her company. *Her* company, she thought with a slight smile. Yes, she had removed her father's stamp on it. It was now and would forever be, *her* company.

A knock on the door interrupted her thoughts, and she sat for a second, steeling her nerve to answer it. A second knock, and she stood up and walked slowly to open it.

"Ah, *chérie*, were you sleeping?" Michel asked moving toward her, his arms outstretched for an embrace. She was still dressed in jeans and a t-shirt from the concert, and said nothing. She moved out of the way and allowed him to enter.

"Sit down," she said. "We need to talk."

Michel sat down, his eyes wide and his heart anticipating bad news.

"I have been doing a good deal of thinking in the past twenty four hours and I've come to the conclusion that I cannot sustain a long distance relationship," she said.

"Oh, Roberta, I feel the same way too, darling," said Michel, his face bright with renewed hope. "I was hoping to convince you to live here in France with me. I think that is the best solution."

"No, Michel. That's not what I mean. I'm going back home, and I am ending our relationship," she said matter-of-factly. "This past week has taught me so much about so many things, and one of those things is that I cannot continue our relationship."

"But why, Roberta?" asked Michel.

"There are a lot of reasons, Michel," she answered. She could have listed them for him; that he had turned against her when she needed his support, that he was too much like her father and she knew she would grow to hate him for that, that she and Evan had met their son and she had witnessed true dignity and grace, that she felt time slipping away, and she could not imagine herself married to Michel, and raising a family, and she knew now that she wanted a family more than ever. But she didn't say any of that, because she was tired, and did not want to hurt his feelings, or get into a long, drawn out argument. "The most important reason is that I cannot sustain a long distance relationship. My business is in Washington, D.C. and I will not move to France."

She watched his face intently, waiting for his reaction. He didn't say anything for a long moment.

"I'm sorry," she said. "My mind is made up."

Michel sat very still for a moment, the hurt and rejection he felt visible on his face. "I am sorry, too, *chérie*." He took a deep breath and reached out to caress her face. She closed her eyes, expecting the familiar tingle that his touch had elicited so many times, but to her surprise and relief, she felt nothing. She took his hand in hers, and squeezed it warmly and with deep affection.

"We will still be friends," she reassured him. "I will be back to continue my work with Cousteau."

She walked him to the door and he hugged her tightly, and then kissed her cheeks in the French way. She watched him walk down the hallway to the elevator and out of her life. She sighed deeply, and then walked across the hall and knocked on the door.

Evan opened it and she fell into him, encircling her arms around his neck, leaning into his body with hers. He folded his arms around her, lightly at first, and then held her tightly as if he would never let go. They stood thus embraced, their eyes closed, wrapped in a lifelong love that could not be broken, knowing they were safe in each other's arms, finally exhaling in long held hope and comfort.

"Let's go home," Roberta said into his ear, and then stepped back to look into his face. "Let's go home and get Cassie, and build a life together."

CHAPTER 52

No One Is Ever To Blame

La Voix de France

Court Finds Nobody Responsible for 1996 Ileana Star Tanker Accident

By Justine Chuchote

NICE, FRANCE, NOV 13, 2006 – Ten years after a horrific accident at sea here that led to one of the most disastrous oil spills in European history, a French court has absolved the defendants of any criminal responsibility.

The court's ruling came 18 months after the trial began amid accusations by citizens, who were first on the scene as clean up began, and whose livelihoods and way of life have been altered for more than a decade, that the trial was fixed, charging that the judge in the case deliberately delayed court proceedings to benefit the defendants.

The judge presiding in the case, Jean-Louis Cunard, concluded that nobody could be held responsible for the environmental damage caused by the spill because the accident was due to the "deficient state of maintenance and conservation" of the tanker. Mr. Cunard was a low-level politician in Paris at the time of the spill, and became a judge five years ago, after leaving a successful career in arbitrage.

Prosecutors had sought prison terms for two officers with RUSoil, and had attempted to link RUSoil to the now defunct tanker owner company, a

Liberian registered Russian company that had declared bankruptcy in 1997, a mere six months after the spill occurred. During the trial, prosecutors had called the complicated ownership scheme a deliberate scam to hide the true ownership of the tanker.

Prosecutors had also demanded financial compensation from RUSoil and the ship's insurers to cover the environmental costs of the spill which had eventually climbed to as much as $350 million, approximately €450 million, as a result of the environmental costs to France, Spain and Italy, where the oil eventually made its way, but the court ruled that no such financial compensation was due because prosecutors did not make their case that RUSoil was in fact, the owner of the tanker. The ship's insurer, Ipswich Insurance, is demanding that it be reimbursed for the €25 million it posted as bail in the case, leaving taxpayers footing the bill for the cost of the clean up.

Theo Koukolous, a lawmaker from France's Green party, told reporters that the verdict would be remembered as a "black day for justice" and described the ruling as a "scandal."

Finale

TENZIN WANCHUK BENT down with some difficulty next to the stream by the little hut, and filled his kettle, the water flowing over worn and gnarled knuckles.

"Water flows over these hands. May I use them skillfully to preserve our precious planet," he said aloud.

He carried the kettle inside the hut, and placed it atop the stove to heat for his tea. He removed the cup, teapot, and the tin of tea, the tin of yak butter, and the bamboo whisk from his leather satchel in preparation.

He pried the lid from the tin of tea with bent and crippled fingers, and pinched some of the dried leaves and put them into the copper teapot. He replaced the lid on the tin of tea and then poured the boiling water from the kettle into the teapot. He opened the tin of yak butter, and scooped a chunk of the thick salty butter with his knife into his cup, and poured the tea over it. He picked up the whisk, and rolled the bamboo stem briskly between his hands, whisking the hot buttered tea to a frothy consistency. He performed each movement with deliberateness, delighting in his heart at each step of the process.

He stepped outside and found his way to an ancient tree stump and sat down, ignoring the momentary pain in his old bones and creaky joints. He drank his tea slowly, savoring each sip, watching his yaks grazing on the alpine meadows. He focused his mind on the sounds carried on the wind and gave a prayer of thanks that he could still hear the joyful tinkle of the yaks bells, the melody from the songs of many birds, the incessant buzz of hundreds of bees, the song of the wind in the trees, and the crashing river in the canyon below rushing over the rocks and carrying life along on its path. *I am present at this moment, in this place of life and earthly beauty. This moment is the axis on which the Earth revolves.*

He contemplated the river below, and the teaching of the Buddha, who says that the dedication of a virtuous act is like adding a drop of water to the ocean. As long as the ocean exists the drop of water exists. He sends out waves of love to the world beyond his mountains, and drinks his tea slowly, living only in this moment, the only moment he will ever need.

The Last Word

Dear Reader:

I presume since you have come to the end of the story that you may be asking yourself, "What progress have we made since 1996, when Roberta's story ends?" It is safe to say, as is the case with most of human progress, it is still two steps forward and one step back, and in some cases, more steps back than forward.

We have made *considerable* progress, due in large measure to a savvier consumer, more industries dedicated to green products and manufacturing, and some innovations that have been spurred by higher goals and stricter laws set by governments. As an example of One Step Forward, Roberta's admonition to the lumber companies in 1984 to begin to practice sustainable development was considered outrageous at the time, yet by 1994, when she and Evan take over her father's PR business, sustainable development was considered both achievable and necessary, mainly from pressure by environmental groups and the public. For an example of Two Steps Back, we need only look at the horrendous man-made environmental disaster of BP's Deepwater Horizon blowout in the Gulf of Mexico in April of 2010, the largest marine oil spill in history. It is estimated that 210 million gallons of oil spilled, and there were indications that the well site was still leaking into the Gulf of Mexico two years later. The greatest tragedy is that the human cost in lives lost and the environmental damage it caused was preventable, and the cost to the environment is still being assessed even now, in 2016, at the time of the writing of this book. Our achievements are continually challenged and threatened. As we see time and again, the rolling back of government regulations to protect the environment are at the core of many political campaigns, and threatens the hard-won progress we've made.

The story of oil's grip on our world is most horrifying when viewed by the geo-political nightmares it causes. Our continuing support, as both individuals and governments, of traditional 19th century energy sources has devastating effects on the planet, on our economies, and on our collective souls. Whether you believe in global warming or not, there can be no doubt that the control these multinational mega-companies have had over our lives with this product has been devastating; the boom and bust economies, bloody wars, stifling of innovation, and social inequality that it creates have wreaked havoc financially, ecologically, and morally. It is almost incomprehensible that the oil-giant Saudi Aramco, when it goes public in 2016, will be valued at $2 trillion! And that's one country creating one company, even with the collapse of the price of oil. To that figure, the largest oil and gas companies in Russia, Brazil, China and the US will add an additional $4 trillion! And these companies continue to lobby for government subsidies and special tax breaks? Who are we kidding?

The precipitous drop in the price of oil since 2014 has roiled economies in oil-producing countries across the world, and they are now coming to the conclusion that they must rethink their futures and broaden their economies into other areas of economic growth. This price collapse has shifted the balance of power. No longer a cartel, the oil-producing countries have turned against each other, and we are witnessing a seismic change in the concentration of power, similar to the end of the Cold War and the fall of the Soviet Union. We *must* keep up the pressure, until we see that our future is based on a much greater mix of clean, alternative fuel sources. The tyranny that petroleum companies and oil-rich nation-states wielded is over. Good riddance to its Fascist, boot in the face strangulation of good ideas, of lies, of choking our air and water, of corrupt governments (including our own) with alternative agendas, and of wars waged to keep it at the top of the list of energy choices we were allowed to have. Good riddance! Good riddance, forever!

What are the alternatives to gasoline powered automobiles? For those unable to walk or ride a bike, and the majority of mainstream buyers who are not on the fringe of the bio-fuels movement, all electric is the only option, and electric vehicles carry their own set of issues – driving range and pollution caused by coal burning power plants, but it is the trade off we make at the moment to break oil's grip on world economies. We must be vigilant in assuring that coal does not become the new oil, and that the U.S. government and other governments support wide-ranging, clean-energy choices within the power supply grid, and that basic research in clean-energy technology continues to have funding. The vision of the future that Roberta described of an earth populated with humans who care deeply for their planet and use their massive human brains to devise ideas and create technologies to live the life we all long for, whisked hither and yon in quiet, comfortable, clean transports powered by clean energy sources that leave no lasting damage, can be achieved! As my simple and wise Buddhist monk says, a virtuous act is like adding a drop of water to the ocean. As long as the ocean exists the drop of water exists. The more drops of virtue we add, the more virtuous we all become. It is only through the action of conscientious people and their governments that environmental firsts (like double hulled tankers) are forced into law. Does the pendulum sometimes swing too far? Yes, it probably does at times, but I for one, would rather err on the side of caution, and put reverence for our planet's fellow inhabitants first. Having a light footprint and a reverent heart must be in every thought and every move we make.

The chat room conversation that Michel witnesses at the birth of The Edenists is a much-needed, past-due examination of how science, religion and business have exploited the long-held idea that man is at the top of the scala naturae, the hierarchical pyramid of social order in the animal kingdom. I reject that thinking as innately flawed for the very reason that it has allowed humans to look upon the Earth and it's fellow creatures as unworthy of our respect and protection, and I prefer to see humans as stewards, the hands that protectively hold the world within. In that chat are scientists, theologians, philosophers, activists, dystopian futurists and progressive thinkers who argue the finer points of how to become reverent of nature in a western world plagued by excess and unattached to the land and the animals that feed us and share the planet. Annran's idea of an empaneled world body of ethicists and theologians to help guide the Earth's nations and its peoples, and enforce punishments for acts of immorality, is the wish for a man-created alternative to the God of old who sees all and punishes the wicked. In the end we must find the god within, and use our own actions to further the cause of compassionate consumerism, and do it every day. What I am calling for in The Outcasts of Eden is a new viewpoint embraced by each individual human being, in which honesty, integrity and reverence for the Earth, rather than selfish gain, are our guiding principles. More Mahatma Ghandi; less Ayn Rand.

Tenzin Wangchuk, the loving monk in the mountains of the Himalayas, is my favorite character. In the Tibetan language, Tenzin means 'Holder of teachings' and Wangchuk means 'mighty'. Tenzin is the mighty teacher, and his thought-prayers and simple way of life as he walks the Earth convey the counterpoint to our fast-paced, mindless existence here in La-La Land, and he is interspersed into the story purposely, and I hope jarringly, to remind the reader that others are already living a life of reverent mindfulness and we can choose a different path, a different way of being, even in western developed countries like the US and in Europe. Just get out of your car and walk, feel your feet touch the grass, and say a prayer for the fact of it.

My final thought to you is simple: I hope you liked the story, and it caused you to think, to pause and to challenge yourself and your perceptions. I welcome your feedback, and hope you will let me know how you feel. Please, do connect with me on my Outcasts of Eden Facebook page, and let others know your thoughts and comments on Amazon. Spread the word.

Sincerely yours in hope,
D J Presson
May 2016

Appendix

Environmental Disasters of Note

Tanker and Oil Well Spills

Dec 1907 - *Thomas W. Lawson*; Est. spill: 2,279,200 gallons in the UK - 7-masted sailing schooner, sank in storm-tossed seas off the Isles of Scilly.

March 1937 – collision between *SS Frank Buck and SS President Coolidge*; Est. spill: 2,731,960 gallons in San Francisco Bay, California.

Dec 1958 – *African Queen*; Est. spill: 6,468,000 gallons in Ocean City, Maryland.

March 1967 – *SS Torrey Canyon*; Est. spill 36,652,000 gallons off coast of Cornwall, England - SS Torrey Canyon, built by Newport News Shipbuilding in 1959 with a 60,000-ton max was later refitted in Japan to a Suezmax Class tanker, capable of carrying 120,000 tonnes of crude. Shipwrecked off the western coast of Cornwall, affecting both the English and French coast, it was the first major supertanker disaster. More than 15,000 seabirds were killed, along with millions of marine organisms. Damage was also caused by the solvent-emulsifiers used to clean up the spill.

1967 – *R. C. Stoner*; Est. spill 6,160,000 gallons in the Pacific Ocean near Wake Island.

1968 – *Ocean Eagle*; Est. spill: 3,696,000 gallons in Puerto Rico.

January 1969 – *Santa Barbara, California*; Est. spill: 2,312,000 gallons spilled into the ocean for 11 straight days. The destruction and pollution of the California coastline leads to reforms in the energy industry.

February 1970 – *SS Arrow*; Est. spill: 3,181,640 gallons in Chedabucto Bay, Nova Scotia.

March 1970 – *Othello*; Est. spill: 18,480,000 gallons in Trälhavet Bay, Sweden.

February 1971 – *SS Wafra*; Est. spill: 8,316,000 – 12,320,000 gallons in Cape Agulhas, South Africa - SS Wafra ran aground while under tow near Cape Agulhas. The ship foundered when the piping that brought seawater on board to cool the engines failed, and the engine room flooded, incapacitating the ship. While being towed, the tow cable broke and the ship was grounded, rupturing all six of the port cargo tanks and two of the six center tanks, leaking roughly 26,000 tons of oil, affecting a colony of African penguins on Dyer Island. The larger part of the ship was refloated and towed out to sea, where it was sunk by the South African Air Force to prevent further contamination of the coastline.

1972 to 1992 – *ChevronTexaco Amazon oil spill;* Est. spill: 52,668,000 gallons into the Ecuadorian Amazon rain forest. In 1993 a number of Indian tribes from the Ecuadorian Amazon filed a lawsuit against Texaco for ruining their rivers and land, causing widespread devastation to the rainforest environment, and creating a dramatically increased risk of cancer for tens of thousands of people. The lawsuit states that Texaco dumped millions of gallons of waste oil products into the pristine rainforest river environment rather than re-inject it back into the well, which is the industry practice in other parts of the world. Water and soil samples taken in the rainforest by toxicologists indicate life-threatening levels of benzene, toluene, xylenes, and highly carcinogenic polycyclic aromatic hydrocarbons. Texaco extracted oil from the Ecuadorian

Amazon from 1972 to 1992 at the rate of 220,000 to 250,000 barrels per day. An estimated 18.5 billion gallons of toxic wastewater products were dumped into the river system or left in open, unlined pits during this time. In June of 1992 Texaco withdrew from Ecuador, leaving many areas still in need of cleanup, and local peoples have still not been compensated. In some villages near polluted water sources, the rate of cancer is 1,000 times higher than the historical norm for the area, and hundreds of open-air toxic waste pits still remain in the jungle.

August 1972 – collision between the *Oswego-Guardian and the Texanita*; Est. spill: 3,080,000 gallons in Stilbaai, South Africa.

December 1972 – *Jawachta*; Est. spill: 4,928,000 gallons in Smygehuk, Sweden.

August 1974 – VLCC (Very Large Crude Carrier) *Metula;* Est. spill: 14,476,000 gallons in Magellan Strait, Chile. With a length of 1,067 feet and draft of 62 feet, Metula was the first VLCC supertanker involved in an accident. As the tanker was passing through the First Narrows area of the Strait of Magellan, an area over three and a half kilometers wide, the ship cut a corner too sharply and hit a 40-foot shoal and became grounded. On the following day, the Metula swung to starboard, puncturing a hole and flooding its engine compartments. Because of the remoteness of the area, no clean up was attempted. Some shorelines formed hard asphalt pavements and a marshland suffered thick deposits of mousse, which were still visible two decades later.

January 1975 – *Jacob Maersk*; Est. spill: 27,104,000 gallons in Oporto, Portugal – The Jacob Maersk struck a sand bar while entering the port of Lexioes, Portugal. The ship exploded and burned for two days, sending plumes of toxic fumes to the sky and consuming nearly half of the oil onboard before sinking.

January 1975 – *Corinthos*; Est. spill: 11,088,000 gallons in Delaware River, Pennsylvania.

December 1976 – *Argo Merchant*; Est. spill: 7,700,000 gallons in Nantucket, Massachusetts.

February 1978 – *Amoco Cadiz*; Est. spill: 69,916,000 gallons off the coast of Brittany, France. The Amoco Cadiz ran aground following a steering failure. The ship broke apart in heavy seas with no recovery of its cargo attempted, spilling its entire 229,000 tons of crude into the ocean. Millions of dead mollusks, sea urchins and other species came ashore from Brest to Saint Brieuc, and 20,000 dead birds were recorded.

January 1979 –*Betelgeuse;* Est. spill: 12,320,000 gallons into Bantry Bay, Ireland.

July 1979 – collision between *SS Atlantic Empress and the Aegean Captain*; Est. spill: 88,396,000 gallons off Trinidad and Tobago. On July 19, 1979, the Atlantic Empress, a fully laden Greek supertanker collided with the Aegean Captain, another fully laden Greek supertanker, in heavy rain and thick fog off the island of Tobago. The ships did not sight each other until they were within 600 yards. Although the Aegean Captain attempted to change course, it was too late to avoid a collision and the two ships crashed with the Empress tearing a hole in the Captain's starboard bow. Large fires took over each ship, and were soon out of control, and the crew abandoned ship. Firefighters from Trinidad and Tobago Coast Guard were able to put the fires out on the Captain, and her crew brought her into Curacao, where her crude cargo was off-loaded. A week after the collision, however, the fire on the Empress was still burning and she was listing heavily, causing an explosion, and increasing the flow of oil into the sea. The ship exploded again the following day, increasing the flow rate to 7,000 – 15,000 gallons an hour. The Empress finally sank on August 3, having spilled 287,000 metric tonnes of crude into the sea.

August 1983 – *Castillo de Beliver*; Est. spill: 77,616,000 gallons. The Spanish tanker caught fire off Saldhana Bay, 70 miles northwest of Cape Town, South Africa. The tanker was traveling through an environmentally sensitive area known for its seabird rookeries and productive fisheries.

July 1984- M/V *Alvenus*; Est. spill: 2,750,440 in Cameron, Louisiana in the Calcasieu River Channel.

November 1988 – *Odyssey*; Est. spill: 40,656,000 gallons. The Odyssey tanker broke in two in heavy weather and caught fire before sinking. There were no survivors among the 27-man crew.

March 1989 – *Exxon Valdez*; Est. spill: 32,032,000 gallons. Exxon Valdez ran aground in Prince William Sound, Alaska on Easter Sunday, March 24, 1989 bound for Long Beach, California. The tanker struck Bligh Reef at midnight local time and spilled an estimated 32 million gallons of crude oil. The Valdez spill was the largest in US waters until the Deepwater Horizon well disaster in 2010. Because of Prince William Sound's remote location, disaster response was difficult and challenged response plans existing at the time. Oil from the spill affected over 1,200 miles of shoreline in Prince William Sound and as far west as Kodiak Island. World Wildlife Fund estimates the total number of animals killed by the spill: 250,000 seabirds, 2,800 sea otters, 300 harbor seals, 250 bald eagles, and 22 whales.

April 1991 – MT *Haven*; Est. spill: 44,352,000 gallons off the coast of Genoa, Italy in the Mediterranean Sea. The ship caught fire and exploded while anchored off the coast. The ship split into three parts in the explosions, one part sank straight away and the remaining two sank during towing. Much of the oil was burned at sea but the slick still covered an estimated 7.5 by 2.5 miles three days after the spill. In the end close to 70 miles of coastline were cleaned, even though booms had been rapidly deployed to protect beaches from the slick. A 43% reduction in fish populations was reported in some areas after the spill.

May 1991 - ABT *Summer;* Est. spill: 80,080,000 gallons 700 nautical miles offshore of Angola.

December 1992 – *Aegean Sea;* Est. spill: 22,792,000 gallons, the tanker ran aground off the coast of A Coruña, Spain due to extreme weather.

January 1993 - MV *Braer;* Est. spill: 26,180,000 gallons off the coast of England near the Shetland Islands.

February 1996 – *Sea Empress;* Est. spill: 22,176,000 gallons off the English coast in Pembrokeshire.

December 1999 – *Erika;* Est. spill: 7,700,000 gallons in the Bay of Biscay, France.

October 2002 – *Limburg (bombing);* Est. spill: 3,757,000 gallons in the Gulf of Aden, Yemen.

November 2002 – MV *Prestige;* Est. spill: 19,404,000 gallons in Galicia, Spain. After suffering hull damage in heavy seas the Prestige was towed, but denied entry, to port in both Spain and Portugal. Towed back into the Atlantic, the ship broke apart and sank in water two miles deep a week later. Oil first came ashore in Galicia, Spain, and then into the Bay of Biscay affecting the north Atlantic coast of France. Seabirds most affected by the spill were Guillemot, Razorbills and Puffins.

July 2003 – *Tasman Spirit;* Est. spill: 9,240,000 gallons into the Arabian Sea at Karachi, Pakistan.

August 2005 - *Hurricane Katrina;* Est. Spill into the Gulf of Mexico and Louisiana Coast: 7,113,876 gallons.

Industrial Oil Accidents

March 1910 – *Lakeview Gusher;* Est. spill: 378,840,000 gallons in Kern County, California, considered the largest accidental oil spill in history caused by an out of control eruption from a pressurized well, lasting 18 months.

1940's to 1970's – *Greenpoint, Brooklyn*; Est. spill: 29,999,200 gallons. Located around Newton Creek, between 17 and 30 million gallons of oil and petroleum leaked into the soil from crude oil processing over a period of several decades.

1950's to 1994 – *Guadalupe Oil Field*; Est. spill: 8,932,000 in Guadalupe, California.

1950's to 1996 – *Avila Beach Pipeline*; Est. spill: 404,400 gallons in Avila Beach, California.

1962 and 1963 – *Savage and Mankato, Minnesota*; Est. spill: 4,620,000 gallons into Mississippi and Minnesota Rivers.

1976 to present – *Niger Delta, Nigeria*; Est. spill: 101,024,000 gallons. The Niger Delta covers nearly 20,000 kilometers of wetlands, and the floodplain makes up nearly 7.5% of Nigeria's total land mass. It is an incredibly lush ecosystem and contains one of the highest concentrations of biodiversity on the planet. In addition to supporting abundant flora and fauna, the area can sustain a wide variety of crops, lumber and agricultural trees, and has more species of fresh water fish than any ecosystem in West Africa. The lack of effective effort by the government to control environmental effects of the industry has resulted in the poisoning of the waters and destruction of vegetation and agricultural land by an estimated 1.89 million barrels of petroleum spilled into Niger Delta.

June 1979 to March 1980 – *Ixtoc I*; Est. spill: 147,840,000 gallons in the Bay of Campeche, Gulf of Mexico. The blowout of the Ixtoc I oil well caused the platform to catch fire. The platform collapsed and the well continued to leak nearly 30,000 barrels per day into the Gulf of Mexico until it was capped ten months later. Ocean currents carried the oil to the shores of Texas. A total of 162 miles of coastline were oiled, endangering coastal marshes, mangroves and beaches, including the only known remaining nesting sites for the criti-cally endangered Kemp's Ridley sea turtles.

February 1983 to May 1985 – *Nowruz Field Platform*; Est. spill: 80,080,000 gallons in the Persian Gulf. Iran's Norwuz oil field in the Persian Gulf was the site of several continuing spills. A tanker hit the platform in February of 1983 causing the first spill; in March of that same year, Iraqi helicopters at-tacked two platforms and the spill caught fire. One of the wells was capped in September costing the lives of eleven men, yet the other remained open until May 1985. Nine men were killed during that capping attempt.

January 1991 to May 1991 - *Gulf War Oil Spill;* Est. spill: 462,000,000 gal-lons. Vast amounts of oil were spilled into the Arabian Gulf when the Iraqi Army occupied Kuwait, destroying tankers, oil terminals and oil wells late in January 1991. The oil slick reached a maximum size of 100 miles X 40 miles and had devastating effects on coral, fish and shellfish in the Arabian Gulf. 30,000 seabirds were killed by exposure to oil, and 800 miles of coastline in Kuwait and Saudi Arabia were oiled. Nearly half the coral in the region suf-fered from the effects of the oil including choking and bleaching, and hun-dreds of square miles of seaweed beds were damaged. In addition to the toxic particulate-embedded smoke that rose into the atmosphere for months, black oily rain from the fallout of hundreds of oil wells set ablaze during the war nearly doubled the amount of oil spilled back into the Gulf.

January 1998 – *Mobil Nigeria;* Est. spill: 1,694,000 gallons.

June 2001 – *Shell Ogbodo, Nigeria;* Est. spill: 2,926,000 gallons.

June 2006 – *Citgo refinery, Lake Charles, Louisiana; Est. spill:* 2,002,000 gallons.

July 2006 – *Jiyeh power station, Lebanon;* Est. spill: 9,240,000 gallons.

December 2007 – *South Korea Oil Spill;* Est. spill: 3,326,000 gallons into the Yellow Sea.

April 2010 to July 2010 – *Deepwater Horizon;* Est. Spill: 215,600,00 gallons into the Gulf of Mexico. After an explosion rocked the oilrig on April 20, 2010 at 9:45 am, the rig burned for two days, finally sinking on April 22. 1,500 meters beneath the rig on the ocean floor, the wellhead had been damaged, and first estimates of the spill rate were 1,000 barrels per day. After underwater footage of the leaking oil were seen in May and June, those estimates were moved to 25,000 barrels per day, and later revised again to 60,000 barrels per day. This amount is equal to an Exxon Valdez disaster every four to seven days. Several attempts by BP to stop the Deepwater Horizon flow failed before it could finally be contained on July 15. (The Ixtoc I oil well in the southern Gulf of Mexico, which suffered a similar blowout in 1980, took nearly a full 10 months to be capped.) The oil slick spread quickly over the ocean surface, covering 580 square miles by April 25 and over 2,500 square miles by the beginning of May. Hundreds of miles of the Louisiana shoreline were contaminated, including several wildlife refuges important for sea turtles as well as hundreds of species of birds. Tar balls from the spill also reached beaches and islands in Mississippi, Alabama, Florida and Texas.

May 2010 – *ExxonMobil, Niger Delta, Nigeria;* Est. spill: 29,414,000 gallons.

July 2010 – *Xingang Port, China;* Est. spill: 27,720,000 gallons into the Yellow Sea.

July 2010 – *Kalamazoo River, Calhoun County, Michigan;* Est. spill: 1,001,000 gallons.

February 2012 – *Guarapiche River, Venezuela;* Est. spill: 12,628,000 gallons.

Chemical, Agricultural, Nuclear, and Mining

The Great Sparrow Campaign – The Four Pests Campaign was one of the first actions taken by Mao Zedong in the Great Leap Forward from 1958 to 1962 in China. The four pests decreed to be eliminated were rats, flies, mosquitoes and sparrows. While the first three of these targeted 'pests' were less damaging, the widespread extermination of the sparrow led to an ecological imbalance that enabled devastating damage to occur by crop-eating insects. The masses of Chinese citizens took the decree from Mao seriously, and mobilized to eradicate the birds by banging pots and pans or beating drums to scare the birds, preventing them from landing, forcing them to fly until they died from exhaustion. During the campaign sparrow nests were torn down, eggs were broken and nestlings were killed. With the rice yield significantly reduced by early 1960, Chinese officials realized that sparrows consumed a large quantity of insects, and ordered the campaign stopped against the sparrow, replacing them with bed bugs. It was too late however, and the near-extinction of the birds from China led to a massive increase in the locust population that swarmed the country. The counter measures used to combat the locusts led to widespread deforestation and misuse of pesticides. Poor weather and drought exacerbated the ecological imbalance, and resulted in the Great Chinese Famine, in which at least 20 million people died of starvation. In an attempt to rewrite history, a television drama that aired in 2009 in China blamed a peasant for coming up with the idea of killing the sparrows.

The Death of Bees – Colony Collapse Disorder is the name given to describe the recent phenomenon of decimating bee deaths. The disorder is largely attributed to the Varroa destructor, a mite seemingly resistant to attempts to control it. A government study has identified multiple factors affecting the honeybee population including pesticides, genetically modified food, viruses, and shrinking habitat. In 2016, a new population study conducted by the University of Maryland in a joint effort with the EPA and USDA found that 44% of the hive populations had died. This is in keeping with a trend of year-round increase in bee deaths of 3% – 4% each year since 2013, and has increased nearly 30% in a decade. A recent study at Royal Holloway University in England has also found that wild bumblebee populations are also declining. In an effort to control the mites believed to be contributing to the rapid decline in the bee populations, chemical companies have created insecticides to remedy the situation, however, unfortunately, none have been effective and may have actually hastened the decline. Studies found that the bees that ingested the insecticide remedies created to counter the mite caused the stomach wall of the bees to breakdown, making the bee more susceptible to spores and bacteria. Although scientists had repeatedly warned that these herbicides were dangerous to bees, the chemical industry trade groups lobbied congress and denied the claims. Another factor that may be contributing to the decline in the bee population is the use of high-fructose corn syrup as a substitute for actual honey to feed the bees kept in industrialized bee farms in Iowa and elsewhere. Large commercial honey factories harvest all of the honey to sell, and the bee is denied access to the natural nutritional enzyme effects of the honey they make. Lack of diversity in plant vegetation may also be a contributing factor, and the USDA has provided funding to cattle farmers to encourage them to plant alfalfa and clover fields for field rotation, instead of genetically modified corn or soybeans, to provide bees with a more healthy, varied habitat. They are hoping that subsequent studies where these crops are grown will show a lessening of bee colony deaths, but it is a race against time, as the Earth cannot sustain any plant life without the tiny pollinators. Buying local honey produced by home producers is one way to change the bee equation. Encourage local farmers to plant non-GMO crops, and support organic gardening at home and on local commercial farms by purchasing organically grown produce when possible.

The Dust Bowl – A failure to apply proper farming techniques coupled with a severe drought greatly damaged the ecology of the Canadian and US prairies, resulting in the Dust Bowl of the 1930's. Insufficient understanding of the ecology of the plains, and extensive deep plowing of virgin topsoil, displaced native grasses that trapped soil and moisture during periods of drought. Between 1934 and 1940 severe drought turned unanchored soil into dust. High winds, common on the prairies, blew the dust into the atmosphere in huge clouds that blackened the sky. These choking billows of dust, called 'black blizzards', traveled across the country reaching as far away as New York City and Washington, D.C. The drought and erosion affected 100,000,000 acres of land in Texas, Oklahoma, New Mexico, Colorado and Kansas.

Dirty Dairying – The term 'dirty dairying' refers to the contamination of water systems from intensive dairy farming practices and the unlawful release of cattle effluent into lakes, streams and rivers. The practice was highlighted in 2008 by the New Zealand government, and has resulted in high pollution levels in several lakes and rivers. New Zealand's Environment Court has collected fines from illegal farming practices in excess of $NZ3 million.

American Chestnut Blight – The American chestnut tree was accidently introduced to the Endothia parasite, a fungal infection, around 1904 from Japanese nursery stock. The fungus killed an estimated 4 billion American chestnut trees. The European Chestnut and the West Asian species of the tree are less susceptible to the fungus. The eastern United States, and especially, the area of the Appalachians, was hit hard by the economic impact that resulted. The wood was used in the region to produce posts, poles, pilings, railroad ties, split rail fences, and the straight grain of the wood was ideal for building log cabins, furniture and caskets. The fruit of the tree was a source of food, and a cash crop.

Dutch Elm Disease – Another introduction to the forests of North America and Europe, the Ascomycota fungi is spread by the elm bark beetle, and originates in Asia. The disease has devastated native populations of elm on two continents, and has also reached New Zealand. The name of the disease is somewhat of a misnomer, and is derived because it was identified in 1921 by Dutch phytopathologists.

Hemlock Woolly Adelgid Infestation – The wooly adelgid is a destructive pest introduced from Japan that threatens the existence of the eastern hemlock and Carolina hemlock. The pest lays egg sacs along the underside of branches and once hatched, sucks sap from the trees. The pest has spread throughout the eastern United States, having been found in eighteen states from Georgia to Massachusetts. Widespread mortality of hemlock trees has resulted in large swaths of dead trees being clearly visible in the mountain ranges of North Carolina and Tennessee.

Deforestation – Forests play a critical role in the cycle of atmospheric exchange of gases that allows our planet's delicate climate control mechanism to function. Tropical rainforest destruction to convert forests to cattle ranching and agriculture, and for exploitation of natural resources such as exotic woods, gold mining and oil is the primary reason. In 2015 and 2016, purposeful slash-and-burn deforestation in Southeast Asian countries resulted in thick, penetrating smoke that affected Brunei, Indonesia, Malaysia, Singapore, Thailand, Vietnam, Cambodia and the Philippines, displacing and killing native animals and traveling across oceans and continents. The reason for the deforestation in these ancient tropical wonderlands is to replace forests with agricultural products, chiefly cocoanut palms, to satisfy the recent craze for all things cocoanut. In addition to slash-and-burn deforestation practices, uncontrolled wildfires burn millions of acres of forestland each year, and in developing countries and the northern latitudes of North America, virgin forests are decimated. It is estimated that between 46 and 58 thousand square miles of forest are lost each year to deforestation. Seventy percent of the earth's land animals and plants live in forests, and certainly cannot all survive the deforestation of their homes. Deforestation deprives the forest floor of sun blocking tree cover, allowing soil to quickly dry out, destroying forest floor eco-systems. Trees also return water vapor back into the atmosphere, which contributes to the delicate balance of heat and moisture exchange that our planet depends on. Agriculture does NOT replace this vital role, and cuts the resulting CO_2, oxygen and water vapor exchange significantly. Additionally, the resulting loss of biodiversity, forest floor organic material, soil compaction and erosion, and the use of chemical pesticides and water supply contamination required for large agricultural enterprises that replace the forests present serious side effects. At this time, only 30% of the earth's land is still covered in forests.

Shark Finning – Shark finning increased in 1997 due to an increase in demand for shark fin soup, a delicacy in China and other Asian cultures, and the practice involves taking all of the fins off the shark, then dumping it overboard to suffocate on the bottom of the ocean. The trade in shark fins is largely unregulated, despite some nations that have banned it. Shark fins are among the most expensive seafood products, and it is estimated that from 26 to 73 million sharks are harvested annually for fins, resulting in a global trading value of over $1 billion.

Love Canal – A neighborhood in Niagara Falls, New York, Love Canal is the site of a toxic waste disposal dump that contaminated the area. Hooker Chemical

Company dumped 22,000 barrels of chemical waste, starting in the 1940's when the canal was drained and lined with clay. The site operated until 1953, when the canal was covered with soil, and vegetation grew over it. Hooker Chemical Company deeded the land to the Niagara Falls School Board for $1 with a limited liability clause against future damages due to contamination of the site. The school board developed the land, and the construction activity breached the containment structures that Hooker had built. The breaches, combined with heavy rainstorms, led to a public health emergency as the trapped chemicals seeped out. Love Canal was the first site on the EPA Superfund list.

Times Beach – A town in St. Louis County, Missouri, once home to two thousand people, completely evacuated in early 1983 due to dioxin contamination, and demolished in 1992. In 1971, Shenandoah Stables paid a waste oil businessman, Russell Martin Bliss, to spray for dust in their indoor arena. 2,000 gallons of waste oil was sprayed, and within a few days birds dropped dead from the rafters and horses fell sick, developing sores and losing their hair. The stable owners blamed Bliss, and removed six inches of topsoil and disposed of it in a landfill. Despite subsequent removal of an additional 12 inches of soil, their horses continued to become sick. Sixty-two horses died, or became emaciated and were euthanized. The stable's owners also became sick suffering from headaches, nosebleeds, abdominal pain and diarrhea. Bliss sprayed other stables in the area, and those owners too, when their horses became ill, removed the top layer of soil in their arenas, dumping it in a landfill. The town of Times Beach hired Bliss to spray twenty-three miles of dirt roads, and he and his employees sprayed 29 other sites across Missouri. The CDC became involved in 1971, and their tests revealed the presence of chemical contaminants including dioxin. The investigation that ensued revealed that the chemical manufacturer NEPACCO was the only company in Missouri that had come into contact with Bliss. The company ceased operations in 1972 when it was taken over by Syntex Agribusiness. In 1979 a former NEPACCO employee reported the burial of toxic waste on a farm outside of Verona, Missouri. NEPACCO had paid the owner of the farm $150 for the use of his land. A total of ninety leaky, corroded drums were found. Nearly ten years after the spraying, the dioxin levels persisted, and it was only because of an EPA document leaked by the Environmental Defense Fund that the residents of Times Beach took action. In

1983, EPA administrator Rita Lavelle was convicted of perjury before Congress, obstructing a federal investigation and submitting a false statement related to the EPA's handling of the Times Beach contamination. The US government paid $33 million to buy out the residential properties and businesses of Times Beach. In January 1984, the federal government sued Bliss, Syntex, and NEPACCO for six dioxin sites in Missouri, and in 1990, Times Beach became the location for a giant temporary incinerator to burn 265,000 tons of dioxin-contaminated materials from across the state, costing nearly $200 million.

Bhopal Disaster – In December of 1984, Union Carbide of India experienced a significant gas leak at their chemical plant in Bhopal, India that exposed more than 500,000 people to a lethal cloud of methyl isocyanate gas and other chemicals. Deaths directly related to the gas leak are estimated to have reached more than 30,000 people, and injuries are estimated at more than half a million.

AZF Factory explosion – In October 2001, three hundred tonnes of ammonium nitrate at a chemical fertilizer plant in Toulouse, France exploded with an equivalent blast of 20 – 40 tons of TNT. The blast measured 3.4 on the Richter scale, making a crater 23 feet deep and 131 feet in diameter. Steel girders from the explosion were found three kilometers away. The cause of the explosion is still unknown.

Mayak Nuclear Waste Explosion – In 1957 a storage tank near Chelyabinsk, Soviet Union exploded, exposing nearly 300,000 people to high radiation levels and killing more than 200. Over thirty small towns and cities were removed from maps of the area between 1958 and 1991.

Three Mile Island – A partial nuclear meltdown occurred in March 1979 at Three Mile Island Nuclear Generating Station in Dauphin County, Pennsylvania. The incident was rated 5 out of 7 on the International Nuclear Event Scale. The accident left the United States shaken and crystallized the anti-nuclear sentiment in the US, and contributed to the decline of new reactor construction.

Chernobyl – In 1986 the Chernobyl Nuclear Power Plant located near Pripyat, Ukraine suffered a catastrophic nuclear meltdown. The disaster killed more than 4,000 people and damage to property was estimated close to $7 billion. 350,000 people were forced to relocate from the threat of radioactive fallout.

Hanford Nuclear – In 1986 the U.S. government declassified 19,000 pages of documents that revealed that the Hanford Nuclear Site near Richland, Washington released thousands of gallons of radioactive liquids between 1946 and 1986. The radioactive waste flowed into the Columbia River.

Fukushima Daiichi Nuclear Disaster – In March 2011, following a major sea-based earthquake and resulting tsunami, the Fukushima Daiichi Nuclear Power Plant in Fukushima, Japan suffered multiple losses of its cooling systems, and a nuclear emergency was declared. It is the largest nuclear disaster since Chernobyl and the plant experienced three nuclear meltdowns and the release of radioactive material. It is only the second time that a nuclear disaster has been given a Level 7 on the International Nuclear Event Scale. The long-term effects of dangerously high levels of radiation exposure by the people of the area are still being assessed and debated. The total emissions of radioactive liquids released into the atmosphere, groundwater and ocean has not been reported.

King Coal – The list of environmental, human health and safety issues related to coal mining is long. The impact to the land and water from the removal process, whether by underground tunnels, open pit mining, strip mining or mountaintop removal mining is highly controversial, but real data on the effect of coal mining on water, air and land is available. Besides the degradation to the beauty of a landscape, coal mining carries with it significant pollution hazards from the solid waste it creates including contamination of water sources and burial of forest eco-systems from valley fills; the practice of dumping the mountain top removal in the valley floor below. West Virginia watershed areas have seen increased sulfate concentrations linked to coal mining, and declines in biodiversity in streams and rivers. Human health is affected by mining when humans are exposed to air-borne toxins and dust from coal. Chronic pulmonary disorders are common in areas where coal mining is the main source of income. Some studies have found that counties in or near mountaintop mining areas had higher rates of certain birth defects. Although reclamation laws require mining companies to reclaim the land, or put it back the way they found it, it is an impossible task. The impact of coal mining is compounded by the burning of coal as a source of energy, and produces airborne particulates of ash, ash slurry, and a toxic desulfurization sludge from cleaning the flues to remove sulfur dioxide that contain mercury, uranium, thorium, arsenic and other heavy metals. Mercury contamination of fresh water fish is directly related to mercury from power plants. In 2008, 1.1 million gallons of ash slurry spilled in Roane County, Tennessee caused by a dike rupture at the 84-acre solid waste containment area, part of the Tennessee Valley Authority's Kingston Fossil Plant, and contaminated the Clinch River and Emory River, contaminating nearly 300 acres.

Death of the Oceans

Coral Bleaching – The loss of coral colonies that form the great structure of reef ecosystems in tropical seas has been reported to be expanding at a new and alarming rate. The symbiotic relationship between corals and algae-like flagellate protozoa that live within the coral reef tissues is causing marine scientist concern. The protozoa are photosynthetic and give the coral its colorations, and it is believed that the corals expel these protozoa when they are under stress. The bleached coral will die unless the protozoa return. Known causes of bleaching are higher ocean temperatures, increases in zooplankton as a result of overfishing, increased solar irradiance, changes in water chemistry, sedimentation, bacterial infections, changes in salinity, herbicides, low tide, cyanide fishing, and certain ingredients in sunscreen that are not biodegradable. Thermal stress on coral reefs is thought to be the primary cause of recent massive global coral bleaching.

Pacific Ocean Garbage Gyre – A large area of the Pacific Ocean where the vortex of currents concentrates small plastic debris, chemical sludge and human non-biodegradable garbage. A similar patch is also found in the Atlantic Ocean. The size of the patch is unknown. The particles of tiny plastic (less than 5 mm in diameter) float below the surface of the water, and various net-based surveys show the abundance of micro-plastic increasing significantly.

Gulf of Mexico Dead Zone – An area of bottom water deprived of adequate oxygen that occurs annually in summer off the coast of Louisiana in the Gulf of Mexico as a result of the drainage of treated sewage from urban areas and chemical run off from agriculture into the Mississippi River and out to the Gulf.

Osborne Reef – An artificial reef constructed of old and discarded tires off the coast of Ft. Lauderdale, Florida in the 1970's. Over two million tires bound with steel clips were dropped 7,000 feet offshore covering over 36 acres of ocean floor at a depth of 65 feet. Ultimately deemed an environmental disaster, a clean up project was begun in 2001, and continues to this day.

Overfishing – The development of state-of-the-art factory fishing technology has created an unsustainable overexploitation of fish stocks in oceans around the world. In a few hours, massive miles-long nets weighing up to 15 tons, are dragged across the ocean floor by deep-water trawlers, and destroy deep-sea corals and sponge beds that have taken millennia to grow. The nets harvest vast sections of the ocean, and though they may target certain fish, will extract all that are entrapped by the vast size of the nets, pulling up far more seafood than humans can consume or use in any form. Some scientists are calling for the end of government subsidies for deep-sea fisheries. Much of the subsidies go to support the large amount of fuel needed to travel beyond the 200-mile limit into international waters to drag the weighted nets.

Important Environmental Milestones

June 1948 – Congress passes *The Federal Water Pollution Control Act.*

October 1948 – 20 people die and 7,000 are sickened in Donora, Pennsylvania, southeast of Pittsburgh, when after sulfur dioxide emissions from a US Steel steel and wire plant descend in the form of a deadly fog. The incident leads to the first conference on air pollution in 1950.

October 1951 – The Nature Conservancy is established in Washington, D.C. with the mission to protect ecologically important lands and waters around the world.

November 1952 – The Paley Commission releases its seminal study, *Resources for Freedom,* which details the US increasing dependence on foreign sources of natural resources and argues for the necessity to transition to renewable energy. This was the first important document to argue for the need for Americans to stop their reliance on oil and the potential for solar energy.

February 1953 – Jacques Cousteau introduces the world to underwater adventure with *The Silent World,* and ushers a new global interest in ocean life.

January 1955 – President Eisenhower speaks to the American people in his State of the Union address on the problem of air pollution, and calls on the Public Health Service to study and implement "effective methods of control".

July 1955 – *The Air Pollution Control Act* passes Congress, the first piece of legislation to address air pollution. However, it puts regulation largely in the control of the states and provides no means of enforcement to the federal government.

July 1956 – Congress, strengthening the federal government's enforcement abilities and control over states' consent where health is endangered, passes an amendment to the Federal Water Pollution Act of 1948.

1960 – Worldwide levels of carbon dioxide climb above 300 parts per million.

1962 – Congress funds a study by the US Surgeon General to investigate the effects of automobile exhaust on human health.

June 1962 – Rachel Carson publishes *Silent Spring,* her seminal work on the effects of the widespread use of the pesticide DDT. Between 1950 -1962 the levels of DDT in human tissue had tripled. Ten years from the publication of her book, DDT will be banned in the US.

1963 – Eighty-three million automobiles roam the highways of the nation, and increasing evidence of a link between smog and automobile emissions will prompt California to mandate that unburned gases be returned to the combustion chambers in all cars, and begins its reign as a leader in emissions standards.

December 1963 – *The Clean Air Act* is passed, allocating $95 million for study and clean up of air and water pollution. The act gives the federal government authority to reduce interstate air pollution, regulate emission standards for stationary pollution sources, and invest in technologies that will remove sulfur from coal and oil.

October 1965 – *The Water Quality Act* is passed, enhancing Federal control over water quality initially set by the Federal Water Pollution Act of 1948. Federal standards become baseline for statewide water quality levels.

October 1965 – *The Motor Vehicle Air Pollution Control Act* sets the first federal automobile emission standards.

October 1966 – *Endangered Species* legislation passes, authorizing the Secretary of the Interior to list endangered domestic fish and wildlife and allotting $15 million a year in the protection of species. The first list of Endangered Species is released in 1967, and includes the United States symbol of freedom, the American Bald Eagle.

August 1968 – Paul Ehrlich argues that the world's environmental problems are the direct result of overpopulation in his book *The Population Bomb*. His dire warnings play a role in bringing the issue of family planning and contraception into the forefront.

October 1968 – The *Wild and Scenic Rivers Act* is passed, providing a system that identifies and adds rivers across the US to a protected list. On the same day, Congress passes the *National Trails System Act,* authorizing similar sets of protections for US trails.

December 24, 1968 – *Earthrise* The crew of Apollo 8 takes the first photograph of the Earth from space. The photograph becomes the iconic image of the environmental movement.

January 1969 – The Santa Barbara oil well blowout leads to reforms in the energy industry.

June 1969 – The Cuyahoga River bursts into flames when oil and chemicals floating on its surface are mysteriously set alight with flames reaching over five stories high.

December 1969 – US Senator Gaylord Nelson hires 25-year-old Denis Hayes to direct a national "teach-in" on environmental issues. Hayes recruits college graduates to come to Washington, D.C. and begins planning the first Earth Day.

January 1970 – Congress passes the *National Environmental Policy Act* due in part to the Santa Barbara Oil spill a year earlier.

January 1970 – Edward Cole, president of General Motors, promises "pollution free" cars by 1980, citing the removal of lead from gasoline and the addition of catalytic converters to stop emissions.

April 1970 – The first Earth Day takes place with an estimated 20 million people across America participating to protest environmental ignorance. In the months leading up to the day, opponents warn that the event is a communist plot because the date of the event coincides with the birthdate of Vladimir Lenin.

June 1970 – The *Natural Resources Defense Council* is established to provide everyday citizens with the tools to draft environmental legislation and lobby for passage.

July 1970 – President Nixon works with Congress to establish the Environmental Protection Agency.

October 1970 – The *National Oceanographic and Atmospheric Administration* (NOAA) is created to monitor and improve the conditions of the oceans.

November 1970 – After Earth Day, Denis Hayes organizes a movement to unseat 12 members of Congress with disreputable records on environmental policy. The movement will successfully unseat 7 of the incumbents, earning the environmental movement significant political clout.

October 1972 – Several measures are passed in Congress in a period of two weeks, The *Clean Water Act,* The *Marine Mammal Protection Act*, and The *Coastal Zone Management Act,* providing key enforcement authority over water quality, natural resource management, and environmental impact on coastal areas.

December 1972 – DDT is banned.

October 1973 to March 1974 – The Arab Oil Embargo against the US. Gas prices skyrocket 400%, prompting immediate research into alternative energy and discussion of energy security in the United States.

December 1973 – Congress passes the *Endangered Species Act.*

June 1974 – Chlorofluorocarbons (CFCs) are identified as destructors of ozone molecules, leading to the erosion of the Earth's protective ozone layer.

December 1974 – The EPA is charged with monitoring water quality standards in every public drinking water system across the country.

January 1975 – The *Eastern Wilderness Act* protects 200,000 acres of National Forests, the first legislation that protects lands that were once logged or inhabited.

October 1976 – The *Toxic Substances Control Act* mandates the EPA to control all new and existing chemical substances used in the US. The *Resource Conservation and Recovery Act* gives the EPA control over toxic waste management. The *National Forest Management Act* gives the Secretary of Agriculture authority to monitor forestlands, and develop standards to manage the National Forest System.

1977 – Governor Jerry Brown of California, and architects of the Office of Appropriate Technology, design the first energy-conserving and self-ventilating building in Sacramento, The Bateson Building. President Carter announces his energy plan including goals to reduce energy demand, reduce gasoline consumption, cut oil imports, increase domestic coal production, and increase use of solar energy, and establishes the Department of Energy.

1978 – The Supreme Court uses the Endangered Species Act to stop construction of the Tellico Dam on the Little Tennessee River by the Tennessee Valley Authority. The court decision, written by Chief Justice Warren Burger, stopped construction of the dam to prevent the extinction of the snail darter fish in the Little Tennessee River. The dam project had already begun construction before the Endangered Species Act became law, and the TVA argued that it should be exempt, but the Supreme Court ruled against them. Two members of Congress from Tennessee, Congressman John Duncan, Sr. and Senator Howard Baker, got involved and an amendment to the Endangered Species Act passed in 1978, which provided a mechanism to allow specific projects to be exempt from the Act. The amendment set up a special committee consisting of Cabinet level members and at least one member of the state affected. The special committee came to be known as the "God Committee" because if they exercised their power to exempt a project from the Act, there were in effect acting like God in destroying an entire species. The committee denied the exemption to TVA a second time and the reservoir project was delayed. Senator Baker tried again, and drafted a special amendment in 1979 that excluded Tellico from the Endangered Species Act entirely. The amendment was attached to an unrelated Bill and passed the House in June by a voice vote, but failed to pass in the Senate. He reintroduced the amendment to the

Senate in September, and it passed on a vote of 48 to 44. President Jimmy Carter signed the bill exempting Tellico on September 25, 1979, at which time the dam was already 95% completed. The gates on the dam closed and Tellico Lake was formed. A small number of snail darter fish were relocated to the Hiwassee River.

February 1981 – President Ronald Reagan cuts the EPA budget by 12% and its staff by 11%. He dismantles the solar panels on the roof of the White House installed by President Carter in 1979.

September – President Reagan cuts the EPA's budget to 44% of its 1978 level. Enforcement cases submitted to the EPA decline by 56%.

May 1985 – *Nature* magazine publishes an article providing evidence of the ozone hole in the atmosphere over the Antarctic. The article creates a new wave of media attention on the stalled environmental movement. This article and the confirmation of the ozone hole by the Nimbus-7 satellite spurs an avalanche of studies worldwide investigating the consequences of ozone depletion on the planet.

September 1987 – The *Montreal Protocol* is signed by the US, Japan, Canada and 21 other countries who agree to phase out ozone-depleting CFCs by the year 2000.

November 1988 – President Reagan signs the *Ocean Dumping Ban Act,* a law that prohibits all waste dumping in the ocean starting in 1992.

March 1989 – The *Exxon Valdez* tanker runs aground, spilling 11 million gallons of oil, killing more than 250,000 birds and covering 1,300 square miles of ocean with oil.

June 1992 – *United Nations Framework Convention on Climate Change* is an international environmental treaty negotiated at the Earth Summit in Rio de Janeiro attempting to set protocols, evaluate mechanisms, and set voluntary limits on greenhouse gas emissions. George H. W. Bush opposed it and lobbied to have all binding targets removed, however the treaty was ratified by the US in March 1994.

October 1992 – The *Energy Policy Act of 1992* set goals, creates mandates, and amends utility laws to increase clean energy use, and improve energy efficiency. Consisting of twenty-seven separate titles, the Act details measures to lessen the nation's dependence on imported energy, promote energy conservation in buildings, and provide incentives for clean renewable energy.

December 1997 – The *Kyoto Protocol,* a treaty among nations setting legally binding reductions in greenhouse emissions to 6% - 8% below 1990 levels, is signed by President William Clinton, however the treaty was not ratified by Congress, and was explicitly rejected by President George W. Bush's administration in 2001.

August 2005 – The *Energy Policy Act of 2005* was a sweeping piece of energy legislation designed to promote US nuclear energy reactor construction through incentives and subsidies including cost overrun support, direct tax credits and loan guarantees. The Act authorized $2.95 billion for research and development for the building of an advanced hydrogen cogeneration reactor at Idaho National Laboratory, and extended the Nuclear Industries Indemnity Act through 2025. It also exempted fluids used in fracking from regulations under the Clean Air Act, Clean Water Act, Safe Drinking Water Act, and CERCLA. It increased coal as an energy source and simultaneously authorized $200 million for clean coal initiatives, repealed the government cap on coal leases, allowed advance payment of royalties from coal mines and demanded an assessment of coal resources on federal lands that are not national parks. It provided increased incentives for oil drilling in the Gulf of Mexico. It directed the Secretary of the Interior to complete an environmental impact statement for a commercial leasing program for oil shale and tar sands resources on public lands within Colorado, Utah and Wyoming. It increased the amount of ethanol that must be mixed with gasoline giving an economic boost to corn, from which ethanol is derived; added ocean energy sources as a separately identified, renewable technology, authorized $50 million annually for biomass grants, authorized tax credits for wind and alternative energy producers; and included provisions seeking to make geothermal energy more competitive with fossil fuels in generating electricity; and required the Department of Energy to report on how to dispose of nuclear waste; provided incentives to homeowners to make energy conservation improvements; required all public electric utilities to offer net metering upon request; and extended Daylight Saving Time by five weeks. The act authorized tax reductions of $4.3 billion for nuclear power; $2.8 billion for fossil fuel production; $2.7 billion for extension of the renewable electricity production credit; $1.6 billion for investments in clean coal facilities; $1.3 billion for energy conservation and efficiency; $1.3 billion for alternative motor vehicles and fuels; and $500 million in Clean Renewable Energy Bonds for government agencies working on renewable energy projects.

April 2016 – In an historic joint statement, President Barack Obama and Chinese President Xi Jinping agree to sign *The Paris Agreement* of the UN Climate Change Conference. The agreement is not presented to the Senate for ratification, and a legal challenge ensues.